Also by Joe Prosit

Machines Monsters and Maniacs Volume I

Machines Monsters and Maniacs Volume II

Bad Brains

99 Town, Book One of the "From Order" Series

7 Androids, Book Two of the "From Order" Series

Zero City, Book Three of the "From Order" Series

Look What You Made Me Do

And coming soon…

The Reality Reaction Team

THEY COME
from
Below

Joe Prosit

Copyright © 2025. All rights reserved.
No part of this book may be reproduced or copied in any form without the written consent from the author. This is a work of fiction. Names, characters, businesses, places, events, locales, and incidents are either the products of the author's imagination or used in a fictitious manner. Any resemblance to actual persons, living or dead, or actual events is purely coincidental.
Author Photo by Cadence Porisch, on Instagram @cadey_photography
Cover art by Nabin Karna.
Contact the author at www.JoeProsit.com or by email at joeprosit@gmail.com.
1st Edition. ISBN 9798336078077

Chapter One
An Unwelcome Guest

On the night of the first snowfall, two things happened. My dad died, and a demon from Hell crawled up my basement steps.

They don't come often. The demons. Most nights I'm alone in this old house. The door leading down to the basement stays latched in its frame. It doesn't sing that slow whining song as it falls inward on its hinges. The only air that moves is my own breath. Most nights I can sit on my couch and read for hours without hearing the dry, hungry, arrhythmic scrapes of claws and talons digging through the wood of each step. Most nights my home is quiet.

But they're coming more often now. The silent interludes are growing shorter and shorter. As I sit in my still home in the dead of winter, I wait for them. The scraping sounds from my stairwell are more familiar to my ears as are the tightening compressions around my spine that accompany them. If I let them come, if they make their way up from the basement and to the surface, they'll wreak unspeakable wickedness. That is why, tonight, while I sit in my living room rereading my third favorite book by HHR Eventide, "Apothecary of Agony," my dad's ax rests against the arm of my couch.

The house is warm. Outside it's cold and dark, but not late. This deep into winter, by six in the evening, it's as somber as midnight. Very little traffic passes by on 7th Street outside my living room window. Thick puffs of snow tumble through the green and red glow of my still-hanging, out-of-season Christmas lights and add another layer to my buried front lawn. My drafty front window cultivates a little more frost. Inside, I'm wrapped up in blankets with a hot cup of tea and a great book. The old oil heater in the basement churns and rumbles underneath the floorboards, but there are no errant noises or spectral strangulations of my spine. Nevertheless, the ax rests at arm's length.

They only come when I'm at my weakest.

To say I'm used to these unholy creatures would be a lie. Whenever I open that door to the basement and catch one of them in mid-creep, the ax shakes in my wet palms, my eyes blur with tears, and my spine compresses down to the width of a single piano wire. I hate them. Those hell spawned abominations. Those amalgamations of humans and creatures and monsters from fairy tales. The things with the horns and wings and hoofs and talons and too many eyes. Slaughtering them brings catharsis, but I wouldn't call it satisfaction. Before they can put their sometimes bird-like, sometimes goat-like, sometimes human-like foot on my kitchen floor, I bury my ax into them. Over and over again till they're rendered to bits and tumble back into the blackness. But I still dread with every fiber of my being those noises and the invisible clenching hands wringing my spine.

The only thing worse than hearing them climb up the stairs would be not hearing them before it's too late. So, I tend to stay away from the TV. No loud music either. I'm being overly cautious; I know when they begin to encroach on the surface. I feel them as keenly as gravity, an ever-growing, unseen force pressing down on me. A feeling radiates within me whenever they draw near, a coming sickness I'm powerless to prevent.

But tonight, it isn't the sound of claws digging through wood treads or the sense of impending spinal injuries that sends my heart thundering away, trying to escape my ribcage. It's the doorbell. I jolt and my book snaps shut in my lap. It tumbles to the carpet while my bookmark still rests on my thigh.

I lost my place. Not a big problem.

I don't get many people ringing my doorbell. I lost my mom to ovarian cancer when I was a kid. My dad died just before Christmas. My only sibling, my sister Zoey, lives two hours south in Minneapolis. No husband or boyfriend or kids to speak of. Just me and my demons, and I thought I had them neatly tucked away in their beds for the night. They never come by the front door anyway.

Always from below.

Unnesting myself from the blankets, I get up and try to peek through the front window to see who rang. Maybe just a FedEx or UPS man who'll leave as quickly as he's come. But there is no truck by the curb, and I can't see around the window far enough to see if there is a package or anyone still on the front step. I check my attire. An unwashed baggy t-shirt that reads, "Woodduck Derby Days, 2021, Woodduck, Minnesota." No bra. Orange pajama pants dotted with jack-o' lanterns more out of season than my Christmas lights. Thick socks with Valentine's Day hearts and arrows I bought last week. Presentable enough.

I crack open the door, and a sharp blast of winter air cuts through what I wear. My whole house is going to drop twenty degrees if it stays open for long. But a kid of about thirteen stands on my stoop. As bundled up as he is, I can tell he doesn't mind the chill one bit. Could live in it all winter long.

"Hi," he says. No "Good evening, ma'am," or "miss," or any other honorific. Instead, he plunges straight into his spiel. "I'm, um, selling pizzas for Woodduck Youth Hockey Association, and I just need to know, like, how many you want to buy."

Quite the salesman, this kid. He'll have a bright future in the timeshare business after he graduates.

"So, where's the pizza?" I ask, not because I want any pizza, but because that's what he is selling and all he has with him is a clipboard and a bunch of glossy order forms. The wind flaps the forms where he doesn't have them pinned down with his big chopper mittens. The same wind finds routes under the hem of my shirt, through the thin cotton fabrics, and up the cuffs of my pajama pants. My crossed arms do little to retain my body heat.

"No, you just order 'em now. We'll deliver them later. I got cheese. I got pepperoni. I got Hawaiian. I got just about everything. You just tell me what kinds you want," he says.

"I don't want any–" I say and stop short when I feel a sharp pang of guilt.

"It all goes to youth sports. I'm in Woodduck Bantam Hockey, and we travel all over, going to tournaments each weekend and this goes towards, um, like, the cost and stuff," I half-hear him say.

"I said I don't want—"

I want to tell him I don't want his stupid pizzas. That all I want is to get back inside and under my blankets and find my place in my book and get back to what I was doing before he rang my bell. But this isn't about whether I want his pizzas or not. It isn't about him not really wanting to sell them either. It isn't about what kind of pizzas he has or if his team will win any games or if he'll even see any time on the ice or just ride the bench all season. It isn't about whether or not I'll eat the pizzas when they finally come; of course I will. And it isn't about the windchill turning my exposed skin to ice. It's about me prioritizing what I have over what his hockey team needs. It's about money. The money I have and the money he doesn't.

"So, yeah. Woodduck Youth Hockey Association is like, um, a five oh see three pee oh, which means it's, like, good for your taxes and stuff. But it's not like you're donating money exactly either cause the pizzas are actually really good. They're McGregor Pizza, so they're, like, locally owned, I guess. So it's like, good for them too," he carries on.

Meanwhile, invisible hands tighten around my vertebrae. I don't know if the footfalls I'm hearing are from my stairs or from inside my mind, but I know something is rising up from my basement with each passing moment. As the junior salesman/hockey player returns to his tried-and-true sales method of rattling off all of the various varieties of frozen pizza McGregor has to offer, I say, "Hold on. I gotta take care of something," and shut the door in his face. The last I hear is Buffalo Chicken, and god dammit, I know I'm going to be eating McGregor's Buffalo Chicken Pizza before spring thaw.

Greed. Apathy. Selfishness. My sins tally up quick. I should be thinking of supporting our local business and youth sports and getting him and his friends as much ice time as they apparently so desperately need. But it's too late for that. A touch of evil is all it takes.

Walking by my couch, I snatch the handle of my ax. I steady myself in front of the old wooden door that leads down to the dark and dank basement and try to scrounge up some courage from the bottom of my guts. I hear them clearly now, the scraps and scratches coming up the stairwell. On the other side of the door, the demon's claws are ripping grooves in the wood treads of my steps. My quivering left hand falls on the doorknob. My right hand grips and regrips the shaft of the ax.

Outside, the kid calls, "So, you still want some, right?"

I throw open the door.

Three steps down is a demon. It's a massive thing, a fur-covered human frame with the head of a wolf, drooling saliva and a fluid black as melted rubber from its elongated snout. Lips curl open like stage curtains to reveal rows of fangs as sharp as obsidian arrowheads. Eyes burn like coals. Pointed ears lie back against its skull. Antlers twisting like fractals rise above its head. The fur is matted with clots of blood or worse. Tails too many to count, barbed like a Roman torture whip, wave from one side to the other. Rather than growling or barking, the demon hisses at me, angry I'd caught it before it could make it above ground. The sound is as sharp and dangerous as a blowtorch focusing its flame into a superheated blue tongue.

Here is the moment I want to run. Every part of my body and mind is telling me to flee. To bolt for the front door, push past the kid on the stoop, and keep running until morning comes. And never come back. That's the only sensible thing to do. That's the thing any sane person would do. But I've done that once before, and I'll never do it again. So help me.

The demon puts a heavy paw barbed with claws a step higher. I step through the threshold and swing my ax in a full arc. The blade impacts where its shoulder meets its neck. Hot black tar erupts from the wound. It screams. I'm screaming too. Its human-like hands, each finger spiked with grotesquely long and lethally sharp nails, lash out for me, but I knock them aside with the ax head before taking another swing. There's more hissing and howling, both from me and it, but I'm careful. Even as I heave and drop the heavy ax over and over again, yanking it free with a puckered sucking sound after each hit, repainting the already-stained walls of the staircase with the infernal creature's steaming blood, I do my best not to give into wrath and hate. I don't enjoy this. This is my duty. My sentence. I'm obligated to be here at the top of my stairs, denying this thing entry to the overworld. I don't do it because I'm angry or bitter or vengeful. I am.

All of those things. But if I'm not careful, if I let those emotions off their tight leash, other things from Hell will follow. So, I stay emotionally cold while I dismember this unholy creation that would kill me, would kill the pizza salesman still at my door, and would escape into town from there.

Once it has been properly rendered to a mangled twist of loosely connected and disconnected limbs, the wolf invader slips and tumbles back into the shadows. Its parts dribble and thump down each wooden tread, the lower parts still tenuously connected to higher parts pulling them down, Slinky-like. No part of it ever shows a will to retreat. It climbed until it physically couldn't, until it lacked the muscles and bones to lift itself a step higher.

Before it's done thudding back into the blackness, I shut the door. If I go back tomorrow, turn on the light, and check for a body, it will be gone. I know this from previous encounters. Only that thick, inky blood will remain on the walls and the steps.

My house isn't big. Only takes me a few steps to bring the ax back to the end of my couch and lean it against the armrest. My book is still lying on the floor. A few more steps and I'm back at the front door. The kid is still there under the shine of the Christmas lights I haven't bothered to take down. He looks cold now. Or maybe just confused and afraid. Not so sure he's going to make his fundraising goals anymore.

In Minnesota when you lose someone close to you this thing happens. Everyone you've ever known and a lot of people you haven't bring you meals. Frozen lasagna in a tin pan. Beef stroganoff in Tupperware. Tater tot hotdish in white and blue Corning Ware with masking tape and the last name of the person who you have to return the dish to on the side. Because they know. Because grief is a swamp. It's thick and you're lethargic and you can't see the bottom. And when you're in that swamp, the last thing you want to do is cook and do dishes. So this is how they show that they care. That they've been there. Not with words but with what people call church basement food. A lot of ground beef and mashed potatoes. Pastas out your ears. Some vegetables. Hearty. Filling. Mostly healthy. Bland. Flavorless. Meals prepared for a family reheated for one. Two months later and my fridge and freezer are still full of them. I swear, if I have to eat another pan of green bean casserole somebody is going to be delivering these same meals to *my* next of kin.

Pizza on the other hand?

"Give me three cheese, three pepperoni, and three of the buffalo chicken," I tell the kid.

Chapter Two
A New Book

     My name is Abby Hendrix, and if you think I'm some Van Helsing-style vampire-slaying demon hunter, you couldn't be any further from the truth. I'm not a world-traveled adventurer. I've never climbed a mountain or gone scuba diving or solved a murder or driven a sports car through the Swiss Alps or even fired a gun. I've hardly left Woodduck. I don't drink or smoke. I've never done drugs. I have zero tattoos. I never asked for any of this. I work in the county's Accounts Receivable office. I drive a hybrid. I like books. I'm boring.

     So I go to bed at a decent time and wake up to my alarm without having to hit the snooze. I get up, get ready for work, and carry my coffee with two splashes of creamer to my fuel-efficient, environmentally friendly, Chevy Volt without any flair or dramatics. If you're looking for a woman with tattoos who likes to drive fast and drink hard liquor and shoot guns and fight bad guys, you should find my sister Zoey.

     So yeah, I might be boring, but I'm not bored. Sure, my car isn't flashy. My make-up isn't lavish or loud. I wear practical clothes for February in Minnesota. Winter boots. Lots of layers. A hat, gloves, and a scarf made from alpaca wool I picked up from last year's Christmas arts and crafts fair. I hide my fears behind dull eyes, but I am very alert and very aware.

The residual adrenaline and paranoia linger in my veins for days after a demon attack. I make a concentrated effort to return to my normal routine. To act kind and pleasant. To be helpful and friendly but not flirtatious. To not get hung up in fear, frustration, anger, and regret. To, in essence, forget what just happened to me while at the same time remaining vigilant. Because it might happen again. The last thing I need is another visit from an unwelcome basement abomination. So as I drive, I do my best to pay attention to traffic, to think about what my workday has in store for me, to focus on my responsibilities, and to keep my thoughts pure.

Woodduck is a nice little working-class town founded in 1870, just twelve years after Minnesota gained statehood. It sprung up from the surrounding forest when the Northern Pacific Railway built a bridge over the Mississippi. By the following summer, the river was full of floating logs and loggers riding them and shoving them to shore and loading them on train cars. A few decades later, iron ore from the Vermilion, Mesabi, and Cuyuna Ranges passed through Woodduck. With the iron ore came money, and for a brief period in history, Woodduck was an up-north bastion of industry and wealth. But the forests were quickly laid bare, the mine was stripped clean, and all the money fluttered away with the unabated windchill. What's left today are either farmers, retirees who escaped from the Twin Cities, or folks who never figured out how to escape to the Twin Cities.

Woodduck is the county seat and the largest town in a thirty-minute drive. Most of the other towns across the county are no more than a church, a bar, a gas station, a city limit sign with a three-digit population, and a dot on the map. We have a high school, a Walmart, a Subway, a regional hospital with a highly accredited cardiac center, and last year, we even got a Starbucks. Everything you need and nothing you don't. All things considered, I'm glad I live where things are reserved and manageable rather than someplace like Las Vegas, Manhattan, or Paris where people hang their indiscretions out to dry. I don't know how I'd deal with the things I'm dealing with in a place like that. Those places would be too overwhelming.

My daily commute takes me five minutes by car. Probably would take me about the same to walk. But I never walk it. For one, it's too cold this time of year. For two... I'm not comfortable whenever I'm between home and work. See, there are no basements while I'm commuting. No place where I can channel the demons and stop them before they reach the surface.

I take 7th Street to Hill Road and turn left toward the courthouse. It rests at the intersection of Hill Road and Highway 210, the only highway that crosses Woodduck. There are stop lights here, and of course I come to a full and complete stop. I'm extra careful during the winter. You never know when you might hit a patch of ice and spin out. A few cars roll by, but my mind drifts to warmer months when all this snow will finally melt and leave the streets a safer place.

Before I lift my foot from the brake, the car behind me squawks. My butt lifts a full six inches off the seat.

It's not just any car. It's Sheriff Graham in his squad car. The squawk, electronic yet bird-like, came from the loudspeaker. The squad car is one of the new souped-up Ford Explorers that came with the equally jacked-up price tag billed to the county. In the frame of my rearview mirror, he gives me a little wave to let me know he's not about to arrest me, but that the light is green, and I should pay attention to the road. It's a friendly we-know-each-other sort of gesture, but it sends my heart into overdrive all the same. I can't help but worry about committing some offense, getting pulled over, and getting a ticket. I want to curse myself out, but I bite my lip and pull onto Highway 210. The parking lot is less than a block away, but my mind is no longer blissfully musing over the inconsequential. Instead, I'm cycling through all of the possible sins and misdeeds I may have just committed.

The Seven Deadly Sins: Pride, Gluttony, Wrath, Envy, Greed, Sloth, Lust. Sloth? No. I don't think so anyway. I run through the Ten Commandments: Idolatry, Blasphemy, Disrespect, Murder, Adultery, Thieving, Lying, Coveting… No. Almost blasphemy, but I didn't swear. I held it in. I don't know where these demons come from, and I'm not particular to any one religion, so I remind myself of the Five Pillars of Islam: Declaring One's Faith, Praying, Giving, Fasting, and Making the Pilgrimage. I mean, perhaps I've sinned by omission, but not by commission. I haven't done the opposite of any of those things. The Five Precepts of Buddhism: Don't Kill, don't steal, remain sexually pure, don't lie, don't drink or allow your mind to be clouded by–

As I come to a stop to turn left into the courthouse parking lot, Sheriff Graham pulls around me and gives me another of those friendly neighbor waves. I hate him for it. For his innocence and ignorance. For the danger he's put us in. No. I don't hate him. I can't hate him. I can't let the demons hear those thoughts, so I replace them with better ones. Sheriff Graham is a good man in a noble profession. He's always been kind to me. He probably just has somewhere he needs to be. That's all.

I park my car in the lot outside the courthouse and prepare for the chill. Sheriff Graham is long gone, so I put him out of mind. My only worry now is crossing the fifty feet through the parking lot to the courthouse front doors with a pure heart. If I can manage that, then I'll have a basement under my feet, and if I conjure up any demons, I can meet them before they have a chance to reach the surface. So as soon as I'm ready to face the cold, I take my coffee, pop open my door, and make my way.

The Woodduck County Courthouse was built in 1922. The year is chiseled on the keystone of the arch above the main entrance. Those indelible numbers are far better evidence of its age than the small brass plaque posted next to the entrance by the National Historical Registry. The architectural style, Beaux-Arts, is common among courthouses, typical even, borrowed from larger and more impressive buildings in places like Rome and Washington DC, but it's still beautiful. I remind myself of these things, not because I'm particularly interested in history or architecture, but because if I'm thinking of these things, I know my thoughts won't be lustful, greedy, or covetous. The steps leading up to the big doors, thank God–

Blasphemy! Get inside, Abby. Just get inside.

– are clear of snow and salted. The pillars on either side of the entrance are Doric, from the classical era. The angelic creatures above them are nude.

Lust. Just a few more steps.

The door is heavy. It catches on a patch of ice as I pull it open.

Come on! Come on!

I check over my shoulder for any bony, fleshless, rotten hands like zombies pulling themselves from their graves–

Fear. Doubt. Faithlessness.

—and the big door gives way. I slip inside. The door thumps closed behind me.

My big, rubber-soled Red Wing boots clop against the rug. I do my best to stomp off any snow because I know how slippery the granite floors get with just a little water. The stomping makes an echoing racket, so I keep it short. No one else is moving through the cavernous hallways. It's quiet now. I'm early.

Still, I'm eager to get to my department. I keep my mind and my eyes down as I pass by Land Services, Community Services, and Administrative Services. My strides are long, and my steps are quick. I ignore the giant historical paintings of European settlers meeting with friendly Dakotah natives. Under my alpaca wool hat, scarf and mittens, my coat, my sweater, and my blouse, I'm sweating. Accounts Receivable is a door past Administrative Services. I push through it and I'm in my department.

"Good morning, Lilith," I call to my boss, Lilith Littlebird.

"Morning," she says from her office and nothing more. She's a quiet, reserved, Dakotah woman who, for obvious historical reasons, doesn't always trust the government. Even though she works for the government. But I get it. As far as I know, she might be a direct descendant of those indigenous people in the paintings in the hallway.

The third member of the team is Hank, a nice enough older white guy who's worked for the county so long, he could be one of the settlers in the paintings. He's at his desk, eyes locked on his monitor.

I don't expect a busy workday, but there are always things to be done. Calendars to check, emails to send, overnight sums to calculate, and books to balance. Most mornings I'd go to Lilith's door and engage in a light conversation with her, sort of "check in" with the boss. This morning, I don't mean to be disrespectful or dismissive, but I'm distracted. My purse and coffee land on my desk. I stride past Hank's workstation, past Lilith's office, to the back of the department. There's an old door there, painted white a long time ago and currently flaking away lead chips. A yellowed notice with the word "CONDEMNED" written in bold Helvetica sits in a document protector taped to the door at eye level. Before I open it, I suck in a deep breath.

The stairwell on the backside of the door is dark and exceptionally deep. But it is also empty. No thin scratching sounds of talons against the metal grate steps. No nails digging into the concrete walls. No black moving inside the black.

No demons.

I ease the door shut and command my throbbing nerves to spin to a soft denouement, like a still-turning record after the last track on an album. When the door latch clacks into place, Lilith says nothing. By now, she's familiar with my "compulsions" and makes nothing of it. I return to my desk.

The workday is slow. As expected. As are most. I like books, but always feel too self-conscious to bring in a book, crack it open, and rest it on my workstation. Hank will play blackjack or Texas hold 'em right on his work computer for hours during the workday. Lilith knows he does it, but when things are this slow, there's not much she can say about it. Still, it's so flagrant, I can't bring myself to occupy the long hours with something as visible as a book. But with my email open on one screen, ready to respond to anything that might need my attention, I allow myself to scroll through book reviews and publishing news on the other.

Today HHR Eventide releases his new novel, "A Black Heart Unbroken." I've read all his books. My dad read all his books. If I had a brother, I'm sure he'd read all his books. My sister on the other hand? I don't think she reads the captions on TikTok. But I'm not about to let her get under my skin. Not today. In a couple hours The Book Bazaar, the independent bookstore downtown, opens its doors and Eventide's latest work will be on the shelves, ready for purchase. Maybe you don't realize how big of a deal that is. HHR Eventide is our generation's answer to Charles Dickens, Nathanael Hawthorne, Edgar Allen Poe, and HP Lovecraft. He is Minnesota's answer to Stephen King. He is the only reason anyone outside of Woodduck County has ever heard of Woodduck, Minnesota. That's right. My favorite author, a legend in our own time, lives right here in my hometown. And Thursday? This Thursday, he'll be at The Book Bazaar autographing copies of his new book.

I'd like to be there when the doors open so I can be the first one in town to own a copy of "A Black Heart Unbroken." But, just like other people, I have responsibilities. I'll get a copy on my lunch break. As long as they're not already sold out. If I don't get my hands on one today, there's a good chance I'll have nothing for him to sign come Thursday. And if I don't get his signature this Thursday? Well, unlike me, Mister Eventide is a rolling stone that gathers no moss. In the two days between launch day and his appearance here in Woodduck, he's speaking in New York, Boston, Philadelphia, and Chicago. And next week he leaves for his European book tour. So it's Thursday or never.

He lives in the old mayor's mansion at the end of Hill Road, on top of the hill. We call it "The Hill" because there is only one hill in Woodduck. There's hardly more than one hill in all of Woodduck County. Plenty of ponds and marshes for geese and ducks as soon as you leave town. Acres and acres of woods for hunting deer. And of course, lakes full of walleye and northern pike. But you won't find any mountains anywhere near here. We just have the one hill, a bit of knoll is all. Just enough of a rise in terrain for it to be controversial when the mayor built his house on it in 1926.

The original owner of the home was an iron ore tycoon and railroad baron by the name of Edgar G. Huntington. Unlike its current occupant, Huntington was a recluse. He chose to build his mansion in Woodduck to escape the bustle and noise of Duluth. Despite his inward-facing personality, he was able to win his first candidacy for Woodduck mayor on name recognition, or by ballot-stuffing, depending who you ask. As mayor, he rewrote town ordinances to best suit him and his businesses. Then he built the mansion on Hill Road to his exacting specifications and made his residence the tallest structure in town. Taller than First Lutheran Church on Fifth Street. And back in those days? That was all it took to upset the good Christians of rural Minnesota.

He lost the next election because of it. People labeled him a godless heathen and quicker than a kid on prom night, his political career had climaxed. Shortly after, his stocks in his iron mining investments tanked. Shortly after that, his affair with a poor, young widow living across town was discovered and further scandalized the town. Not long after that, he shot his wife and four children inside the home before taking his own life. His last act was to hang himself from the mansion's highest chimney for everyone in town to see. Even in death, he put himself above the bells of First Lutheran.

And ever since, the rational, reasonable, logical, and stoic citizens of Woodduck tend to glare at the mansion on top of Hill Road and whisper the word, "haunted."

The home is of the Flemish Renaissance Revival architectural design. It features a turret, seven gables, and two tall and slender chimneys that rise high above the roof peaks. Like the courthouse, the mansion was placed on the national historical registry and therefore, was well maintained and preserved for the decades it remained empty. The grounds are hidden from view by the hill and the surrounding forest, but the folks in the historical society reported that the property contains servants' quarters, a pool house, and a sprawling courtyard full of hedges, statues, and fountains. Every dozen years or so, a proposition fails to turn the estate into a museum. Always a matter of money. That was until HHR Eventide moved here from Duluth a few years back. There was some debate about turning the mansion over to another private owner and what this eccentric, New York Times A-lister might do to it, but it's always a matter of money. We watched as remodeling and moving trucks pulled up to the old residence. We all speculated what might be happening inside and hoped to catch a glimpse of the man himself. One day, all the workers and movers left, and it became clear that the man himself was already inside, occupying the hundred-year-old home, and all that was happening inside now was the tapping of fingers on a keyboard.

I don't care much for geology, architecture, or history, but I'm keenly interested in all things Eventide. And the data mining and trivia collecting keeps my mind on innocent, pure things.

Behind me, Lilith sighs.

My shoulders spring around my neck. I didn't hear her come up behind me, but I assume she sighed that way because I'm at work and she is my supervisor, and she caught me in the middle of some very non-work-related internet scrolling.

"That guy's kind of a creep," Lilith says in that mousey quiet way of hers.

"I don't know. Don't you think he's kind of intriguing in a mysterious sort of way?" I say, not wanting to outright argue with my boss.

"I know he's supposed to be, like, our hometown boy and everything but... People talk about him like he's Stephen King or

Nathanael Hawthorne or Edgar Allen Poe. But those guys? Those guys are from New England where there's real ghosts and they burnt real witches. How's some scrawny pale white guy from the Midwest supposed to be as good as those guys? I mean, those guys are all scrawny white guys too, but..."

She's reading my monitor. About Eventide. I'm equally embarrassed by being caught absolutely not working and upset that she has the gall to say something so unfair about our resident horror wordsmith. I minimize the window but can't help but say something.

"HHR Eventide is the best writer this state has ever–"

"Sinclair Lewis? F. Scott Fitzgerald? Will Weaver? John Sandford? Laura Ingalls Wilder? Tim O'Brien? Hell, Garrison Keillor couldn't keep his hands to himself and even he was better than that weirdo," Lilith says. And then, as if she hadn't just made the most scandalous statement I've ever heard, she abruptly changes the subject. "You applying for the position at the library? You'd have his book by now if you worked there."

Despite her taste in literature, and despite being nothing you'd expect from a regular boss, Lilith is great. She isn't saying I'm not doing well here in Accounts Receivable, or that she doesn't want me as a member of the team. But the window to apply for the Assistant Head Librarian position at the County Public Library is closing tomorrow, and she knows it would be a better fit for me. Knows it pays more too. I'd be an idiot not to at least apply. And she's right. Besides, you know what the Woodduck County Library has that the courthouse doesn't? Brand new copies of "A Black Heart Unbroken."

But you know what the courthouse has that the library doesn't?

A basement.

"Just saying," Lilith says over her shoulder on the way back to her office. "Also, I need my Corning Ware back as soon as you're done with it."

After Lilith is gone, I turn in my chair and eye the old door leading downstairs.

Chapter Three
The Full Amount

Because of the extreme cold and the limestone geology, it's not uncommon for cities and towns in Minnesota to hide a network of underground tunnels just below the frost line. Deep underneath St. Paul, a man-made labyrinth connects the State Capital to other government buildings, hotels, up-scale restaurants, and some say, gangster-era speakeasies, and long-defunct cathouses. Political corruption and organized crime have a long history in St. Paul, so I have no doubts. There are also tunnels in Rochester between the university and the Mayo Clinic. New Ulm boasts an "underground city," although the only thing down there are old steam pipes. Duluth has passages between downtown businesses and hotels. When Minneapolis shot up out of the prairie, rather than tunneling underground, engineers built human-sized hamster tubes connecting the city a floor above street level. So it should be no surprise that Woodduck, even as small as we are, has its network of passageways.

Rumors at work say they connect the courthouse to the Sheriff's Department, the county jail, and the school district's administration building. If they lead to other locales, no one knows, and no one's allowed to find out. If construction plans were ever drawn up, the Records Department won't admit to having them. In addition to the "CONDEMNED" sign in the document protector, there used to be a padlock and a metal hasp screwed into the frame, but those screws rusted out and worked their way free a long time ago.

Maybe no one else has, but I've been down those steps, just like I've been down the steps of my basement in search of things not from this plane of reality, living or dead. I've never found either below the courthouse, but that doesn't mean I won't someday in the future. If that sounds like a curse, it's not. If I have any errant thoughts here while at work, those horrors will be confined to the passages and funneled to the stairwell right behind my desk, where I can stop them. If my wandering mind gives way to lust or greed or envy or hate while there's no basement under my feet, they'll still rise, but from where I have no idea.

All the same, I'm typing my information into the online application on the county's jobs website. I uploaded my resume last week. Even got a glowing letter of recommendation from Lilith. Not because I'm planning on applying. But because it's a good habit to keep my resume current, and as a test to see if I could apply. To see what the process feels like. And now, it's done. All that's left to do is a single click of a mouse. The cursor hovers over the "Submit" button. My hands sit folded in my lap. My email inbox sits empty. The doors of the library and The Book Bazaar are open for business. What I don't know is if copies of HHR Eventide's latest magnum opus remain on the shelves.

I can't submit that application. There is no way I can conscionably leave my position here at the county courthouse to work blocks away from my house and any known entrance to the tunnels. I want to be there at the library, surrounded by thousands of books set in distant lands, far removed from the icy wasteland and mental torment of living with the memories of what I've seen in this town. Maybe, I'm relegated to a sedentary, boring life in Woodduck, Minnesota. But books change all that. There's an energy old books give off. An aura of endless possibilities. A million unbroken promises of freedom. Inside a book, I'm free to go anywhere, see anything, do everything, and be whoever I want. Amidst all those books, I'm free of the guilt, of the regret, of the shame of having accomplished so little in my life. Standing between shelves and shelves, I'm relieved from the trappings of my life. Because around me, isn't just the potential for living a different life; there's the ability to dive into a thousand lives.

I can visit the library. When I'm pure of heart. When I don't have to worry about what might come up from below. I don't need to work there or at The Book Bazaar or anywhere other than here. I go to close the window of the online application, put one hand on my mouse, and grip the edge of the desk with the other.

"What up, sis?"

It's Zoey. Of all people and of all places, my sister stands before me, here at my place of work.

My grip on the mouse eases. What I realize only after the button clicks back up is that I just submitted my application for Assistant Head Librarian to the county's HR department. A pop-up window tells me, "Thank you for your interest in joining our team!" Out of habit, my teeth sink into my lower lip, and I blow out the first f of a four-letter word before I stop myself. I can rescind the application. I can call them and tell them to delete it. I can intentionally bomb the interview. I can just not show up. It's fine. It means nothing.

Zoey, on the other hand, always means trouble.

"Hi, Zoey. Didn't expect to see you all the way up here. At my work," I say.

She is dressed in a midnight black suit with a scarlet blouse under the jacket. A single button holds the jacket together, tight against the shape of her torso. Her chest is prominent, but so is a smaller lump on her right side. A handgun, I know. Her lips and fingernails are painted sanguine red. The nails roll from pointer to pinky across the surface of the customer counter just above my desk, making a high-pitched snare roll. A pair of silver reflective aviator sunglasses is perched in her hair, which is pulled back into a ponytail so tightly, I worry her roots will rip right out of her scalp. Her eyes gaze off in the distance and her jaw masticates a wad of highly odorous cotton candy-flavored chewing gum.

"I haven't seen you since…" The funeral, I decide not to say.

"Yeah, well, you know how I just love to visit our hometown." She lacquers her words in sarcasm, just like she always has. "But I'm actually here on business."

I smirk. "Am I like, wanted for murder, or something?"

Zoey works for the Minnesota Bureau of Criminal Apprehension which, she never allows me to forget, is a big deal. See, I thought that every law enforcement agency in the state was a bureau that deals with the apprehension of criminals, but the BCA, as she likes to tell me, is like Minnesota's version of the FBI. Just like HHR Eventide is Minnesota's version of King or Lovecraft, I suppose. When the local police departments and sheriff's departments and the state patrol need assistance with DNA evidence or forensic psychologists or hostage negotiators, they call the BCA. Now what my sister actually does with the BCA, she's never made clear. Because I suspect, if she did, it wouldn't be so impressive. Or maybe she'd have to kill me. I don't know.

"No," Zoey said. "Believe it or not, Abbs, the BCA has zero interest in anything going on in your life. Zero. Interest. The reason I'm here is because I need to renew my federal background check, and apparently, the birth certificate I originally submitted isn't the official birth certificate. So, I need my real birth certificate. Not the pretty one with all the laurel leaves and the foil stamp, but the actual, legal, birth certificate that comes from the county, not the hospital," Zoey says.

I take in a breath to tell her exactly what I was about to tell her before she went on her tirade about which birth certificate she needs.

"And before you tell me that birth certificates aren't your department," Zoey cuts me off. "Let me tell you that I've already been upstairs to the Records department. And what they told me is that I need to see you so I can get this slip of paper initialed saying I paid the fee for having them generate a new, official, birth certificate."

Between her red nails, she swings a manilla sheet of paper my way.

"So if it weren't for that slip of paper, I suppose you would have just gone right upstairs, got what you needed, and left town without ever saying 'Hi,'" I say.

She doesn't roll her eyes, but I can see her repress the urge. "Look. Let's not make this a thing. Can you just initial off on this so I can get what I came for and we don't have to see each other again till the next funeral?"

Harsh. Cruel. Intentionally rude. But that's my sister. I take the slip of paper and mumble, "I can't imagine what funeral that might be." With Mom and Dad already in the ground and without any aunts or uncles we ever knew, or husbands or kids... Who do we have left to mourn?

"Twenty-eight dollars and seventy-eight cents," I read to her what is clearly printed on the card.

"Seriously?" Zoey says, locking eyes with me for the first time since she arrived. "This is for, like, official government business. Can't you just waive the fee?"

I glance around the office. Hank is ensconced in his Texas hold 'em. Lilith is entrenched in her office, probably scrolling through Amazon. The stamp that the Records Department will look for when I send Zoey back upstairs, not an initial, just a rubber stamp, sits on my desk. The door behind me stays closed. The stairwell stays silent. For now.

"Zoey..." I sigh.

"Abby," she growls back, playfully, as if her frustration is a joke and not genuine. "It's twenty-eight bucks. Who's going to care about twenty-eight measly dollars? Just..."

She lets her sentence hang, wanting me to complete it with the obvious "initial it," conclusion. And you know what? I would love to stamp it for her and get her out of my hair. Because my boss isn't paying attention. There is no comprehensive database that compares every replacement birth certificate issued with every fee paid. The whole bureaucracy is a thinly veiled honor system. The quickest and easiest way to be done with Zoey is to gently stamp her little slip of paper and send her on her way so she can go on and spend her time doing all those big deal, big agency, cop sort of things like arresting terrorists and busting drug rings or whatever it is she does down in Minneapolis.

But there's a steel coil tightening around my back. The scraping sounds of talons against steel steps will come next if I let them.

"Maybe we can waive the fee," I smile. "Let me ask my supervisor."

"No– Just– Fucking aye, Abby. Just let me pay the fucking thing," she's saying, realizing I'm not going to allow this to be a "between us sisters" kind of deal and that I'm already calling for Lilith.

It takes a minute for Lilith to extract herself from her office. Meanwhile, Zoey and I share a wonderfully awkward moment glaring at each other through narrow eyelids.

"Lilith, can we waive records fees for state employees if the records needed are for official business?" I say.

"This is for a birth certificate," Lilith reads the slip quickly but takes her time reading the tension between Zoey and me.

Zoey has already produced a credit card and holds it between her fingers tipped in red, wanting to pay the twenty-eight dollars and seventy-eight cents now and spare herself the embarrassment and the hassle.

"So, the thing is, birth certificates are considered personal documents. And since it's a personal document, we can't waive any of the fees," Lilith says to Zoey coolly, professionally, quietly. Then to me, "Charge her the full amount."

"Thought we might share a little professional courtesy," Zoey says, her credit card still hanging from a cliff. "But that's okay. I'm sure when you're ass deep in meth labs and human traffickers you won't mind paying the Minnesota Bureau of Criminal Apprehension a twenty eight dollar fee so we can do our job."

As if she's paying me a bribe. As if I'm doing anything but my job. I say nothing. I run her card. I stamp her slip. I hand it back to her and say with a smile, "All set."

Now it's Zoey's turn to smirk. "We should do this again sometime. You know I always love our sister time together."

Then she's gone.

But you know what? So are the shrill sounds of claws against steel and the squeeze compressing my spine.

Chapter Four
A Coming Storm

Each day, from eleven thirty to noon I have a lunch break. Most days, I take it at my desk. It's safest that way. But today isn't most days. I watch the minute hand as it creeps closer and closer to the bottom of the hour. When it seems to die at the five, defying gravity and refusing to move any closer to the six, I lose my patience.

No. I don't lose my patience. I look to my supervisor for leniency after years of dutifully taking a shortened lunch break at my desk. With my coat, scarf, gloves, and purse already in my hand, I rap on the frame of her office door.

"Hey. Sorry to interrupt," I apologize.

She mumbles something that is either, "No inconvenience at all" or "Don't inconvenience me long."

"Sorry. Do you mind if I run into town on my lunch break? There's something I want to pick up before they sell out," I say.

"Don't think I don't know what you're looking to pick up during your lunch break. I know you want that new book. And also, you're already in town. If you run anywhere at all, then you'd be out of town," Lilith says. "You really are a townie, huh?"

"So... should I eat at my desk then?" I ask.

"Aren't you listening? No, you shouldn't eat at your desk. Go get your book already. What kind of prison do you think I'm running here?

It's not like the people of Woodduck are breaking down the doors to come and pay their parking tickets," Lilith says.

I glance quick, so fast no one notices, at the door leading downstairs. Silence. "Okay. Promise I'll be right back."

With her chin in her chest, she shakes her dead. Then waves a hand at me like she's shooing me away. "Go already. And take your time for once. You're allowed a full lunch break, you know. You're making the rest of us look bad."

If it warmed up during the four and a half hours between when I arrived at work and when I make my way down the steps of the courthouse, I can't tell. There's a big difference between sixty degrees and seventy degrees, but once it gets to ten degrees on down? It doesn't really matter. Especially if you're bundled up properly. Sure, your hair will freeze if it's wet, and your nose hairs freeze if you're not wearing a scarf, and if you are wearing a scarf your breath will get your eyelashes wet and then they'll freeze instead of your nose hairs, but that happens whether it's ten degrees or negative twenty.

And Lilith has a point. Woodduck is one of the smallest county seats in the state. What I think of as "into down" is the three blocks of "downtown" that consist of the old, shut down Paramount movie theater, an ancient hardware store, a consignment shop, Schmidt's Dentistry and Orthodontists, Woody's Tavern, The Book Bazaar, and empty storefronts. In the time it would take me to walk to my car, I can be halfway to the bookstore. And a walk will do me good. I don't exercise enough. And doesn't it say in The Bible that the body is a temple to the Lord?

I never settled on a religion. Probably because Dad was never religious. Out here, way up north and away from the big cities like Bemidji, Brainerd, St. Cloud, Duluth, and the Twin Cities, it isn't like I have a lot to choose from. I can either go to First Lutheran or go with the Catholics to St. Augustine's. There are no mosques or synagogues or Buddhist temples in town or Wiccan prayer circles hidden out in the woods. As far as the people of Woodduck are concerned, Woody's plays both kinds of music (Country *and* Western), and the churches cover both religions (Catholic *and* Lutheran.)

At this point in my life, it feels silly choosing one or the other, as if these two available options are the only options when deciding my eternal fate. Like going to the county art fair after seeing just two paintings and having only seen these two paintings my whole life, choosing one of them and declaring with utmost certainty that this one is the best painting in the world across all of human history. Except, there are no eternal prizes for picking the second-best religion in the world. You either get it exactly right or you go to Hell.

But that kind of thinking is too close to blasphemy. Blasphemous to which God, I have no idea. Best not to waste time trying to puzzle that out. In the short term, if it's a sin to "Have no other Gods before Me," then having any god is like playing Russian roulette. So, I don't play.

These thoughts occupy my mind while I penguin-walk across the train tracks and through the canals of the semi-shoveled sidewalks toward downtown. They're not the purest of thoughts, so I don't want to dwell on them, but they're also not the irrepressible greed that resides just below my consciousness. There's a hungry desire to get HHR Eventide's book in my hands. There's an envy that would come if I don't get my hands on a copy. There's a thrill I get from looking at his author photo on the inside jacket and peering into his deep-set eyes and his solemn countenance and those lips that hint of knowing terrible and wonderful things I could never imagine. There's a lustful warmth repressed inside of me when I dream about slipping into his imagined worlds. I'm tempted to go there, but there's no basement under my feet where I can trap the manifestations of these thoughts, so I vanquish them from my mind. All the same, I'm like a guided missile that has locked on to the heat signature radiating from The Book Bazaar.

I turn the corner onto Main Street and see the signboard for The Book Bazaar hanging under its sidewalk canopy. I hurry my steps. Hurry too much on icy concrete, and I'm liable to land on my tush, so my steps are short and quick. The soles of my boots never rise more than a half inch above the surface. Glancing through the storefront window, my heart skips a beat as I see HHR Eventide himself, larger than life, with an aloof smile on his face and a hardbound copy of "A Black Heart Unbroken" in his hands, offering it to me as if I could reach through the glass and take it from him. It's only for a moment, but in the moment before I realize I'm only looking at a cardboard cut-out, my veins flood with adrenaline and dopamine and all of those other feel-good chemicals that lure my mind and soul into greedy lustful places. But it's only a display. An advertisement. Across his double-breasted suit is printed, "The Master of Midwest Gothic Presents: A Black Heart Unbroken," and below that, in smaller font, "Available Everywhere on February 10th. In-store book signing on February 12th."

Today is February 10th. The day. I pull open the door to The Book Bazaar, half expecting to find a greedy mob of fans all fighting over the last copy. But the store is quiet. A bamboo flute, soft, sparse drums, and a traditional Chinese stringed instrument I don't know the name of play from the speakers. There's no crowd, and there's no table stacked high with copies of the book either.

I'm too late.

They're all gone. The people. The books. The whole show. Gone without a trace. The circus came and went so quickly there isn't even the scattered residue of ripped tickets and crushed popcorn kernels. I'm breathing heavily from my rushed walk, from the shock of seeing what I thought was Eventide himself, and from the sudden realization that I'm going to have to go without my book while all the rest of Woodduck read theirs.

Wrath.

"Jane," I call my friend's name before even looking toward the register. Jane has been the owner and sole proprietor of The Book Bazaar for as long as I can remember. I know she'll be standing behind the counter before I even look. She practically lives in this place.

Jealousy.

Instead of Jane, there is a massive, gray, long-haired Maine Coon that looks as much lion as house cat sitting like an Egyptian statue on the counter. His name is Oy, and his stillness unsettles me until he finally flicks away an itch in his ears. If it weren't for seeing both Jane and Oy together, I'd suspect that the cat is her witchy familiar. The way Oy hops off the counter, landing behind it with a heavy thud, just before Jane emerges from the back room with her nose in a book does little to disprove this theory.

Jane Straub is an eclectic woman with a habit of wearing shawls and bobbles and big hoop earrings. Her parents were Sixties flower children. How she has a name as plain as, well, Jane, and not Sage or Sunset or Starchild or Rainbow, I'm not sure. She's a book lover just like me but with a wealth of idiosyncrasies I can only dream of. She's free in all the ways I'm not. Along with books, she sells crystals and tarot cards and incense and all sorts of other odds and ends. But she was raised around these sorts of things, so for her, the mysterious and mystical are the norm.

And the book she's reading, it's not just any book. It's *the book*. She slips a scrap of paper between the pages, already a third of the way through the thick tome, and meets my eyes before saying, "Sorry, Abby."

Covetous.

"They're all gone? Already? All of them?"

"Oh, no. It's not that," Jane says. "Our delivery was late. They were supposed to be here yesterday. But they promised me they'll have two hundred copies here by tomorrow. I asked for more, but they gave me some nonsense about sales trends and order history. But they better get here. Mister Bigshot Eventide is taking a break from his grand globe-trotting world tour and coming here in two days. And if I don't have any books..."

"But you have a copy," I say.

Oy emerged from behind the counter and is now making figure eights around my ankles. He purrs like an idling dump truck. Most days, I'd hoist the massive cat into my arms. Today, I have other things on my mind.

"I couldn't wait," Jane says and gives me a squint that tells me she feels bad but not too bad for getting her copy before me. "Had Jason put a copy on hold for me at the library as soon as I found out our shipment wasn't coming in on time. Picked it up first thing this morning."

That would explain the thin plastic cover over the dust jacket and the additional barcode sticker on the back. I notice these things now that I'm at the counter. Can hardly pull my eyes away from the book. It lays face down, the cover hidden from me, but that's fine. I've seen the cover before in all the ads and reviews. But I haven't seen the back cover and the blurb printed there in white letters over a black background. Above the smaller text, big and bold and right at the top, it reads, "Demons Are Meant to Be Played With." Jane rests her palm on the book as if she suspects I'm going to snatch her borrowed copy and run out the door with it. Or am I just projecting my greed onto my friend?

"So?" I ask her. "Is it good?"

"Oh my god, Abby! It is *so* good!" Jane gushes. "You should go get yourself a copy from the library too. Just to tide yourself over until our shipment comes in. And please, read it as fast as you can because I am going to need to talk with somebody about this book. And I mean soon!"

Oy lets out a loud whine, either concurring with Jane or complaining to me for ignoring him.

"You think they still have copies left? Over at the library?" I say.

"They might. Jason wasn't letting anyone reserve them ahead of time. He said the demand was too high and too many people put books on hold and never get around to picking them up. I don't think that kid likes Eventide. Said he plagiarized from other cultures or some such nonsense. Anyway, I had to promise that I'd be there as soon as the doors open this morning before he'd make an exception for me," Jane said.

"And your delivery guy is coming tomorrow?"

"No later than tomorrow. Maybe even today. Tell you what. I'll send you a text as soon as they come in," she says and gestures to her phone. Unlike most people, I hardly ever see Jane looking at her phone, but I trust her.

I check my phone. No missed calls or texts. And I still have twenty-five minutes of my lunch break left. The library is in the opposite direction of the courthouse. Another five or ten minutes by foot. But I'd have to walk five or ten minutes back to work to get my car anyway. I can hoof it. Ten minutes to the library. Two minutes there. Ten minutes back. I can make it.

"Okay, Jane. Send me a text as soon as they come in. I want to own a copy but…" my eyes drift back to her copy.

Envy.

"It's really good. Like, his best yet," Jane says, not helping.

"Okay," I smile. "See ya."

If I could run the whole way from downtown to the library, I would. But I'm bundled up in my big down coat that hangs to my knees and all the alpaca wool covering my head and hands. If I try to move fast,

I'll look like an insane sleeping bag come to life, hopping down the street. Or I'll slip on a patch of ice, break a hip, and give myself a concussion. Then I'll be laid up in the hospital and still won't have a copy of "A Black Heart Unbroken."

When I call to them, the demons find a way to the surface. If I'm not at work or at home, they'll still come. Maybe up someone else's basement. Maybe right through the frozen ground. My only shot at stopping them is to channel them to a stairwell where I can stop them. Do the tunnels lead to the hospital? New construction that far from downtown? I doubt it. No way those old tunnels trail all the way out there. Besides, it doesn't matter. I'm not breaking a hip or concussing myself. But I am definitely making it to the library. Slow and steady. Slow and steady and pure of mind and soul.

Seven minutes later, I push through the doors of the Woodduck Public Library, hip and head still intact, demons still lurking deep below, and with plenty of time. The place is nearly as empty as The Book Bazaar. School is in session and anyone who's ever been in a public library knows that kids are ninety percent of their customer base. The only other customer is a weathered old man, most likely jobless, probably homeless too. He hunches over one of the ancient computers, hopefully job-hunting and not hunting for a way to bypass the firewall and get to a porn site. Warming up from the cold at any rate.

Libraries play a critical role in any town. They are an invaluable resource to people who can't afford books or an internet connection or heat. Yet, our county board hasn't found a need to raise the library's budget for the past decade. They're always short of funding and short of staff. Which inevitably means cutting programs, services, and personnel. I bet with my insider knowledge of the county's accounting and budgeting practices, I could find ways to address that.

Jason is behind the counter. He's maybe old enough to drink and looks the part: A ratty pair of Converse high tops, jeans, a baggy white Adidas hoodie that hasn't seen laundry day since he'd last seen his mother, the retreating scars of teenage acne, and a messy head of hair. As the Junior Librarian, he's basically been running the place since Wendy, the former Head Librarian, keeled over at the age of ninety eight, and Margret, the former Assistant Head Librarian and an octogenarian herself, took over Wendy's spot. That left the position of Assistant Head Librarian vacant. Jason would be a shoo-in, but he's a college kid, and I think he only took his current position as a way to continue his studies during a skip year. A bright, young kid like him has to have bigger ambitions than being a small-town librarian, right?

If I say these things with a hint of malice, as if I hate the old man or the elderly ladies or the young upstart with no plans to stick around, it's only because I'd rather be here so much more than the courthouse. The library has a smell, a peace, a consistent environment of order and education and purpose I've never found anywhere else. And all the books and all the stories. Even the non-fiction encyclopedias, travel guidebooks, and foreign language dictionaries permeate with prospects for adventure. So maybe if I'm being honest with myself, maybe it isn't all Zoey's fault I clicked that "Submit" button this morning.

Maybe this place has a basement after all. Hidden in the back, a stairwell tucked out of sight.

I don't know about that, but I see what they do have.

On a round table right between the front doors and the counter are stacks of HHR Eventide's "A Black Heart Unbroken." One copy is propped up on a stand to show off the cover behind the library's glossy clear plastic jacket. The front of the book is brilliant red. The title is at the top. At the bottom is "HHR Eventide." Dead center is a biological heart with all the atriums and ventricles and veins and arteries. What those veins and arteries connect to, rather than human lungs and muscles, are red things that are maybe organic, or maybe mechanical. The cover artist is an art student out of Portland, Oregon by the name of Delmar Lulipe. I know this because I read an article specifically about the cover art. The artist took inspiration from turn-of-the-century medical diagrams, HR Giger who inspired the biomechanical aesthetic of the "Alien" movie franchise, and Ralph Steadman who is most closely associated with his splattered Indian-ink drawings in books by Hunter S. Thompson. She combined all of these influences into an image that is medically professional and sterile, yet grotesque and chaotic. HHR Eventide worked with her directly to achieve this single image that is truly wonderful and horrific and appalling and alluring. And that's just the cover.

The book is in my hands now. I don't even remember how it got there. I must have picked it up, but I'm not touching it yet. The damn alpaca mittens are keeping me from it. I peel and shake them off, flinging them to the floor. My numb and tingling fingers grip the library's plastic jacket. It's not enough. I crack the spine and let my fingertips run over the words and paragraphs of a random page halfway through the book. I only allow myself to glance at the words, afraid to stumble across spoilers, before I snap the book shut.

I march to the front counter, already digging through my purse for my library card.

"Morning Jason," I say.

"Hi, Abby," he says and sets down his book. A paperback. Not a college research textbook. Last I heard, he was still working on a master's in anthropology with an emphasis on ancient Persian Zoroastrians or some such. There is a textbook on the counter as well, tagged with endless little sticky flags and graffitied with lines and lines of yellow highlighter, but that isn't what he's been reading. The book he is reading is a dog-eared trade book that he sort of makes a tent out of by setting it open-side down, about three-fourths of the way through. And what trash is he reading when he could be reading Eventide's latest masterpiece? Stephen King's "Four Past Midnight," which, to me, on today of all days, feels traitorous. Like wearing a Green Bay Packers jersey to a Viking's game at US Bank Stadium.

I slide what I am sure is a much more superior book on the counter for him to scan. Jason hesitates. His lips tighten, holding back an opinion maybe. Regardless, his laser gun beeps once at the barcode on the book and again at the barcode on my library card. The computer does the rest, and I know in my heart of hearts that I could be excellent at this job.

"So, did you submit your application?" Jason asks me as I'm about to leave.

"Huh?" I say. My attention is on the book.

"For the Assistant Head Librarian vacancy?" he asks. "The gals were saying you'd probably apply for it."

"Um…" I debate what to tell him. I'd rather tell him nothing, but certain words are spinning in my mind like lemons and cherries and bars on a slot machine. Words like Greed, Envy, and Deceit. So, I tell him the truth. "I did, actually. Just this morning."

"Good for you. And I should tell you, just, like, full disclosure, I sent in mine as well," Jason says, and I immediately hate him for it. His confidence. His false friendliness. His smooth-shaved youthful looks. The way he's ready to crush my dreams under the sole of his trendy tennis shoe with a smile on his face. "But good luck though. You'll probably get it anyway. You're in here almost as much as I am."

"Yeah," I say, which is safe. Not a lie or an insult or an attack. "Gotta go. Good luck to you as well." That part. That feels like a lie as much as wishing someone good luck can. I don't want him to have good luck. I want him to have terrible luck. I want him to take his Persian anthropology research studies and his stupid, old, tattered Stephen King book and I want him to go back to whatever college he came from and never come back. I want him to have an accident that renders him incapable of getting the job I need. I don't want what's best for him. I want the worst for him.

No. No, I can't think those things. Shouldn't even feel those things, but I can't help that. The demons… I have to get somewhere where I can cut them off. The courthouse. Or home. Somewhere where I can keep them underground. I'm on my way out the front door, scooping up my alpaca mittens off the floor on the way, when I stop.

"Jason?"

He looks up from his paperback. "Yeah?"

"Is there a basement in this building?" I ask and realize that I don't know if I'm asking so I can go and slay something that might be working its way up those stairs as we speak, or for future reference. Or if I'm subconsciously hoping something does come up from below while I'm not around. A terrible thought, that last one. I want to take it back immediately, but you can't erase a thought once you've conjured it up. Especially thoughts evil enough to delve into the recesses under this town and reach the things that dwell in those infernal depths.

"A basement? No. I don't think so. Why? Is there a tornado coming or something?" he jokes.

"Never mind," I say, trying to smile it away. It was a weird question to ask and all the charm in the world won't blot it out. I wave with one of my mittens, say, "Bye," and I'm out the door.

A basement. A basement. I have to get to a basement. I wince at the sensation of a ghost reaching through my clothes and the skin of my lower back to clench my vertebrae tight in its icy cold, bony fists. A demon is coming.

Chapter Five
Guarding the Gate

Outside the library, on the corner of 3rd Street and Hill Road, the intersection feels oddly empty and barren. The wind is just as cutting as it has been all morning. My borrowed copy of "A Black Heart Unbroken" is solid under the cushion of my alpaca mittens. My cell phone is buried in my purse, counting the minutes and seconds until the end of my lunch break. To the north, Hill Road lays a straight path back to the courthouse. If I followed it south, I'd come upon 7th Street in four blocks, and my home just three more blocks to the west. There, not only is there a basement, but also my ax, still leaning against my couch, ready for action. I look that way.

Beyond all the streets and avenues and turn-of-the-century homes, at the end of Hill Road, is Woodduck's one and only hill. A sundog of icy, airborne particulates halos the sun that looms above. Below, nested peacefully in a copse of oaks and maples is the seven gabled, Flemish Renaissance Revival mansion of Woodduck's only resident celebrity and literary genius, HHR Eventide. I can see through the midday haze the two slender chimneys above the gables, the taller of which had once been decorated with the corpse of the original builder, homeowner, and town mayor: Edgar G. Huntington.

And if I went there and used the heavy cast-iron knocker mounted to the front door, would Eventide himself answer the door and invite me inside? Chances are he's still in Philadelphia or Chicago or some other big, important city. Does he have a butler? A maid? Anyone in there besides him and ghosts? The idea of retaining servants seems preposterous in our modern day. But the idea of him stepping away from whatever new masterpiece he's currently working on to come to the front door seems equally improbable. If I did go there, and say he did open the door for me, what then? Surely there is a basement inside the manor. Would he show me to his wine cellar so I could murder a demon right there inside his home? And if he did, and if I did, what would we do then?

Standing stationary in the cold, I peel open the back cover of his book. On the inside jacket is his picture. A beautiful man. Tall and slender with those deep-set, almost hollow eyes... I could gaze into them for hours. His image is like a drug to me. I can imagine such wonderful things...

My mind strays. The jealousy of seeing Jane with her copy of his book still lingers. I'm disgusted by the advantage Jason lords over me simply by working there. He's young. He can take the low-paying job as Junior Librarian and be completely content with a paycheck that would put me on welfare. All the while, he's earning himself a favored spot in line for my dream job. And what is this new sensation rising from inside me as I look down Hill Road and dream of Eventide's photograph inside the book? I know the name of the sin, but I won't speak it.

Work is four blocks away, but there is no ax there. My home is six blocks away. But I'm also on my lunch break, and if I don't make it back to work on time, what will Lilith think? And what ill-formed breed of demon will my selfishness beckon?

"Car's still at work," I say aloud, reminding myself that I'd put myself into this situation and that I'll remain in this situation until I get back where I came from. I have no choice. I turn away from the hill and the mansion at its summit, point my feet north, and head for the courthouse.

Along the way, I keep my eyes on the sidewalk and do my best to keep my thoughts away from Jane, from Jason, even from Eventide. I need to find neutral thoughts. Safe thoughts. Factoids. Trivia. Data. The music in The Book Bazaar. I liked that music, but I don't know the name for it.

Don't even know the instruments it used. Something Chinese in origin. Traditional. I should research that. Commit to memory the history and the styles and the most popular song names, if there are song names. There was no singing that accompanied the instruments this morning in the shop. Maybe the genre is made up entirely of instrumentals, like European classical music.

  I blink my eyes and see Eventide's. His black pupils are like gravity wells, pulling me in. His knowing lips hide a thousand thoughts and a million words. His heart... Is it as black as the one on the cover of the book? Or does it drum inside his chest like mine? If we pressed our bodies together, could I feel his pulse sync up with mine? Our blood gushing over rapids like two rivers nearing a confluence?

  No. Stay pure. Stay chaste. Lilith won't care or notice if I'm five minutes or even fifteen minutes late. That's not what has me in a panicked rush. I have to make it back in time to catch the demon as it makes its way up the steps. It's coming. We commune, me and the dread thing. There is a connection like a tow rope pulling me along, bringing me to the exact place where I don't want to go. Toward the tunnels below the courthouse. I called it and it responded. And now it draws near. If I'm not back in the courthouse soon, what will it do to Hank and Lilith?

  And if I do make it back to work in time, what the hell am I going to do to it?

  I'm crossing the tracks. No trains in either direction for long flat miles. Then Main Street. There is a crosswalk at Highway 210. Legally, traffic has to yield to me, a pedestrian, and although normally I wouldn't trust it, I'll stroll straight through traffic if it means getting back before the demon reaches the surface. When I step off the curb, I speed up. Almost running. When I reach the far curb, my eyes are scanning the steps for patches of ice like the watchmen onboard the Titanic. My lungs are pumping geysers of steam into my face. Icicles weigh down my eyelashes. My black heart is thrumming. I'm focused on the slick steps leading to the big double doors. I don't see the workman making his way up the steps, hauling a heavy toolbox as he goes, until it's too late. We collide and bounce off each other, almost losing our balance. His toolbox crashes against the granite. Screwdrivers and wrenches and things I don't know the names of clatter and rattle down to the sidewalk.

"Oh. Sorry! So sorry!" I say, but I don't slow down. I'm walking backward up the steps while I apologize.

"Nope. That was my mistake. Didn't see ya coming there," the workman says. He's not angry with me, not like he should be. Not like I'd be. Instead, he's smiling. His clean and pleasant face is warm and forgiving, happy even. As if he's completely immune to any negative disposition whatsoever. That honest grin of his disarms the whole situation, assuring me he's not upset. "Where's the fire, anyway?" he jokes.

"I– I'm on my lunch break," I don't lie. "I have to get back."

I leave him there to pick up his tools. I know I should stay and help him and maybe offer a genuine apology. I would like to do that, to pick the brain of a man so unfamiliar with anger and frustration, but I don't have that luxury. There is something that needs my attention desperately bad. I race up the steps, rip open the door, and scuttle inside.

My boots are wet. The granite floors are polished smooth. I don't bother with the rug. Still clutching my library book, I bolt straight for Accounts Receivable. As soon as I'm through the door and into our department, I drop the book on my workstation.

"Sorry I'm late," I say in the general direction of Lilith's office. I don't know if I'm late or not. At least as far as the clock is concerned. What I do know is that my spine is twisted in knots and claws are scraping against metal steps behind the door at the back of the room. It is a dry, sharp sound, with high-pitched grating vibrations. Peeling off my mittens, I abandon them on the floor for the second time in one day. My hat too. I'm sweating from head to toe. In front of the door leading down into the tunnels, I hesitate.

Lilith never responded when I apologized for being late. Hank hasn't looked up from his Texas hold 'em. The office is quiet except for a few things I hope only I can hear: my rapid breaths, my faster heartbeat, and the shrill of claws carving gouges into the steps on the opposite side of the door. With my hands empty, with my brow soaked, with the icicles quickly melting from my eyelashes, eye to eye with the Condemned notice, I twist the knob.

That's all I have to do. The weight of the door pulls it inward, revealing to me and only me, what is coming up.

It's already more than halfway up the deep and long stairwell. A three-headed thing, all shadows for a body, but with the head of a bull off its right shoulder, the head of a goat off its left shoulder, and something close to human in between. The extended bullhorns of its right head force it to list to the right where its goat horns stand vertically rather than horizontally. Three long tongues wag at me and lap up saliva. The tongue of the human head is forked and longer than the others. The menagerie of creatures takes a step closer. The black talons of a raven clink against a dirty metal step.

And here I stand with nothing to defend myself. Of course, I've played out this scenario in my mind prior to today. I inventoried the office for any usable weapons a long time ago. The best I could come up with was the fire extinguisher and the AED in the hallway. But it's going to take more than a blast of white powder to send this horror back to Hell. And there's no chance I'm getting close enough to this thing to apply the AED stickers to try zapping it to death. As if this isn't something of death already. As if it doesn't dwell in the realm of the dead. As if it isn't death's master. As if I can move an inch without surrendering the realm of the living to its steady advance.

But I conjured this thing with thoughts and desires. I can banish it just the same. It is a beast born of my sin, my corruption, my lies, and my weaknesses. So, it stands to reason that the truth, goodness, and mercy I have inside of me can send it away just as effectively. If I have any truth, goodness, and mercy in me.

I've leaned heavily on Christian lore to categorize and name these demons. And just as I've memorized the Seven Deadly Sins, I can also recite the Seven Heavenly Virtues (charity, chastity, diligence, humility, kindness, patience, and temperance,) and the Fruits of the Spirit (love, joy, peace, forbearance, kindness, goodness, faithfulness, gentleness, and self-control,) along with a several other articles of faith of other religions. But more than all the rest, I have committed to memory and can quote even under the most stressful conditions First Corinthians Thirteen verses Four through Eight. I like lists. And if there are no other weapons or tools available to me, perhaps this simple list and definition of love will work.

I close my eyes, stand firm at the top of the stairs, and whisper as quickly as I can, "Love is patient. Love is kind. Love does not envy, is not boastful, is not arrogant, is not rude, is not self-seeking, is not irritable, and keeps no records of wrongs. Love does not delight in evil but rejoices in the truth. It always protects, always trusts, always hopes, always perseveres. Love never fails."

I breathe in deep, tasting the demon's stench, but keep my eyes closed.

"Love is patient love is kind love doesn't envy doesn't boast..." Rushing the way I am, the words slip from my memory, but I find them again. "It isn't proud, isn't rude, isn't self-seeking, isn't irritable. It keeps no records of wrong. It... It... Love doesn't delight in evil," I say, but lose my place again.

My eyelids fly up at the sound of another set of talons landing on another step. The beast is only a few feet away from me now. Its fiery eyes stare into my flawed soul and see my weakness and cowardice. It's going to kill me. I know this. But I grab the frame of the doorway tight, determined to stop the thing I called up from the blackness physically if I can't do it spiritually.

I start again.

"Love is patient," I say, and hear the words for the first time that day. Patient. *Patience.* It's worthless just to spit out words without understanding their meaning. I have to embrace them. I can't just say things about love. I have to feel love. I have to reject the thoughts that got me in this situation and surrender to the beliefs that will get me out of this situation.

The demon is only inches away from me now, but I keep my eyes clamped tight. Its three mouths push hot, oily, wretched breaths into my face. Still, I remember to be patient, and I start over.

"Love is patient. Love is kind," I say, giving each sentence its own time and breath. "It doesn't envy or boast. It isn't proud or rude or self-seeking." I know I'm not reciting the passage verbatim, but that doesn't matter. I'm saying them as I feel them. As passionately as possible, imagining the way the Apostle Paul felt when he first wrote them down twenty centuries ago. "It is not easily angered. It keeps no record of wrongs. Love does not delight in evil."

At the word evil, the bull lets out a huff from its nostrils, the goat grinds its teeth, and the human growls. I ignore it all and keep my eyes shut.

"It always protects, always trusts, always hopes, always perseveres…" I'm crying. I'm crying because either the last line in the passage is true, or I'm about to die. Beyond my eyelids, I sense that the human head has unlocked its jaws and is ready to sink long, inhuman, canine teeth into my neck. My body shakes. My tongue is heavy and numb inside my mouth. My cheeks are wet. I speak the last line. "Love never fails."

There is a moment of silence. For the span of a heartbeat, I wonder if I'm dead. If death can be this quick and painless and silent. I open my eyes.

The empty stairwell pours down into the tunnels below and is eventually swallowed by the darkness. In the metal steps are the smallest traces of the three-pronged feet that cut fresh scars through the old paint and grime. Nothing else.

The demon is gone.

I lose my grip on the door frame. My knees buckle. My butt comes within inches of the floor before I catch myself against the wall. Vertigo clenches my vision down into a narrow tunnel no wider than the staircase leading below the courthouse. My whole body is drenched in sweat, but I'm alive. And the demon is back where it came from.

Chapter Six
Islands of Light

From far away, through the thick medium of air as viscid as swamp water, just over the high-pitched ringing in my ears, I hear someone call to me. A man. Dad?

"Hey, there," the voice says. "You need a hand?"

I focus on breathing because right now, that's all I can control. With breathing comes other things to hold onto. Bits of physical reality for my hands to cling to like the wall and the frame of the closed door. Also, bits of reality for my mind to cling to like the sound of that voice and the weight of my Red Wings against the cracked tile floor. My vision, seized tight like a cramp, begins to loosen. More and more of the office comes into view.

"Ma'am?" I hear that distant voice again. It's not my father's. He's dead. I haven't forgotten that much. Or the role I played in his death. This is a different voice, although similar, with that same downhome casualness. "Should I come back there?"

I stand up and my head only spins for a few seconds. Then everything seems to right itself and I can take in the office again. Hank is still at his desk, focused on his monitor full of playing cards and bet totals. Lilith is still in her office, equally unfazed. At the front counter, just beyond my desk, is a man. The workman I'd bumped into on the front steps.

He wears a tan duck coat with a dark brown collar and a Minnesota Gophers beanie with a maroon and yellow pom pom ball on top. That heavy toolbox that puked half its contents on the courthouse steps what feels like an eternity ago is resting on the counter. When he recognizes me, he grins in a way completely foreign and alien to me. It's free of sarcasm or superiority or hidden intentions. When was the last time I saw someone smile simply because they were happy?

"Hey, it's you," he says. "Did you find that fire you were after?"

"Huh?" I ask as I reestablish my sense of balance, place, time, and reality.

"Oh. I was just saying that 'cause of how you came rushing in here so fast. You know, how we bumped into each other outside like we did," he says. He's plain but handsome. He has some scruff on his chin, not a beard but not unkempt either. His eyes are crystal clear and blue like sunlight reflected off a lake. No dread or torment or weariness in them.

"Abby? Is that you?" Lilith calls from her office but doesn't come out. "Did you get your book?"

"Yeah, I got my book," I say.

Hank looks up from his monitor, notices me and the man at the desk for the first time, and seeing that I'm handling our first customer of the day, returns his gaze to his game. But it's as if Hank and Lilith have returned to the same dimension I occupy. Or rather, I've returned from a dimension occupied solely by me and the thing that had been in the stairwell. I am with humans again.

"You okay?" the man in the duck coat and beanie asks. "You're sweating pretty good there."

"Oh," I say and squeegee a good amount of the sweat from my forehead into my hair. "It's just hot in here."

"Well, you are wearing a coat," he says.

"Am I? Yeah, I guess I am," I say, dumbly. "Um... Can I help you with something?"

"Oh. Yeah. That's why I'm here now that you mention it," he says, just as dumbly. Why else would he be here if not to be helped? "Woulda been here sooner but there's not like a front desk for me to ask for directions so I went to the licensing office and they said before I can get started I need to see the records department. Sos..." and he says "So" that way. With an "s" on the end. And just like that, I've decided that I like this guy. He rambles on. "Sos, I'm wandering around and eventually I make it up there all the way on the second floor and I'm waiting in line and let me tell you, the lady in front of me? Boy howdy, she was not a happy camper. Just cussing up a storm, let me tell ya. Sos anyways, after all that was over, they sent me down here to you folks. Now, I know you're not exactly the maintenance or building and grounds department or whatever it is you call yourselves here but–"

I stop him because if I don't, I don't know if he ever would stop himself. And because I have a suspicion who the angry woman on the second floor might be. "You can just tell me what you need. I'll be happy to help."

"Oh. Sure," he says. "Electrician. Somebody called from this building and said you're burning through lightbulbs faster than a Vegas casino. Breakers tripping all the time. Surges in the power, which usually means faulty wiring and as old as this place is… Well…" and I can tell that whatever he's about to say to me is funny to him. "Just make sure you don't have any building inspectors come and take a look at this place!"

"Okay," I say and smirk even though I don't get the joke. As he continues, I take another moment to appreciate his plain but honest features. A shapely face. Clear eyes. Cheeks still red from the cold. When he talks, the little pom pom on his hat bounces, which undermines anything seriousness he might be talking about.

"Sos anyways, I already took a look at all the subpanels and those seem up-to-code well enough. Modern breakers and whatnot. The wiring leading into the boxes is older than all-get-out but still in decent shape. Sos now I'm gonna have to take a peek at the main breaker panel and they tell me that that's in the basement, and apparently, the stairs to get down there are in this office?" He finishes with a question mark. Asking if what he was told is true, if the main breaker panel is downstairs from this office.

I know that it is because I've been down there. I don't know much about electrical work, but I know enough to recognize the gray steel box with all the switches inside. I know exactly where it is.

My first instinct is to lie, but I don't have the chance.

"Abby, you've been down there," Lilith says from behind my back. I didn't notice her leaving her office. Never notice her coming up behind me, she's so quiet.

"What did you say your name was again?" I ask him.

"Oh," he says and points to the patch sewn onto his coat that reads "Eric and Sons Electric." "Names Eric. Eric Erickson of Eric and Sons Electric. Junior. The first Eric is my dad but he doesn't get along so well anymore and my brother, well he never wanted to do anything with the business anyways so really it should just say 'Eric's Electric' since it's only me around here."

"So, Eric?" I ask.

"Yeah, that's me," he smiles that genuine smile again.

"So…" he leaves the second "s" off for once. "Where's this basement at?"

As charming as his ah-shucks demeanor may be, the last thing in the world I want to do is reopen that door. I look over my shoulder, wishing the door away or at least trying to come up with a passable lie. But Lilith is there, and she's already laying a finger in the direction of the stairwell.

"You shouldn't go down there," I say. "There's rats."

"Well, you should call an exterminator to handle those guys," Eric says. "Could be they're chewing on the powerlines. All the same, I better have a look-see. Don't want this place burning down around your head and shoulders!" Another line that he tells as a joke, regardless if anyone laughs or not.

Dread has devoured any humor I might have held inside me.

"You can show him, Abby. We can cover for you for a bit up here," Lilith says as if she's doing me some favor. As if there is some massive workload that takes the whole team to handle. As if our most difficult assignment isn't fighting off the boredom.

"That'd be great!" Eric says. "You know, I used to be a little bit scared of the dark. One time, when we was kids, my older brother, the one I was telling you about, he brought me down into the church basement and was telling me this story about how they took the naughty kids and walled them into the foundation. And Mike, that's my brother's name, he knew enough about electrical work by then that he'd explained to his friends how to flip the breakers and son-of-a-biscuit! Let me tell you when they cut the power–" he chuckles at his own joke again, and I feel obligated to laugh along with him.

"Yeah, I bet," I say.

His disposition, as bright as a spring day, melts much of the horrors lingering in my mind, but I'm still trying to come up with lies and excuses to keep us from going down those stairs. Lead in the walls. Asbestos. A gas leak. Anything better than rats! But Eric is already picking up his toolbox and walking around the counter for the back of the room. All I can do is follow him, whether I want to or not.

"Let me get the door," I say.

"No. Please. Allow me," he says.

"No. Really. The doorknob is tricky," I lie again, but win our little fight over who can be more polite.

A white lie. Just like the lie about the rats. Told to protect us. Nothing so severe as to call up evil wretches from the darkness. As I tell myself that, I hope I'm not telling another little white lie.

The knob twists without any hitch or kink. The door eases inward and I'm afraid to look.

"Oh geez," Eric says, the fear obvious in his voice. "It's darker down there than an Amish fashion show at midnight."

If one of us is a liar, it's not Eric. The light of the office only penetrates down maybe a half dozen steps before dying to the dim. From what we can see, there's no three-headed demon and no blood stains the shade of molasses either. Just a plain boring, metal staircase flanked by gray bricks on either side. I notice the scrapes left by demonic claws in the rusted, paint-flaking steps, but does he? Below the limits of the light, there's nothing, as if going any further equates to stepping out of reality and into an empty and infinite vacuum.

"There's some lights down there," I reassure him. And myself. "The old kind you turn on by pulling a string. Maybe that's something you can fix while you're here."

"Yeah. I think that'd be a good idea," he says, following me down the steps where the three-headed thing had just been. "Genius idea even."

I don't know all the rules with the demons. I've killed enough to know that when I kill one of them, that particular demon doesn't return. They're never the same, but they never run out either. After all, they are

Legion. When one of them retreats, like what just happened, how far does it retreat? Is that three-headed fright with all its horns and tongues still here in the tunnels, waiting in the shadows, lurking just beyond the light? We feel our way through the black to the bottom of the staircase.

The fear in my nerves doesn't make it any easier to find the pull string of the nearest lightbulb. Once I wrangle the old length of twine from the abyss, I hesitate. If I pull it, will I be face to face with another hellspawn? And what if by some hellborne magic, I can see it, but Eric can't? No doubt it could still tear him limb from limb or perhaps kill him in some other more subtle yet equally diabolical way; he'd just never see it coming.

It's a debate over what I fear more: the unknown horrors waiting in the darkness, or the stark terror of seeing what is down here with us. Eric is waiting, and I heard the waver in his jovial voice as we came down the steps. And I hear his fear now in his near-silent breaths. I give the string a gentle tug.

A dusty sixty-watt bulb snaps to life, and light shines on an empty stretch of hallway. All cinderblock walls, concrete floors, and conduits and pipes running overhead. The smell of burning dust on top of the bulb mixes with the tang of earth and the dryness of concrete dust. But there are no monsters.

"Okay," Eric says, the relief obvious in his voice. "Alrighty then. Let's just see what we have here."

And only then does he have the wherewithal to pull a flashlight from his toolbox. It's one of those new flashlights with an array of tiny LEDs, much brighter than the single incandescent lightbulb softly swinging on a cord above our heads. It blinds me for a moment as he whips it up to inspect the conduits. Pointed the way the beam is, it does nothing to pierce through the gloom further down the tunnel. While he examines the plumbing and electrical over our heads, my eyes and ears do what they can to anticipate what might be waiting for us wherever the wiring might lead.

"Just need to follow this conduit…" Eric says, keeping the beam of his flashlight trained on the guts between the overhead steel rafters, not watching where he's going, just following the old pipes.

The hallways aren't climate-controlled by any furnace or AC unit. They don't need to be. This far underground, below the frost line and surrounded by bedrock, the tunnels stay a constant, cool fifty degrees year-round. It could be a sweltering hundred-degree day in July or a negative thirty-degree night in February and the tunnels will remain right around fifty degrees, only fluctuating a couple ticks on the thermometer either way. That might make the tunnels alluring to some, a cool place in the summer and a moderate place in the winter, but not me. Not knowing what I know and having seen what I've seen.

Just as we move beyond the reach of the old bulb, we come across another. I tug on the cord, and we stand in another small island of light. When we turn a corner, just a few feet ahead, we're once again left with only the cold shine from Eric's flashlight. I wish I had grabbed my cell phone from my purse before coming down here. That way I could have my own light source and keep it aimed in front of us as we outwalk another island of light. But it's too late for that now. I'm completely reliant on Eric's light and the far-too-seldomly placed bulbs installed whenever these tunnels were last maintained.

"Here we are," he says.

The beam of his light waterfalls from the ceiling, along a wall covered in thick aluminum pipes, to several large gray metal boxes which I'm sure he'll tell me is the main panel. While he opens the box and examines its contents, I continue further down the hallway, my hands and palms outstretched and waving slowly through the air, hunting for the next cord for the next lightbulb.

"Oh yeah. Oh criminy. These things are ancient," Eric is saying behind me.

My hands grope through the blackness. There has to be another bulb here soon. I look back the way we came to measure the distances between each of the previous bulbs, and when I do, one of them bursts. Tiny bits of glass tinkle to the concrete, and we're left with a long and black leap between our intermittent islands of light.

"Just a surge in the power," Eric reassures me. Did I squeal or yelp when the bulb popped? I may have. "Problem is some of these old fuses are way overloaded. And them being fuses instead of circuit breakers, well, that's a whole other problem. You know my uncle used to take a penny and put them in those old round fuses. Dangerous as all heck, but it worked."

"I'm going to find another light," I say.

He returns his attention back to the panel and goes on about how outdated they are with the same fascination an enthusiastic coroner raves over a case of tapeworms bad enough to kill a man. Meanwhile, my hands continue to flail in the dark. I'm certain I'm near the spot where another light bulb ought to be. Still, there's nothing. Nothing but an electric buzz more felt in my veins than heard in my ears.

"Yeah, this is going to be a good amount of work," Eric is saying. I'm not paying attention. "New circuit breakers. More circuit breakers. Might as well install a whole new panel box while I'm down here. These ones are pretty old and rusted. Oughtta run new wiring while I'm at it."

Rather than my hand touching the string of another lightbulb, my foot kicks into something round and dry. It clatters down the tunnel, rolling and spinning across the gritty surface. The noise is enough to scare both of us, and this time I definitely let out a yelp. Eric spews out another one of those pseudo-swear words. He hangs onto the "f," and for a moment I think he's about to drop The Bomb. Instead, he says, "Fffffor Pete's sake."

"Sorry," I say.

"That's alright. Just gave me a start is all," he says. "Hey, yous guys should do like a Trick or Treat haunted house come Halloween. Wouldn't have to decorate or nothing."

"Yeah," I laugh because that's what his rambling is meant to do, defuse the tension. I'm still wondering what it was I'd kicked. It rattled against the concrete, dry and hollow like a human skull. A length of string brushes against my face, interrupting that rather unpleasant line of thinking. I back up and my hands find the twine quickly enough. Another held breath and I pull the cord. The bulb glows orange on another stretch of empty hallway. Whatever I kicked, it's beyond the reach of the bulb's shine.

Eric's attention is back on the panel. With a heavy sigh, he sums up his diagnosis. "This is gonna take me a few days."

"I'm sorry, what?" I ask, only a portion of the implications of what he said registering.

"Yeah. I mean, maybe if my dad and brother were here like the name of the company says we could knock this out in two, three days," he tells me. "But being that it's going to be just me down here… Probably be a full week or so."

"You can't be down here by yourself," I say, too suddenly and too sincerely.

He smiles at that. "Believe you me. The last thing I want to be is down here all by my lonesome, but I'm no superstitious little kid still afraid of the dark, ya know."

"Can't you just, you know, do a quick fix?" I ask. "I can stay down here with you for a little while but…"

"No, no, no," he says, phony machismo covering for his obvious fear of this place. He has no idea how afraid he should be. "I can handle it. And there's no way any of this is going to be a quick fix. Everything down here is so old, if I left any of it the way it is I could lose my license. Who's your building inspector anyhow?"

I shrug.

"I mean, if you want to stay down here and keep me company…"

I laugh at that. Not because anything is funny but because I'm nervous and some stupid part of my brain wants to pretend I'm not nearly as terrified as I am. But also, because, if I could, I would absolutely stay down here with this kind, handsome, folksy electrician with an easy smile and an obvious fear of the dark. But coming back late on my lunch break and spending a week away from my desk are two different things.

"Um. Well. What do you have to do today?" I ask as if tomorrow these tunnels will be any safer.

"Not a ton, honestly," he says. "I'm going to have to go back to the shop and get some parts and put in some orders before I can get started. You guys are probably going to want a quote too. Should I include wiring in some light switches down here while I'm at it?"

"Yes," I say with no hesitation. "And brighter ones too. Do that first actually."

"Okay," he says and that smile returns.

Maybe he's happy that I don't want him to be down here alone, or maybe because he wants better lighting down here even more than I do. Or maybe he's just always happy. His bright blue eyes lift my spirit.

Suddenly, I'm not thinking so much about what I kicked or what else might be down here or the tightness of my back. Suddenly, the only thing I want is more of him. To steal some of his innocence and use it to erase all the guilt and shame and fear in my life. I want to move in close to him and suck some of that joy straight from his lips.

"Alright. Well, let me do some more looking around down here and I'll write something up. I'll be fine down here doing just that today. Shouldn't take me more than a few minutes. Sound good?"

It doesn't. Not exactly. But it sounds better than him being down here indefinitely. "Okay," I say.

And having said that, there's not much more to say. I should go back upstairs now, in any normal scenario, and let him do his work. What else can I say to convince him to leave this place, abandon whatever money the county promised him to fix these power surges, and never come back down here? Nothing. That's what I can say, and that's all I do say as I walk backward away from him, toward the way we came.

"Just a few minutes," he promises.

"Wait," I say. "I should give you my number. Just in case the power goes out or you get turned around."

"Okay," he says, and that easy smile returns.

I read off the numbers to my cell phone, and he plugs them into his.

"Text me so I know you got it," I say. So I have his number too, in case something, anything happens. And maybe for other reasons.

"Done," he says and flips his phone around to show me that he's sent me a text that reads, 'This is Eric,'" and nothing more.

"Okay," I say, and now I have run out of things to say.

I make my way back to the staircase. My nerves shiver each time I step out of an island of light and into the ocean of darkness between the glow of the bulbs. Glass crunches under my boots where the bulb broke. When I turn the corner and I'm out of Eric's eyesight, I run.

Chapter Seven
Sister Time

The rest of the time Eric is in the tunnels, I'm a saint. Mother Teresa, Gandi, and Woodduck County's Employee of the Month all wrapped into one. I find projects to keep me occupied. I'm super polite and accommodating to anyone on the phone. I look for ways to be friendly toward Hank, even though he seems to want nothing more than to win his stupid casino computer games. I clean the coffee pot. I follow Paul, the janitor, through our office space and put new liners in all the trash cans so he doesn't have to. I wish him a good afternoon by name when he leaves. I do everything but look at my newly borrowed copy of HHR Eventide's "A Black Heart Unbroken."

The tension in my back that comes with encroaching demons is absent, which eases my anxiety, but doesn't erase it. The text Eric sent me never came through and I'm sure the soil and thick concrete between the tunnel and the surface are to blame. Of course there isn't cell service down there. But I'd feel a demon come before it reached him, wouldn't I?

What was I thinking of leaving him down there alone?

I can't go back down those steps, not without a good excuse, so I prop open the door leading to the basement with a trash can, and when I hear heavy boots tromping up the metal steps, I close my eyes and pray it's Eric.

"Okay," he says to the whole office. "Yeah. This is going to be a doozy."

My cell phone buzzes, and, sure enough, his text message finally comes through.

"So I'm gonna level with ya. Whoever cuts the checks for the county probably isn't going to like the number at the bottom of the quote I'm about to send," Eric says. "But I'm also here to tell ya that if we don't do the work, there's a good chance this whole building is going to burn to the ground, like, any day now."

"But it's all concrete and granite," I say.

"Sure. It's a concrete box…" Eric leads me, "…full of carpet and furniture and curtains and paper and people…"

"So you'll be back tomorrow?" I ask, already knowing the answer.

"It might take me a while to draw up the new wiring plans to get everything back up to code, but yeah, probably late tomorrow afternoon I can get to work," he says. "Did you get my text?"

I check my phone and confirm. "Yeah. I did."

"Cool," he says. By now he's brought himself and his toolbox around the counter and is back on the customer side of the counter. "So if I need anything…"

"Yeah." I return his smile. "Just shoot me a text if anything comes up."

"Cool," he repeats, and for a short while, I allow myself to believe that everything is what I have never been. Cool.

The rest of the workday passes without further incident. At quitting time, I collect my coat, hat, mittens, purse, and my copy of "A Black Heart Unbroken," and shuffle to my car.

At five o'clock, the sun is already touching the treetops on the western horizon. Soon it will be all dark and I'll be home with my book, my ax, and my basement. I don't drink anymore, but with a nice cup of tea, I'll have everything I'll need for a perfect evening at home.

What I'm going to do about Eric and the work he needs to do in the tunnels, I haven't quite figured out. Maybe I can convince the buildings department that whatever the price is on Eric's quote, it's too high. Surely the wiring isn't so bad that a granite courthouse that has stood for over a hundred years is going to go up in smoke if we put off upgrading the electrical for another six months to a year.

When I pull into the driveway, I admonish myself for still not taking down the Christmas lights, but I don't do anything about it. I'd have to drag a ladder out from the garage and trust it on the icy concrete. It's cold out, and if I'm being honest with myself, I kind of like how they turn the front yard into a kaleidoscope each night. Then I'm in my kitchen and I'm wishing the boy with his hockey pizzas was here now so I could have an easy dinner. But he's not, so instead of buffalo chicken pizza, I warm up some soup and start the electric kettle to make tea. I change into my pajamas. I eat my soup on the couch. Eventide's latest novel waits next to me.

My dishes are in the sink and my tea is on the end table next to my ax before I set the heavy book in my lap. Only silence rises from the basement. My back relaxes. All the ghosts rest. All the demons remain deep below. I crack open the front cover.

My doorbell rings.

For the second time in as many days.

But things have gone well since this afternoon, and I'm feeling optimistic. Maybe the hockey kid is back with my pizzas. I set my book aside, unfurl the blanket from my lap, and walk to the door. As soon as I twist the knob, the person on the other side shoves it wide open.

Zoey, looking half-frozen in her business suit and high heels, pushes past me and into my kitchen. Her shiny new blood-red Chevy Camaro is parked on the street, barely visible behind the mounds left by the snowplows.

"It's fucking freezing out there!" she swears and rubs her arms to warm herself.

I shut the door behind her to keep out the cold. As manic as her nature is, she doesn't allow a moment for me to say a thing.

"Okay, so before you start, I already know what you're thinking. 'What the hell is she doing here?' Well, let me tell you, this was not my plan."

"Okay..." I say.

"My plan was to come into town, say hi to my sister, get my damn birth certificate so I can prove to the government that I'm alive, and get back to my apartment for dinner," she tells me. "But apparently Woodduck County has other ideas."

Because of course they don't have an extra copy of her birth certificate just waiting for her up in the Records Department. Of course they'd have to have a new one printed. Of course that was my sister Eric saw yelling and swearing on the second floor. And of course, she would come here when they told her she'd have to come back tomorrow.

"But never fear," she says, "I come bearing gifts," and pulls a bottle of expensive-looking whiskey from a brown paper sack. "I'll get some glasses."

"Zoey..." I whine, but I know there's no stopping her. I can tell her I quit drinking till I'm blue in the face and it won't make a difference. She is a juggernaut, not just with me, but with everything she touches. Her car has no brakes, and I mean that metaphorically, but if she hauled me out to the speed machine parked in front of my house and showed me it only had one pedal, I wouldn't be surprised.

"Oh, don't 'Zoey,' me," she says as she ransacks my kitchen for two tumblers with the same finesse she'd exert on a drug raid. When she finds two short glasses with faded cartoons of Snoopy and Charlie Brown painted on them, not ideal for pounding whiskey, she turns to me and shifts her expression to one of sincerity. "Besides, I felt bad after this morning. I was rude. I shouldn't have asked you to compromise your integrity, especially at your place of work."

I can't tell if she's faking the sincerity or if she's being genuine. That's the thing about people like Zoey. You trust the biggest liars because they're good at it. When my shoulders slump, that's all she needs to know that she'll be spending the night. Her face lights up, and she goes to pour us both a drink.

"It's been too long since we've had some decent sister time anyway," she says. "And I know a lot of that is my fault. I'm the one who ran off and put everything into her career and only comes back home for funerals and birth certificates..."

Something about the irony of that catches me and I laugh as she hands me the novelty glass which is, as far as I can tell, full of straight whiskey and three ice cubes.

"What?" she asks.

"No matter how far you run, everything begins and ends in Woodduck," I say.

"Tell me about it," she says. When we clink our glasses Snoopy and Chuck smooch.

"Listen, Abbs, I didn't pack an overnight bag. Do you have some pajamas I can change into? This suit might look nice, but these pants have been climbing up my ass crack like an itsy bitsy spider up a waterspout all fucking day."

"Yeah. Sure. You know where to look in my closet," I say.

She goes, sipping her drink and shouting, "Praise the fucking Lord!"

While she's back in the bedroom, I move "A Black Heart Unbroken" off the couch and to the end table. Doubt I'll read a word of it tonight, which sort of makes my whole mad run through town today a waste of time. And if I hadn't gone on that journey, I probably wouldn't have had to face down the three-headed thing after my lunch break and probably would have felt a lot more relaxed with Eric this afternoon. Why am I not surprised when all the blame for my bad day leads back to Zoey?

I find the TV remote and turn on something dumb but visually stimulating, one of those shows featuring people falling off big foam obstacles into muddy water. I take a sip of what she's poured, and it burns like gasoline from my lips all the way down to my guts. I'm about to cough or gag or throw up as she trots back from the bedroom. I repress my reflexes.

She's wearing my pajamas, so how she looks so much better than I do, I have no idea. Zoey is older than me by six years. With her in her thirties and me still in my twenties, you'd think I'd finally be the sexier sister, but one look at her and I know better. Her body is fit, trim, perky…

She gestures to the end of my couch. "What are you, Paul Fucking Bunyan, now?"

The ax. Hopefully, I won't need that tonight, but then again, the first sin ever committed was fratricide.

"Never mind that," I say and haul it away so she doesn't ask any more questions. What is the right word for a sister killing a sister anyway? It's not fratricide. That's for brothers. Sororicide? I suppose that would be it.

"Oh my god, I love this show!" Zoey yells from the couch.

I take another pull from the drink and let it burn me from head to tail. A sweet and smooth bourbon. I wasn't always a teetotaler. Wasn't it the Son of God himself who turned water into wine? Besides, I'm in for a long night.

By the time I start my second drink, Zoey is starting her fourth. And when she tops off her glass, she adds no additional ice cubes. Just more whiskey. So now there's no ice cubes to dilute it and she's drunk. Her butt drops next to me on the couch. Whiskey splashes over her hand. The show switches to commercials.

"Why are we so different do you think?" she asks. "I don't mean that in a mean sort of way. But just... Why?"

"I don't know," I say. "You kind of just went and did your thing."

"And you chose to stay here," she summarizes my life in six words.

"Things aren't so bad here," I say. The lies are tallying up today, but for whatever reason, I haven't felt the threat of encroaching hellspawns since my lunch break.

"No. You're right," Zoey sighs. "We had some good times when we were kids. Dad gave us a lot of leash to run with."

"Especially those long summer nights we stayed out after dark," I say. "Playing hide and seek..."

"...throwing things at cars..." Zoey adds.

"...riding bikes..."

"...making out with boys..."

"...sneaking into abandoned houses..."

"Those houses weren't abandoned, Abbs," Zoey reminds me. "They were for sale. We were breaking into brand new houses and just occupying them like we were the new homeowners."

"Yeah, but it wasn't like we vandalized them or anything," I say.

"You always had a good head on your shoulders. As for me? I don't know how I left this town without a record," Zoey says.

"You and your friends... You guys were always so much cooler than I was," I say.

"Well, you were six years younger than me. It would have been a little weird if you were drinking cheap vodka and making out with boys the same time I was," Zoey says. "And don't tell me you didn't do those things after I left."

"By the time you left, Dad wasn't doing so hot. I was more of a parent to him than he was to me," I say. "And after I graduated? I felt bad just leaving him here, all by himself with nobody to look after him."

"Dad was a grown man," Zoey states what I already know.

"Yeah, well, he was our dad," I say, lamely.

"He was a drunk, a lay-about, a recluse…" Zoey says.

"You don't mean that," I say, but the alcohol has me feeling weak and I don't say it with any passion.

"You can believe whatever you choose to believe, little sis," Zoey says. "But you want to know why I left here and never came back? It was because there was nothing left for me to come back to."

That stings. Sharper than the bite of the whiskey.

"What I mean is, by the time I was in high school, Mom was gone, and Dad was so far into the bottle… I wanted nothing to do with what was going on in this house," Zoey says. "But you… Even after what happened to Dad, you still didn't move. Not even one block away. Still live in the same house, even after what happened here. Doesn't it bother you? The memories of how he died?"

"It's not so bad. Really," I equivocate. No. I don't equivocate. I lie. Yes, it bothers me. Yes, there are nights when I still see him there in his recliner at the far end of the couch. Yes, I keep the rug there because there are still stains on the carpet. Yes, it bothers me the hell out of me, is what I don't say.

"So why do you stay here?" Zoey says, seeing right through me. There's a little slur in her words, which makes me suspect that if I tried to articulate all my reasons, I'd slur too and come off sounding like an idiot.

I'd love to leave this town and never look back. Travel the world and actually physically see all the places I've only read about. But I have my reasons for staying here. All the normal boring reasons like the low cost of living, knowing people in town, having a job that I don't hate, and the fear of the unknown. Those kinds of reasons, and a much darker and immediate reason. Because whether I like it or not, I see myself as something of a guardian of the surface world. Because I've arranged my life in a very specific way so I can keep the demons down below. I am a watcher on the wall, a guard in the tower, a defender at the gates. And people like Zoey and Eric aren't making my job any easier. I can't say all of that to Zoey, of course, but I have to say something.

"I don't know," I qualify my answer, a habit I hate about myself. "Maybe that's just how I was raised."

Zoey blows a long raspberry. "Raised? We were *raised?* By who? The cancer took Mom out of the picture while you were still in kindergarten. And as for Dad? He didn't raise me as much as he gave me the motivation to leave. He was a drunk, Abby. He never paid any attention to us. Never brought us to basketball practices or band recitals or attended any parent-teacher conferences. All those things we did? We did by ourselves. I bought clothes with babysitting money. I bought us McDonald's when the frozen pizza ran out. And when I wanted something more than I could pay for? Well, I'm just happy the FBI doesn't review Walmart security footage from Woodduck, Minnesota when they do their background investigations. Cause I got a lot of shit back in the day for free ninety nine.

"And I know you dealt with the same shit. For fuck's sake, the only reason I felt bad about leaving this town was you, Abbs," my sister said. "At least with an older sister, you had somebody looking out for you. After I left, well, obviously things didn't get any better. So. I guess. What I'm trying to say is… I'm sorry. I shouldn't have left you here like I did. I should have taken you with me."

I shook it off. "You're making it sound worse than it really was. Dad drank and all that. But he never hit us. Never did anything sexual. Wasn't mean or verbally abusive, not to us anyway. He was just dealing with his own demons." Grief. Depression. Anxiety. Post-traumatic stress from his time in Iraq and Afghanistan. He never told me about what happened over there, but it seemed the only time he was happy was when he was at the VFW with other, old army guys, drinking and swearing. I got the idea that some of the things he saw over there followed him back home. Old, ancient things that had been buried under dunes of heavy sand and crawled all the way back to this very house where they germinate in our basement until they ripen into fully formed demons. Demons which I then inherited after his death.

"I'm sorry I left you here with him," Zoey repeats. "But I'll never forgive him for what he did."

The word "suicide" lingers in the air, unspoken.

"It's too bad what happened to Mom. It really is," Zoey says. "I know that fucked him up just as much as the deployments. I'm not saying he had life easy. But to say he raised us?" Zoey slurs. "My point is, little sis, Mom and Dad didn't raise us. No one did. We were raised by wolves."

I don't respond because I know there's no winning this debate. So instead, we sit on the couch and watch more stupid TV and sip our drinks and let the alcohol numb the pain. As Zoey's intoxication lulls her to sleep, she scooches closer to me, and before I know it, we're snuggled up together. As if we're real sisters who swap gossip and do each other's nails and all the rest of those things we've never done. I could resent the fact that the only time she's affectionate is when she's drunk. That would be the logical emotion to have. But these moments are too few and far between. So, when she rests her head on my shoulder and between snores mumbles, "Love you, little sis," I whisper back, "Love you too, big sis."

And the whiskey is working its trick on my inhibitions too. Because I want to explain myself to Zoey, to anybody, really. Without qualifications or apologies. Without white lies or half-truths. I hate the idea of relying on alcohol to get to a place where I'm emotionally vulnerable enough to tell the truth. After all, if Dad had figured out how to have real conversations without leaning on a bottle for support, maybe he would have gotten some help and maybe he'd still be around. And how Zoey doesn't see that, how she is so ready to drown her emotions in booze astounds me. We are victims of this drug. So why go back to it? And she has the gall to ask me why I stay here as if I'm the cowardly one still clinging to this town like a kid clings to her mother's skirt. She's the cowardly one, clinging to booze and fast cars and dumb guys who never stick around for long and a career that takes up all her time. She's the one who lacks the guts to stay in one place and stare down what really killed our Dad.

Because, "It wasn't suicide," I whisper only loud enough for Zoey to hear with her ear so close to my lips. But she's asleep and I know it. It's another brand of cowardice on my part. Confessing only when I'm certain my confession will fall on deaf ears. "I know he died with a hole in his head and a gun in his hand. And, yeah, I know it happened right over there, in the shadows, in his recliner in front of this TV. I remember finding him there, like that. Can't get the image out of my head. And yes, it bothers me every single day. What you don't understand is maybe his finger pulled the trigger, but it wasn't suicide."

It was just me and him in the house. And yes, Zoey, you're right about me doing most of the parenting by then. He had fallen asleep in the recliner that afternoon, so when I left that evening, I didn't disturb him. He was snoring, only a little louder and more ragged than Zoey is snoring now. Figured he'd be fine while I went out for dinner with coworkers. I don't even know why I checked the door to the basement. Maybe I heard the sounds of the demon's claws or felt the wringing of invisible hands around my back, not that I knew anything about demons back then. Whatever the reason, just before stepping out, I opened the door leading to the basement.

And that was when I saw a demon for the very first time.

At first, I thought it was a man. Some disfigured home intruder that had slipped into a storm window to find a place to sleep for the night. That alone was terrifying enough. But its handsome face, chiseled like a statue, was the only feature that was even vaguely human. Horns corkscrewed out from its temples, turning in tight twists across the span of the stairwell so the tips nearly scraped the walls. Black, wet, matted fur covered its shoulders. It was nude below its chest. A long penis swung against its thighs like the clapper of a bell. Wet and dripping viscous tar made splat splat splats when it dribbled onto the stairs. The demon moved slow as if each step was forced and painful. Hooves stomped against the wooden stairs.

This was no human being. It was a nightmare. An apparition. A hallucination. A thing that couldn't possibly be real, yet something that could certainly inflict great harm.

So, I did what anybody would have done. I told myself that it wasn't real, I shut the basement door, and I ran. Did my best to convince myself it was some hallucination or trick of the light. Did everything I could to forget all about it. And in the process, I let it come up from Hell and left our dad to deal with it.

If the demons make it to the surface, I don't think they always come to simply murder. They infect us. They taint us. They corrupt us. They ply our weak mortal minds into doing terrible things. The same sins that beckon them to the surface, they turn back on us. We are both addicts and victims of our worst inclinations. That night, the demon of apathy and sloth and selfishness and shame and self-hate climbed up our basement stairs and possessed my father. The demon killed him as much as the gun. And all I would have had to do to stop it was... anything. Literally anything at all. I could have screamed. I could have woken him up. I could have stood my ground. I could have used Dad's gun to blow its head off. I could have chopped it to pieces with an ax. Instead, I ran.

And when I came home and found Dad dead in his recliner, I knew it was my fault. I called 911. Sheriff Graham was the first on scene and pulled me away from the horrible thing my eyes beheld as if I was Lot's wife, turned into a pillar of salt, incapable of ripping myself away from the thing that was destroying me. I remember him telling me over and over again, "It's not your fault. It's not your fault." Those specific words. The very words I knew not to be true.

Since then, as a penance, I've been set as a watchman at the door between our world and Hell itself. And I don't complain. But I really wish I could tell someone about it.

"A demon killed Dad," I whisper to Zoey, but not so loud as to wake her up. "It came up from Hell, and when I had the chance to turn it away, I ran. I let it have its way with him while he slept. What happened to Dad, it was my fault.

"I want to leave," I go on. "God, how I'd love to leave this town and never think of the things that happened here ever again." I don't want to look into the dark corner of this room and see him sitting there, limp and lifeless and bloody and pale. I close my eyes and see his head tilting up to the ceiling and his wrist draped over the armrest, the gun still dangling from his fingers. Each time I see it, the memories are as fresh and crisp and terrible as if it just happened. Every time.

I remember a time not so long ago when his chair was still there, blood stains and all. It stayed there for a little while after he died because getting rid of it felt like getting rid of him. A little more of him. As if he hadn't been robbed from me wholly with a single squeeze of a trigger.

It wasn't until the night of the funeral. After Zoey left for the Cities. I was here alone, drinking to wash away the pain. In my double vision, I fixated on that recliner still sitting in the dark corner of the room, sort of like I am now. I was drunk, so emotions came easy. I was angry. I was frustrated. I was cheated. The ghost of his corpse still sat in that chair, as vivid as the night he died.

I did the only thing I could do. I went to the garage and found Dad's old ax hanging from a pair of nails pounded into the garage wall. I snatched it from its place, brought it inside, and loosed all my rage. The padding and the springs absorbed the first blows. The pine frame cracked and splintered underneath. As for the metal armatures and hardware, l spun the ax head around and bashed those pieces with the blunt end. I smashed the chair into the floor until it was nothing but shreds and pieces. All my anger and sorrow and sense of injustice, I poured into that old piece of furniture. I directed everything I had into that recliner. I swung and chopped and swung, numbed by booze, blinded by tears, and deafened by my own screams.

Didn't see or hear anything else, but I felt that now-familiar twist in my spine long before the demon reached the top step. When I opened the door to the basement, I didn't care if I was hallucinating or not. Can't even say what it looked like. If it had horns or wings or talons or tusks… I couldn't tell and didn't care. All that matters was that it was there. I wasn't afraid. No. I was grateful for that demon. I needed it there to be a victim of my rage. I wanted it there. Compared to that demon, the recliner got off easy.

After that night, the ax stayed next to the couch.

"I don't blame you for leaving," I tell Zoey. "I would have done the same thing. But I can't. Not anymore. Not ever."

It's not late, but the second glass of whiskey is enough for my head. Tomorrow, I'll wake up with a headache and a rot in my belly. The TV shows have only dwindled in intelligence, so I find the remote and the racket and flashing images die. I'm left in the silence of my house and my watch post. The green and red Christmas lights paint the living room like a vaudeville circus. No ringing from the doorbell. No scratching from the basement steps. At least there's that. I lean my head back on the couch and the sum of all those regrets and desires rise over the cusp of the levee. Tears stream from the corners of my eyes.

From below, Zoey's stomach makes an odd, gurgling noise. She burps in her sleep. Then her eyes blink open and she's pushing herself off of me.

"Ugh. Shit. Where's the toilet?" she mumbles.

"You know where–" I start.

"I'm gonna puke," she announces. Then she's up from the couch and staggering around the living room. "I'm gonna throw up. Give me a bucket. Where's the fucking sink?"

"No! Not in the sink!" There are dishes in the sink. I prepare my meals around the sink.

I grab her by the shoulders and corral her toward the bathroom. Her body convulses and bucks. Little spurts of vomit jet out of the corners of her lips and spritz the carpet. As soon as we're in the bathroom, I try to ease her down, but her knees crack hard against the floor. She flings the seat open just for it to bounce off the tank and smack her in the back of the head. She doesn't seem to notice, but I lift it off of her and try to gather as much of her hair as possible so it doesn't fall into the blue water and–

Zoey retches, and up comes a whole stomach's worth of bile and booze and stomach acid and whatever she had for lunch. Subway maybe? After the first surge is up and out and floating in the toilet water, she's huffing and sucking in air.

My cell phone rings. Of all the times for my phone to ring, why now?

"I'm good!" Zoey shouts, her words echoing from inside the bowl. "I'm okay. Go get your phone."

"You sure?"

"Yeah, I'm sure. Awwww, gawd," she says and dry heaves. Then, she yells, angrily, as if the ringing of my phone has done this to her, "Go get your phone!"

I leave Zoey with her face below the rim of the toilet and get over to the end table where my phone vibrates and rattles against the wood. Picking it up, I see Eric Erickson is calling me. Why would the electrician from work be calling me now, well after regular business hours? If something came up and he can't make it to the courthouse tomorrow, surely, he could have waited until morning to tell me or whoever it was at the county that hired him. I hesitate to even answer. After all, I'm dealing with things here. Zoey, dry-heaving in the bathroom, won't let me forget that. Still, there's a thrill in my chest that gets the better of my brain and before I know it, my thumb has tapped the "Answer" button.

"Hello?" I say.

"Awww gawd, Abby!" Zoey cries from the bathroom. "There's more! I'm–"

And then I hear that wonderfully delightful sound of bile and a half-digested cold cut exiting her body and splashing into the toilet water.

"Hi. Abby?" I hear Eric say.

I'm rushing back to the bathroom to help Zoey with her hair while saying, "Eric! Hi. I didn't expect to hear from you so soon."

"Ugh. Shit," Zoey is saying. "Fuck. Fuck me. I think I'm good now."

"Yeah, sorry to call you kind of late," Eric says. "Is it a bad time? Do you got a minute?"

"Yeah, no. Of course. What's up?" I try to sound cool.

"Nope. Not done yet," Zoey says. As she retches up another gallon of puke, I'm leaning as far away from her as I can while still holding her hair, hoping the noise doesn't span the distance between the toilet and the phone's speaker.

"Okay. Cool," Eric says, oblivious to what's happening on this end of the line. "So, this might come off as kind of forward, but I'll be honest with you. I've done the whole dating thing and being coy and all the nonsense for a while now, so I'm just going to be straight with you. If that's okay."

"I think that's it," Zoey says through a hoarse throat. "Abby, you're pulling my hair."

"Um… Okay," I say to Eric because too much is going on for me to think of any real response.

"Yeah. Okay. Here goes." I can hear Eric building up his courage for what is both obvious and impossible. "Sos I feel like we kind of hit it off today and tomorrow night Woody's is doing a meat raffle and's got two fer one domestics, so what do you think if me and you meet up someplace after work tomorrow night? Say for a beer or whatever?"

More dry heaves from Zoey, which still require her to plant her face below the rim and me to hold her hair but are thankfully much quieter.

"Um… Like on a date?" I say.

"Well, yeah, if you want to call it that, I guess. But it doesn't have to be anything serious," Eric says. "There's a pull tab box at Woody's I've had my eye on. It's getting low but all the big winners are still in the box, sos how about we swing in and split a pitcher and see how it goes? Whattaya say?"

"Yeah. Sure. That sounds… cool," I say.

"Alright. Yeah. Great then. Alright. See you then," Eric says. "Or, well, I suppose I'll see you at the courthouse tomorrow too."

"Yeah. For sure. See you then," I say, doing my best in this clumsy exchange. Despite Eric's straightforward approach, it feels no less awkward than being asked to slow dance at a middle school spring social.

"Yeah. See ya then," he says and mercifully ends the call.

Meanwhile, Zoey has collapsed sideways off the toilet and is leaning against the bathtub. Her scalp and forehead are wet with sweat. Her lips and chin are wet with throw-up. Her eyes swirl before uncrossing and meeting mine.

"Why are you smiling?" she says. "Did somebody just ask you out?"

I clutch my phone tight and nod vigorously.

"That's my baby sister!" she shouts and shoots her wet hand up for a high five. Regardless of whatever is making it glisten, I smack it.

Chapter Eight
Date Night

All day long, I'm dreading Eric showing up to the office. Because when he shows up several things might happen, none of which will be good.

First and most inevitably, he'll go back down into the tunnels where he'll have no cell phone coverage, and I'll have no ability to keep him safe from the demons.

Second and almost worse, I'll either have to confirm the plans we made last night and commit to meeting him at Woody's where I know there will be drinking, an irresistibly charming man, and no basement…

Or, third, I'll cancel on him, go straight home after work, sit on my couch with my ax at the ready, and finally get started on my book.

That's what I should do. That would be the smart thing to do, but that's not what I want to do. Eric is sweet, and if I cancel on him, I don't know if I can come up with a believable excuse that won't crush him. After all, he stuck his neck out asking me out last night, and it's not like I don't like him. I do. He's kind. He's cute. He's funny, or at least he thinks he's funny, which is somehow much more charming than if he were an actual comedian. He's an old-fashioned townie, happy with meat raffles and pull tabs. The kind of guy Lilith rolls her eyes at. He works with his hands and can make sure the lights always stay on. In a lot of ways, he reminds me of Dad. Dad when he wasn't so far into the bottle. The dad I remember playing dolls with on the carpet and scribbling crayon drawings together on the dining room table. Dad during the good memories that Zoey can't seem to, or chooses not to, remember. Or maybe just an idealized version of the dad I never had. The dad I wish he'd lived to become.

But also the complete opposite of Dad. Someone open and optimistic and bright and happy. Someone the world never got a chance to grind down to all his worst facets. Someone not like me. Eric is the kind of guy who could make Woodduck feel like home again. Or maybe I'm building him up too much in my mind. Gluing expectations onto him that he can't possibly live up to.

Not that I deserve any of that. Because the truth is, I made the bed I'm sleeping in. My actions, or my inactions, have led to the mess I'm in. If I were strong enough, if I was pure enough, if I was brave enough, things would be different. Why would a guy like Eric want to be with a woman like me anyhow?

Zoey and I said our goodbyes this morning, promising each other to "do this again soon." Although I have to admit, I don't know what "this" is. Dumping our emotional baggage on each other while in various states of consciousness until one of us pukes in a toilet? I can think of other things I'd rather do. But she has plans to swing into the courthouse as soon as she's ready, pick up her birth certificate, and head back south. No reason to hold our awkward goodbyes at my place of work. So, we do it before I leave for work, while she's still hungover and I still have fog in my vision.

Which leaves me alone with my thoughts and my worries. Eric said he had to draw up some plans and make some orders this morning and wouldn't be around until the afternoon. I was going to use my lunch break to run over to The Book Bazaar and buy my own copy of "A Black Heart Unbroken." But if I do that, there is a chance that Eric will show up and go down into the tunnel while I'm gone. He'd be helpless without me around to keep him safe. So, I'll have my lunch at my desk. I can pick up the book after work, before the date. If there is a date. If I don't cancel beforehand.

In the meantime, I do my best to focus on my job. I'm churning through spreadsheets and data, creating reports no one is asking for, which, even if anyone ever looks at, will offer little insight on how to better manage the county's fees and revenues. But let no one say I'm not being diligent and hardworking and virtuous, and that Woodduck County isn't being financially transparent. Because a big part of my strategy is to give the demons no reason to come crawling up those stairs behind me.

But something is pulling me away from the numbers and functions on the monitors in front of me. A nagging thing I can't pluck from my mind and discard. Something red and irritating only partially protruding above the skin like an ingrown hair my tweezers can't get a hold of.

I try not to think about the night when I found my dad dead in his recliner. As soon as I do, the image of him sitting there, limp, and lifeless returns in complete clarity. No details left out. I'd prefer to jab a steak knife into my thigh rather than intentionally remember that night. But there is one detail I've tried not to forget.

When I first came home, before I pulled my car into the garage, when that first snowfall left me with the impression of innocence before the fall, I noticed tracks leading from our front door, down the walk, and beyond the curb where they were swallowed by the slush of the street. Work boots with big waffle treads cleanly pressed into the otherwise unblemished snow. I remember thinking that Dad must have gone for a walk. Of course, I forgot all about the prints after finding him the way he was. How could I think of anything besides how quickly the man I'd known since birth had been reduced to a horrific, traumatizing mess of body and blood?

I didn't recall the tracks until later. After I called 911 and Sheriff Graham and EMS and everyone else showed up. Sheriff Graham, he pulled me out of the house and was holding me in the driveway as I sobbed and wailed under the red and blue lights of ambulances and cop cars. All those lights, they were starbursts in my vision, but I wiped my tears away and saw clearly for one brief moment. Over the leather shoulder of Sheriff Graham's jacket, I saw those footprints again. In my hysteria, I fixated on them.

A single set of tracks, starting at the front door and leading away from the house.

For a moment, I allowed myself to believe it wasn't suicide, and it wasn't the demon I'd seen in our stairwell. That it had been a normal human murderer. That whoever left those marks had killed my father. But there was no evidence of anyone coming inside the home. Only leaving.

In the days and weeks that followed, Sheriff Graham was exceedingly patient and tolerated my irrational pleas. Told me that maybe someone had come to the front door, rang the doorbell just for no one to answer, and left, laying his departing prints overtop of his arriving ones. Maybe a visitor came just as it started snowing, stayed long enough for some snow to accumulate, and then left. Maybe I imagined the footprints entirely. There are a thousand reasons that could explain what I saw that day. None of which satisfied me.

The police report. The coroner's report. Fingerprints on the gun. Powder burns on my dad's hand. The line between the entry wound in his mouth and the exit wounds in the top of his head. All the evidence I'd taken in with my eyes besides those lone tracks in the snow. They all collaborated: The cause of death was a self-inflicted gunshot wound.

My dad died alone. By suicide.

So who left our house that night by the front door?

A question I could never let go. Even as the rows and columns and numbers of my latest spreadsheet paint my dull eyes an electronic gray.

Around two in the afternoon, my phone buzzes next to the empty sandwich bags of my brought-from-home lunch. It's a text.

"Hey its Eric. Wont make it to the courthouse this afternoon. A customers furnace went out so I'll have to pasteurize that. Should be there tomorrow."

Then after a very short pause, he texts, "*Prioritize"

"OK," I type back. It's easy to hide my overwhelming relief via text.

"We still on for tonight?"

And here's my chance to get off easy. All I have to do is a little wiggling of my thumbs and I can let him down softly and avoid both of the things I was dreading today. Won't even have to look him in the eyes when I crush his hopes. I start typing.

"Sorry. Something came up." But what? What in my boring, isolated life could possibly come up? I delete the text and try again.

"There's something I have to tell you," I type and then immediately delete again. There is too much I'd have to tell him. Too many things I can't explain, and he couldn't possibly believe.

"Maybe we should just stay friends." Delete. That one is the stupidest response yet. It wasn't like going out for pull tabs and beer equaled anything more than friendship. And the thing is, up here in Woodduck, there's not a ton of opportunities for starting relationships. I'm sure where Zoey lives, it's as easy as opening up Tinder or Bumble or any of those other apps and swiping until you find someone to share a night with. Up here? At my age? Everyone has either gotten married and had kids or moved away. Going out with Eric is by no means an act of desperation, but I'm well aware that if I turn him down, I'd be burning one of the very few bridges off my island of isolation. I'm also well aware that if I don't turn him down, I'll be opening myself up for him to crush my soul someday down the road.

There is no good answer. No viable excuse. No real reason to say no. So, after what I hope isn't too many times of those three little dots appearing and then disappearing on his phone, I hammer, "Sure. What time?" into the keyboard and hit send before I can change my mind.

"Hows 7?" he is quick to reply.

I text him a thumbs up because even just texting with him has me nervous that I'll screw something up.

Leaving work, on my way home to get ready for the first date I've had in years, I forget all about stopping by The Book Bazaar.

Maybe I should have shown up late. Fashionably late as they say. Maybe I should have called Zoey for advice on when to arrive, what to wear, and what to say. But who am I kidding? It's going to be another six months to a year before I see her again. So, I wear jeans and a nice but uninteresting blouse and walk into Woody's ten minutes early, because punctuality is a virtue.

What my virtue earns me is that wonderful feeling of telling the server that I need a table for two, that I'm waiting for someone else to show, and then sitting all by myself suffering through the very real possibility that I only needed a table for one all along. When my server meets another server at the little touchscreen where they punch in the orders, I know they're talking about the poor woman at Table Nine who's being stood up and how it's a waste of available chairs. How, if it wasn't for that solitary woman, they could seat four at that high top.

Did I hear Eric right last night? A lot was going on during that call, but I'm pretty sure he said "Woody's." And when I check through the text messages, I see that, yes, we agreed to meet at seven, and it's only six fifty-three right now. But nowhere during our texts did we mention the location. Should I text him to make sure I heard right and that he's not waiting for me at some other bar in town? It isn't like there's a lot of other options. Maybe Walter's Supper Club? The VFW? Subway? I check the time again. Six fifty-seven. Seriously? Could he not show up three minutes early to keep me from enduring this self-inflicted anguish?

But I remind myself, tonight is all about endurance. Sustaining a sociable exterior while maintaining a virtuous interior. Getting by. Suffering through. Weathering the storm. That's the goal. Never mind all the other goals a normal person might have when it comes to dating. Impressing the other person, starting a healthy relationship off on the right foot, maybe even getting laid… all of those things sound beyond fantastic. But I'm also keenly aware of the lack of accessible basements not just in this building, but in any building in a three-block radius.

Woody's is a nice place. Despite it being one of the only three bars in this town, I haven't seen the inside of the place in a long time. It's been renovated since then and feels more like one of those modern, urban, hipster breweries than a small-town dive bar. It was a small-town dive bar, and for the majority of my lifetime, it was a dump. Wood panel walls. Lopsided pool tables. Crushed popcorn kernels all over the floor. Old taxidermy. Big, vinyl, beer banners adorned with bikini models who would never be caught dead in a town like Woodduck. But not anymore. Artistic, historical black-and-white photos of Woodduck during its logging boom and iron mining heyday hang on the walls. A neon sign spelling "Woody's" in glowing cursive gives the place a lively Americana vibe. The ancient, felt-worn pool tables are gone along with the vinyl beer and bikini girl banners. In their place are big oak picnic tables, a pair of cornhole boards, a shelf full of board games, and a big stack of those oversized Jenga blocks. There's a small stage in the corner, and a man with a beard and an acoustic guitar is playing cover songs about trains by Cash, Dylan, and Marley. The place isn't packed but populated by more than just barflies. There's a family here, complete with a pair of kids playing with those Jenga blocks. And the food actually looks good! Through a window to the kitchen, real cooks in white uniforms work the grill instead of just a bartender forced to operate a fryer. The whole atmosphere is bright and communal and social and fun.

Dad would have hated this place.

All the same, I'm tempering my optimism and reminding myself that I might be, at this very moment, getting stood up. I keep in mind that even if I don't get stood up, the worst may come true and I might unleash literal, not metaphorical, *but literal hell* upon this place. I about have myself convinced that the best thing to happen just might be getting stood up when Eric walks through the door. He's wearing the same coat he wore yesterday, a flannel under it, a pair of jeans, and the smile that might be sewn to his face. He's casual, relaxed, and happy-go-lucky like a yellow lab. When he spots me, he gives me a little wave and heads my way. His easy temperament is already melting the tension.

"Sorry I'm running late," he says as he sits down at the high top table across from me. "That customer's furnace was a real antique, let me tell ya. Took me a bit to get her back up and running, but no worries. Ol' Miss Andersen will be nice and toasty warm for the rest of the winter."

"I thought you did electrical work," I say.

"Yeah. Nah. Little bit of everything. Especially with older clients, it's as much of a favor to them as real business. But that old bird, she doesn't have much, so I try to do it for as little as possible. And whatever I eat for fixing her furnace on the cheap, I'll just upcharge the county for swapping out their old fuse boxes to make up for it," he says and gives me a subtle look that lets me know there's something of a joke in that.

His eyes, there's always something of a joke in those blue eyes. Like they've never known melancholy. I find myself wondering how things as simple as eyes could express so much personality and history, and then I wonder what he sees in mine. And then I realize that he's waiting for my response. That I've lost myself for a moment.

"Charge them whatever you want," I say, shaking away the fugue. "I think you've earned it for having to work down in those tunnels."

"Those are creepy, huh?" Eric says. "You know, I've never really been comfortable in the dark. I think I told you that story about how my older brother Mike got me good by flipping the breaker in the church basement, right?"

"Yeah," I say. "My older sister, she's a character too."

And just like that we're swapping childhood stories and telling jokes as naturally as if we'd known each other for twenty years instead of two days. I tell him about the time Zoey tricked me into eating dog food by putting it on top of my ice cream. He tells me about the time when he and his brother got into real big trouble by borrowing their dad's tools and breaking into the old Paramount theater just to swap out the bulbs and get the old marquee up and running again. When the server comes, she's outgoing and polite and asks what I'd like, and I tell her whatever Eric's having. She comes back with two giant frosted mugs of light-colored beer with green olives floating in the foam. Maybe I quit drinking for a while, but I can recognize a Minnesota martini when I see one. The beer goes down easy, and I find myself mesmerized by the olives bobbing and sinking like bathtub toy submarines. And by Eric's simple charm.

"How have we never met before?" I interrupt him mid-story. Rude, but the question came at me suddenly and demanded an answer.

"Run in different circles, I guess," Eric says. "I left town right after high school and just came back last year to help Dad out with the business."

"I'll leave Woodduck. One day," I say but don't elaborate.

All my fear and guilt and regret remain far away. That is until I hear myself laugh at one of his lame jokes. I've never liked my laugh. A boy in high school called me a donkey just once, and that was all it took to hate it ever since. And when I hear it now, the hee-haw hee-haw of it, I hate myself all over again. Not because of how I sound. Or, not *just* because of how I sound. But because I know I don't deserve this. I shouldn't be here. I shouldn't be as carefree and casual as I am. Cause most often, the harbinger of demons isn't the sound of claws climbing up the steps as much as it is the pang of guilt in my heart and that twist of my backbone. The ache of shame. The feeling of injustice I don't acknowledge just so I can keep on going with my life after abandoning my father to that horrid thing that came up from the basement. I know if I'm out on the town, drinking, laughing, flirting, having a good time, that means I'm not at my watchtower. That I'm recommitting my original sin of neglect and selfishness and cowardice. And like a self-fulfilling prophecy, the knowledge of my wrongdoing only deepens the severity of my sin. The longer I sit here, smiling and giggling and batting my stupid eyes at Eric, the more the sin festers.

God, I want to ignore the feelings building up inside of me. I want to be numb from it so I can't feel the corkscrew twisting into my spine like it's ready to rip a vertebra out like a cork from a bottle. I want to be like the people around me. I want to live a life free of consequences. I want to be normal. I can't begin to describe how bad I want to give in to all my worst desires and stay here with Eric and drink and get drunk and let him bring me back to wherever he lives and let him do whatever he wants to me.

And then I add a new sin to the list. I'm hungry for his physical body. I'm horny. I'm wet for him. It's been far too long since I've been with someone, and once the possibility of scratching that primary itch has entered my mind, there's no getting rid of it. It's not even that I want to get laid so much as I want to be the kind of woman who gets laid. I want to be as driven and willing to go out and get what I want as Zoey. I want to be as laid back and casual as Eric. I want to forget the past and what evils might lie in wait in the future and just be here and have fun and let my desires and emotions take me where they may.

I can't stay here but I can't escape either. The truth is, either I'm going to sprint out the door and deal with my demons, or spend the rest of the night with Eric, wherever he chooses to take me, and let the rest of Woodduck deal with whatever comes up from below. But if I do the right thing and grab my ax from the car and find the nearest basement, what can I tell him? How can I leave without hurting him and embarrassing myself? Even if it's the opposite of how I truly feel, running out the door will send a very clear message that I'd rather be anywhere but here.

"Sos I says to him, I don't care if we have to work all day. We're gonna be done by quittin' time!" Eric puts the punchline on a joke, but to say my attention was waning is more than an understatement. I laugh anyway and hate how my fake laugh sounds so much prettier than my real one.

Maybe Eric will be heartbroken if I leave. Maybe he'll brush it off and find another lady friend as quickly and carelessly as Zoey finds her bed partners. By now, it's clear that none of that matters. Either I leave here, and leave right now, or unspeakable horrors will surface, and when they do, people will die. I check my phone for text messages that aren't there. I look around for the server so I can pay my half of the tab. I fidget. I check my phone again.

"Everything okay?" he asks, but I can barely hear him over the imagined sounds of talons climbing up steps. Claws, evil and strong, are ringing my vertebrae dry like a damp rag.

"Yeah. No. I'm having a great time. It's just..." I search for answers but knowing what I know, that hellspawns are, right now as I sit at this table, far too close for comfort, I can't come up with a single excuse. "It's just..." I check my cell phone again, implying someone is contacting me with some emergency.

"If you gotta go, that's okay. I mean we just got here but–"

"Yeah. I gotta go. Sorry," I say, already gathering up my coat and purse. There's no time. I can feel those evil beasts rising up as if the whole town is ready to boil over with them. I can't delay another second. "Another night. I promise. It's just that..." and I'm already away from the table calling back to him over my shoulder. "Something came up!"

I stiff him with the bar tab. Add another misdeed to the list. I only had a few sips anyway. The upside of that is that I'm in no way intoxicated for what I have to do next. I'm as clear-headed as I've ever been. Rushing to my car and falling into the driver's seat, I see the handle of my ax resting against the passenger's seat. It's ready. I'm ready. Now all I have to do is get to a basement in time to do what I do best.

Chapter Nine
The Courthouse at Night

The pressure grinding away my spine and the urgency coursing through my veins tells me I don't have much time. The thin tires of my Chevy Volt hatchback spin on the ice as I back out of the parking space and try to go forward. I'm doing the math in my head. My work is three blocks away. My house is eight blocks away, with as many stop signs between here and there. The difference might only be a minute. Seconds even, but every second counts. When I slide to a stop in the slush at the intersection of Main and Hill Road, a force pulls me north like a magnet to a loadstone and I know which way I'm going. Without a turn signal and without coming to a stop, I veer right for the courthouse. The rear end of the car slips and skids as I turn, but I stay on the gas. As I bear down on Highway 210, I'm looking both ways but I'm not stopping here either. In front of the granite edifice where I work, the tires slip, and I bury the front headlight in the snowbank.

Because the car stopped moving, the gas engine cut out. It's quiet for a moment.

No lights shine from inside the old Beaux-Arts courthouse. The key to the front door is on my ring. I grab my keys and the ax. There's no movement outside of the courthouse, which is good. If the demons have made it up the tunnels, my best bet is to contain them inside the building. If I can stop them, everything will be okay. Trudging up the steps in my boots, careful of the ice, I'm trying to creep and not let them know I'm coming. The keys jangle against the metal door frame as I unlock it. The heavy door thuds loud behind me. So much for stealth.

Inside, the air is stiff with silence. Outside, the wind found pathways through my alpaca hat and whistled in my ears. The rustle of leafless oaks rattled like bones in a coffin. But in here even the dead don't stir.

I peel off my mittens and hat and drop them where I stand. That's become habitual now. My coat is next. It might be negative twenty outside, but I feel like I've stepped into a furnace. The wide corridors are dark. The "EXIT" signs reflect off the polished granite floors, painting the interior a hellish red. Slowly, clutching my ax tight, I make my way toward the Accounts Receivable office. The familiar, oversized oil paintings of the history of Woodduck loom over my shoulders. The eyes of white settlers trading with Dakotah Indians follow me as I go. The wet rubber soles of my boots squeak against the smooth granite. I try to change the way I walk, but it's no use. Still, I stifle the noise of my own breathing and creep to my office doors.

They're supposed to be locked anytime the department is empty. I have the key ready to unlock it, but as soon as I rest my weight on the handle, it unlatches and eases inward. Not a great sign. The department is dark. Hank's monitors glow blue with a screensaver. I move toward the back, thankful that enough ice and water have come off my boots to walk without squeaking each step along the way. I slip around my desk so I can see the door to the stairwell from a distance. It's wide open. The depths of its maw are impenetrably black.

My nervous hand digs my phone from my purse. The unlock button is stubborn with my wet thumbprint. My eyes flick back and forth between that pitch-black stairwell and the keypad as I hammer in the PIN. My phone unlocks and I find the flashlight app.

"Please oh please oh please, still be down there," I mutter because I know I've called them up. There's no doubt in my mind about that, and for once I'm praying to find something there, something terrible and gruesome and murderous halfway up the steps. I tap the flashlight icon and aim it down.

Electric white light stabs into the black. Nothing.

"Oh fuh… Oh shiii… Oh no no no." I never swear. Never. At least not since Dad died, but I want to swear now. Zoey reintroduced those words into my vocabulary. This is her fault.

Lowering the beam of my flashlight only gives me more reason to cuss. Something has left fresh scrapes in the flaking paint of the steps. And there are black droplets splattered against the tiles as if the demon bled creosote while slouching across the office.

The black splotches lead me out of the door I just entered and back to the main corridor. A mound rests motionless in the center of the hallway near the entrance. It's small. Small enough to be the body of a child. Denial hits me first. Then shock like ice water doused over my head that runs in rivulets all the way down to my feet. A dread that I'm already too late and the demon has already killed. But the pile in the hallway is just my discarded things. Nothing more evil than a coat, a hat, and a pair of gloves. Yet.

Because I know something came up from the tunnels, and I know it's still here. I can feel it in my bones. It's tugging me along like the thread of sutures pulled from a not-yet-healed wound. As much as I'd like to ignore it and pretend there's nothing inside this old building and go back to Eric and apologize for running off, I know there truly is something to fear. A demon of my own making. A demon only I can unmake. Following that impending sense of doom, I retrace my wet footsteps back toward the front entrance of the courthouse. My boots are dry now and silent against the granite. I grip and regrip the wooden shaft of the ax as I cross my discarded coat, hat, and gloves. The grain of hickory feels good in my fingers. Much better than the clench strengthening its grip on my back.

A rage builds inside of me. I've always retained the upper hand with these demons. I've never let one past me. Never surrendered the surface to one of them. Besides the one that killed my father. But never since then. Now, at least one of them has emerged from its abyss and is stalking through these corridors. A thing that doesn't belong in this world. Maybe more than one thing. But I swear on my life I'm going to put them all back to bed.

Something screeches or squawks up ahead. In the dim red glow of the EXIT lights, I can't see it, but that something is clicking sharp and slithering wet just beyond my vision. The clatter of scalpels on a stainless-steel table accompanied by the slurping of an afterbirth squirming free from the womb.

I quicken my pace, taking longer strides. It's around the corner, headed toward the back of the courthouse. There are exits there as well. Too many exits now that I think about it. It's a big building and I'm sure fire code mandates all these doors, but they're not doing me any good now.

I'm almost running when I turn the corner, only reigning in my strides to stay silent, hoping to catch this unholy beast by surprise. When I turn the corner, it's not waiting for me in ambush. It's running from me. Or crawling. Slithering. Not out a door but up the stairs. There, on the second landing, before the flight doubles back to the second floor, I spot something twisting and swirling through the thick granite banisters. Something black and wet and long. The phalange touches the hourglass-shaped banisters like a tongue running over teeth, tasting each one as it goes.

From the foot of the stairs, I see that trailing tongue-like appendage, but I can't see what it's connected to. Forgoing any pretense of stealth, I charge up the stairs, my boots hitting hard against the steps. I'm eager to draw its attention, to stare it in the eye, to put it back in its place. Am I afraid? God damn right, I'm afraid. But I've earned my sentence of defending the surface from these demons. And at this point, death is not the worst thing I could suffer. It's failure.

When I start up the second flight, hoping to catch a glimpse of this thing before I'm facing it, tooth-to-ax, it's a step or a slither ahead of me again, disappearing around the corner and only trailing its black mamba-like tail behind it. Terrified but undeterred, I chase it up to the second floor. When I reach the top and once again turn the corner into the second floor's central corridor, I see it fully, bathed in the red glow of the EXIT lights, and any courage I have drains away like water from a bathtub.

The leviathan takes up the whole width of the corridor. It glistens like molasses but is plated in segments of hard carapace. How many limbs it has, I have no time to count, but it's way more than four. A dragon-like head sways on the end of a neck that is at least ten feet in length, hoisting the head high so it brushes the ceiling. It has no tongue or teeth as far as I can tell, but a beak like an eagle, large and sharp enough to snap my torso in two. That tail I'd seen earlier dances behind its mass like a king cobra rising from the wicker basket of a snake charmer. The demon is ready for me, and all I have to use against it is a stupid ax.

And my rage.

This is the thing that has trapped me in my own town, has kept me a prisoner in my own home, has turned me into a recluse, has stilted my career, has isolated me from my sister, and has killed my father. It or one of its ilk.

Claws like a lobster's tip the snake-like limbs. They dance and spread open so they can snap through me when they strike. When one of them lashes at my head, I swing back. My ax blade cleaves into the limb just beyond the claw and sinks through the plate armor and into flesh. That towering head screeches loud enough to make my ears bleed. Its voice is impossibly high pitched, yet gravelly, raw, and full of fear. The thing squirms back another ten feet away from the stairwell, me, and my ax.

The ax head drips melted tar onto the clean granite floor. The claw dangles from its wounded limb on threads of sinew, not severed, but no longer useful. Its other limbs gyrate as if waiting their turn to launch a strike. Its head hangs back, afraid to come near me and risk its long scaly neck. This is the largest demon I've ever faced, and I have it on the ropes. Despite all its lethal appendages and razor-sharp beak, it's cowering from me.

It lets out another shriek, this one shorter and not so tormented, but not at all pleasant. It slithers back another five feet.

"Come on!" I yell at the thing, taunting it, urging it to make a mistake and send another lame, single attack. Because there's no way I can withstand an attack if it sends all of those claws at me all at once. The only way I can keep this up is if it attacks piecemeal, only daring one part of itself at a time. If it commits…

It's a trick. A feint. Never before has any of these damnations shown fear. Never have they withheld their advance for the surface. Never before has one backed down. And this one isn't either. It's not backing down; it's holding back. This monstrosity isn't afraid of me and my stupid ax. It's drawing me deeper into the second-floor corridor. I'm being lured away. From downstairs. From the front door. From the stairwell where this thing came. From where others might come. And it's doing it on purpose. As it continues to slip and slither backward, I stop my feet. When I take two steps back, that dragon beak hisses at me. Now it's the one beckoning me to fight, and I know engaging with it is exactly what I shouldn't do.

The idea of turning my back to this creature is not a welcoming thought. If it wants, it could shred me to pieces as fast as wheat in a threshing machine. But I have to get back downstairs and block the front door. Because now that I'm paying attention, I feel the sensation of at least one other demon coming up from below, lurching toward the exit and the outer world. I should have been paying attention! I shouldn't have allowed myself to become so distracted! How did I let this abomination outsmart me? How could I have been so stupid?

I can't show my hand before I make my move, but undisciplined, I throw a glance over my shoulder. The leviathan bellows another high-pitched keen, and for the first time since I spotted it, it draws closer to me. No more waiting. No more feigning ignorance. I know what it's trying to do, and it knows what I'm about to do. So I do it. I bolt.

Holding the ax one-handed, I rush down the stairs like floodwaters pouring over a dike. It's all I can do to land my feet in the middle of a step so as not to snap my ankle and crash in a twisted pile on the landing. When I grab the round, granite newel post and whirl to the lower flight, I see the demon not far behind me. Almost in striking distance. And the way it's built, just a hub of tentacles, not something that moves on legs or feet, it has no need for stairs. Instead, it spills over the railing from one flight of stairs to the next, trying to cut me off. But I'm already running and falling to the first floor. I don't let go of my ax, because the truth is, once I make it to the front door, there will be another demon there for me to fight. At least, I hope.

I wheel around the corner to the main corridor of the first floor and see it. The second of the two demons. The one that the leviathan at my back doesn't want me to notice. The one trying to escape the courthouse for the wider world.

This fresh spawn from Hell crawls over my discarded coat, hat, and gloves. It is a thick, almost shapeless thing, like a ribbed, pale sausage. A thousand tiny bug-like legs protrude from all over its skin like prehensile in-grown hairs emerging from festering pores. It turns what should be its face toward me. I can't tell if it has any eyes or ears or nose. Its whole end is a round, puckered, sphincter of a mouth. When the orifice opens, concentric rings of teeth click and clatter against each other. It squeals at me as if the only sound it can make is a whistle strained through the fat of its throat. I have no idea where I might sink my ax and have any effect, but I can't let it out of the courthouse.

"Stop right there you bitch!" I scream at the thing while running from the leviathan pouring down the stairs behind me.

The slug of a demon at the door bunches itself up, squeezing that pale skin into rolls. Then it punches forward through the courthouse door and propels itself into the night.

I'm not far behind. The door closes between us for just a moment before I'm there to shove through it, following the demon out into the night. Reckless, but I don't care. I can't let my mistakes, my flaws, my sins infect the rest of my town. I can't let these things go and do to Woodduck what they have done to me and my father.

Outside, the windchill bites into my skin but nothing else. I fly down the steps. My neck twists in each direction searching the streets and sidewalks for the foul beast. The highway slips into darkness to my left and right. Hill Road is bare for as far as I can see. My car sits on the other side of the snowbank. My feet carry me past my car and into the middle of the highway. Nothing. Fear compels me to check my back. The leviathan hasn't followed me out here, and I don't see it beyond the glass doors of the courthouse either. It's as if, suddenly, I'm the only one that's come near the courthouse all evening.

The soft sounds of Woodduck at night return, just audible under the raspy noise of my panting breath. Wind rattles leafless trees. A transformer buzzes overhead. Nothing else. Wandering into the street, I keep spinning to search each direction for something, anything, to prove what I've just experienced isn't entirely hallucination. Standing there without a coat or hat or gloves, clutching an ax that's still dripping the molasses-like blood of the leviathan, I look absolutely and legally insane, ready for the institution.

I spot movement. A woman. She's walking along the sidewalk in front of the courthouse, far from the light of the front steps but visible in the dim despite her dark clothes.

"Hey!" I call to her, not to ask her if she'd seen anything. It was obvious she hadn't by her calm and quiet demeanor, but to warn her about the things lurking in the night that could slaughter her in a moment's time.

"Hey! Stop!"

I run toward her, paralleling her route along the sidewalk as I sprint down the middle of the street. She doesn't turn my way, not until she's about to be swallowed by the shadows of a pine tree between her and the streetlight. Only then does she bring her two feet together, pivot, and face me.

It's Zoey. My sister is dressed in the same clothes she wore yesterday. An all-black business suit with a red blouse underneath, aviator sunglasses perched in her hair, superbly underdressed for the weather. But she shows no susceptibility to the cold. She meets my eyes, smiles once, and backsteps into the gloom.

"Zoey!" I cry to her, more afraid of where the demons might dwell than ever before.

I have to climb over the snowbank to reach the spot where she disappeared. Snow slows my progress, fills my boots, and numbs my bare hands as I go. By the time I get to where she stood and peer into the murk, I'm panting and the mist from my breath hinders my vision. Trotting deeper under the pine, it becomes clear there's nothing to see.

They're gone. My demons. My sister. All of them.

Chapter Ten
The Man in the Seed Jacket

The next morning I'm standing at the top of the stairs that lead down into the tunnels like a detective standing over a crime scene littered with corpses covered in bed sheets. Only in my case, there's no evidence. Yes, there are a few of those opaque drips on the tile, but they're thinned out and dried up. A tilted cup of coffee could have left them as much as a grotesque hell-born slug or a giant armor-plated sea monster. As far as the pool of tar the leviathan left on the granite floor when I chopped into its limb with my ax? Nothing to show for that besides a fresh shine and a "Wet Floor" sign. Did Paul mop up that noxious mess, put out a sign, and call it good?

I hope he at least used some bleach.

I bring my ax everywhere now. I don't care about appearances. It rests against my desk this morning, even while I stare into the labyrinth below Woodduck. If I thought another demon might be waiting for me beyond this door, I'd be holding it in my hands. But I know there's nothing approaching through the tunnels. That squeeze around my spine is conspicuously absent. The weight of it is missing. The crush of it is gone. Imagine a migraine you've had for days or someone constantly stepping on your foot, instantly and inexplicably lifted away. That's how it feels looking down these steps. There is nothing where I know pressure should be. And that provides no relief whatsoever.

Last night, after I lost sight of Zoey, I went back inside the courthouse to search for the remaining demon. I stalked through every hallway and corridor. I checked every door. I went back to these very steps and scoured the office for any signs that the thing had returned this way. But there was nothing. The leviathan, I am sure, escaped. Perhaps through any one of the other exits in this building.

And what's worse, I know now, is those two aren't the only demons loose in Woodduck.

I called Zoey last night and again first thing this morning. No answer. I texted her. Left voicemails begging her to call me back. Still no response. Now that she's back in the Cities at her oh-so-important job and not drunk on my couch, I'm forgotten.

So how did I see her last night? Or, a better question, how did that gargantuan slug of a demon slip away from me so quickly? And why aren't the Sheriff's Department and the BCA and the goddamn Minnesota National Guard not currently surrounding the escaped leviathan and shooting it with machine guns and bazookas? The same reason why no human was in the house when Dad died.

Because something clawed its way up from the basement, but that same thing was wearing boots when it left. Because when they make it outside, the demons shape-shift.

The slug, the leviathan, the humanoid goat-headed abomination I first saw climbing up my basement steps? They're out in Woodduck, right now, disguised as one of us. May in this very building. They could have gone to Lilith's house, or Hank's house, killed them, taken their place, and be in this office with me right now. I have to track them down and kill each one, but how I'm going to do that, I have no idea.

I stand in front of the open door, gazing down into the void. Vaguely audible words heard as if they were spoken underwater come from the customer counter. Only after the man dings the little hotel lobby bell am I able to break away from the view of the empty staircase.

He's a big guy. Over six feet and stocky. An old corn-fed farm boy. His push broom mustache hangs over his lips. His cracked and calloused hands rest next to the bell. Tight pupils fix on me behind squinted lids as if snow blinded. He's an edifice in a green Northrup King seed coat and a stocking cap. Even so, my eyes focus more on the ax leaning against my desk than the man standing beyond it.

"Hello? Yeah. Hi. I need to make a payment for a building permit," he is saying.

"Sorry," I say and shut the door to the tunnels. "Do you have an invoice from Land Services?"

The man is unfolding a sheet of paper from the pocket of his seed coat and grumbling about jumping through hoops when my phone vibrates.

I tap the screen. There's a text message from Jane over at The Book Bazaar. "Are you coming to get your copy? The shipment came in but they're going quick."

"Just a minute," I say to the man at the counter. Then I'm tapping away at the screen, messaging Jane, "Be there soon. Is the signing still happening today?"

"Just chatted with THE MAN myself. Should be here around 3, but I doubt there will be any books left by then."

"Be right there," I text her back, and then, just when I'm about to put the phone down, I realize that if I'm not here, Eric can't be here either. There's no way I can let him down into the tunnels without being around to keep him safe. Behind me, the door to the tunnels is closed. The stairwell beyond the door is quiet. That pressure that twists around my spine is absent. For now. Real quick, I pull up my chat thread with Eric and hammer into the keyboard, "Sorry about last night. Emergency. We should meet up again soon. Also, don't go into the tunnels today. Not safe."

"Ma'am?" the gentleman with the invoice for his building permit says.

"Yeah. Sorry," I say and process his payment. I don't know if I ever look him in the eyes or read what his building permit is for. It doesn't matter. These kinds of transactions are routine, mindless work. He's taken care of and gone shortly after. My mind is on so many other things. Last night. Zoey. The three escaped demons. Who the two other demons might be posing as besides Zoey. Eric and the date and how he'll respond or if he'll respond to the cryptic text I just sent. Eventide's book signing. And on finally getting my hands on my own copy of "A Black Heart Unbroken."

After the man has left but before I sit down at my desk, my feet carry me to Lilith's door.

"Hey. Hi," I say but her eyes never leave her monitor. "Say, do you mind if I take an early lunch? I have some PTO scheduled for this afternoon so I can make it to the book signing across town, but I have something I have to take care of first. Hank can cover down for me while I'm out."

"Uh huh," Lilith says and nothing more.

"Great. Thanks," I say. Then I call to Hank across the office, who manages to glance my way. "I'm going to be out of the office for, like, a half hour. Can you cover down for me?"

"Yep. I'll get right on it," he says and returns to playing his games.

Maybe we're all zombies. Maybe, the three demons have possessed all three of us. It's a strange idea, so I cast it aside.

I gather my keys, phone, hat and gloves, coat, and ax, and head out the door. I have no clue who the demons might be. I have no trails to follow. I have no direction to go, so for the time being, I stick with my regular schedule. And today is the big book signing at The Book Bazaar. It might sound like an exaggeration, but to say that all the demons of Hell can't keep me away from meeting HHR Eventide is pretty accurate, all things considered. A moment later, I'm headed to my car. I know I'm pushing it at work. I know I'm distracted. Thinking back, I should be ashamed of my lack of customer service I provided the big gentleman with the building permit, push broom mustache, and seed jacket, but today, those sorts of things don't seem to matter. I have to make time for the things I need to accomplish. Like getting my hands on and purchasing my copy of Eventide's book before Jane runs out and I have nothing for him to sign at his event later this afternoon. In no more than two minutes, I've made the trip from the courthouse to Main Street. I roll by Woody's, the Paramount, Schmidt's Dentistry and Orthodontists, and Jane's storefront looking for an empty spot to park. The cardboard Eventide still stands behind the glass. Surely, I'm not too late this time, not right after getting Jane's text. Finding a spot in front of the old hardware store, I park and get out.

The wind bites as I make my way along the sidewalk, but it doesn't bother me. It's a short walk. It would be anyway. But then I see the man who'd just been at my customer desk with a building permit. There's no mistaking him. Weathered face. Big mustache. Even bigger frame. That violently green, Northrup King, rain jacket. He's walking my way, undoubtedly headed for the hardware store. That alone is no issue.

"Oh. Hi again," I say, trying to make up for my less-than-stellar customer service earlier.

He does that thing that old men do, bobbing his head but uttering no audible reply. That's fine. I didn't figure we'd ever become best friends. Besides, he has nothing to do with what I need to accomplish today. He's of no concern to me, whatsoever.

Until I see him again.

A half a block later I spot the same man walking in the opposite direction with his back to me. I recognize that god-awful seed jacket first. It's an ugly, vinyl, green thing with a big "NK" Northrup King logo on the back. A common free-be giveaway to farmers who deal with the big agro corporations. I can't help but notice the jacket and the size of the man… or thing… wearing it. He ducks his head a bit when he walks under the sign hanging from The Book Bazaar's eave. When I spin around, I see the same man again, the one who just walked by me and gave me that reserved nod, slipping into the hardware store.

No two people could match that description. Not with that corn silo body and that old jacket. But I'm not dealing with two people. These aren't identical twins. No more than the woman I saw outside the courthouse last night was the same woman I shared a couch with the night before. They look like two instances of the same person, each walking in opposite directions, but I know better.

I'm frozen in place in front of the orthodontists, halfway between the hardware store and the bookstore, paralyzed with indecision.

Two large men in green seed jackets. One is real. One is a demon. The one behind me is already in the hardware store where a human who just pulled a building permit is likely to go. The other one beyond The Book Bazaar, he stops on the sidewalk and looks back my way with a glare as numbing as Novocain to the brain. Then he slips into an alleyway.

"I see you, you son of a bitch," I say, emitting puffs of breath as I do.

Now I know two of the three skin suits being worn by demons loose in Woodduck. And one of them is right in front of me.

I didn't bring my ax with when I got out of the Volt. Wasn't planning to chop up any demons while book shopping in front of Jane, but that was a mistake. I double back, running now, sliding into my car, throwing open the door, and dinging the car next to me. I grab my ax and storm down the sidewalk, as fast as I can move in my boots and layers, like a meth'ed out lumberjack, right past The Book Bazaar.

The alley is empty aside from the dumpsters, pallets, milk crates, trash, and grayish, compacted snow. It butts up to a brick wall and back entrance of whatever building faces the next block over. There, it splits to the right, the way I came, and to the left behind the abandoned Paramount theater. From there, it feeds into Woody's parking lot. Nothing moves but a blown scrap of paper.

When I reach the end of the alley, something topples off a stack of clutter in the direction of Woody's.

I follow the sound, peering around dumpsters and down other branches of the alley as I go. My boots slip through the snow. Nobody shovels or plows back here. The snow has been trampled and packed down over the course of the winter, turning it into dirty, uneven, icepack. I run as fast as I can, hauling my ax with me. The steam is pumping faster and faster out of my lungs and into the frozen air.

When I reach the back of Woody's, the alley opens into a larger parking lot. There's a smattering of old cars parked on a frozen mess of slush and ice and snow. A woman in a Woody's server uniform steps out the back door with a bulging black garbage bag. She swings it, getting ready to heave it into a dumpster.

"Hey!" I shout at her.

Her head spins my way. The garbage bag collides against the rusted green dumpster, mid-heave. A flow of orangish clumpy fluids pours out of the bag like water from a faucet.

"Have you seen a man?" I call to her rushed, impatient, and out of breath.

"Jesus, what'd he do to you?" she asks, eyeing my ax and dropping the bag of slop into the pooling puddle of stinking fluid.

"A big guy with a mustache and an ugly green jacket?" I ask.

"You need me to, like, call the cops?" she asks but doesn't answer.

I'm about to respond when I hear a car door slam from across the parking lot. Turning away from the server, I see him. The man in the green seed jacket. No. That's not right. I see the *thing* in the green seed jacket. He's climbing into a rusted-out farm truck with a bed full of snow and scrap metal, a vehicle that matches the style of the jacket.

"Hey!" I yell as I sprint away from the server.

He sees me before he gets into the driver's seat and stops to stare at me. I come from the front of the truck and shoulder shut the driver's door to remove that barrier between him and me. He takes a few steps back, confusion swimming in his eyes.

"Are you one of them?" I demand, still clutching the ax but not cocking it back for a swing. Yet.

"What in Christ Jesus?" the man– the thing *pretending* to be a man, says.

"Where did you come from?" I ask more specifically. With each step forward I take, he's taking two backward. "Did you come from below?"

"I came from your office!" the man bellows.

"Not good enough!" I yell, because sure, he could have just come from my customer counter after paying for his building permit, or he could have come up from the tunnels and through my office last night. So I ask him, pointedly. "From my office or under it?"

"Hey, should I call the police?" the server is asking again, but this time, I don't think she's asking me.

"Lady, you ought to put that down if you know what's good for you," the thing in the green seed jacket says. "I know Lilith and some of the others up at the courthouse there. If they hear you're out threatening folks around town…"

My eyes catch a glimpse of his right wrist protruding from the sleeves of his long johns, flannel, and the jacket's green cuff. The wrist is thick and hairy and not exactly clean, but there's no wound there. No scar.

No sign of having a lobster-like appendage all but lopped off just last night. I check the other wrist and it's equally intact. Then I check his eyes.

He's a big guy, so he doesn't surrender to fear easily, at least not externally, but I see it in his eyes and his posture. Sure, he's big, but a crazy woman with a sharp ax can do a lot of damage to a person of any size. Also, he's big enough to know that he can do a lot of damage if he has to do something about a crazed woman with an ax. The fear of either of those things happening, of me hurting him or him having to hurt me is genuine. Because he is a man. Not a demon. I don't know how I know, but I can tell. Which means…

"It's the other one," I tell him as if that's an explanation. "The one in the hardware store."

I turn away and run back toward the alleyway. The server and the oversized human in the green seed jacket are watching me go as if I'm crazy. I don't have to look behind me to know that. Of course, they are. And that server, is she already pulling out her phone to dial 911?

"Don't call the cops!" I yell over my shoulder. "Everything is going to be fine!"

Because of course they should take my word for it, the strange woman brandishing an ax and sprinting through back alleys on a freezing cold Thursday morning. Not that it matters. Let her call the cops. I have to get back to the hardware store and trap the demon inside. But I can't get any traction on the ice-layered alley, so like a rat in a maze, I slip and skid around a corner and back onto Main Street's sidewalk, right in front of The Book Bazaar. Some guy is coming out of the store and when I plow into him, his freshly purchased copy of "A Black Heart Unbroken" goes spinning through the air like a wounded duck and crashes into a snowbank, open and with the pages resting against the grimy snow. The receipt, which Jane had tucked between the pages, flitters off toward the hardware store. The man takes a good look at me. I take a good look at the book lying in the snow. For a moment, I have an almost irrepressible impulse to snatch the book out of the snow and claim it for my own, but both my hands are holding my ax.

I bolt for the hardware store, disregarding the man and his damn book.

"Sorry about that," he calls after me, even though it was my fault. And then, completely misunderstanding my intentions in the most positive way possible, he says, "I don't really need the receipt."

I bust into the hardware store like a SWAT team. The kid behind the register jumps and drops his phone. By now, I'm struggling to catch my breath and resting my fists holding the ax against my knees. Still, my head is up and on a swivel. My eyes scan the aisles for the thing in the green seed jacket.

"Um..." the kid says. "Is that a return?"

"Huh?" I ask.

"The ax," the kid points. "Are you looking to return that?"

"What? No! Have you seen a guy in a green jacket?" I ask.

"Like a golfer?" he says.

"Not a golfer," I say. He's clearly no help, so I'm moving again, stalking through the narrow aisles of tools and plumbing parts and bins of nuts and bolts. The kid behind the register and I might be the only two people in the store. If the thing in the green seed jacket is here, I don't count him as a "person." I know better now. I let the wrong one get away. This one, this version, I know it's the leviathan from last night. But I'm moving quickly through the maze of aisles and I'm not finding it.

The kid from the front calls, "Can I help you find something?" He's probably seconds from calling the cops, and in a town this big? It won't take Sheriff Graham or one of Deputy Ruiz long to get here.

When I look to the front of the store, I see past the kid at the till and through the big storefront windows. And I see *it*. Not the kid and not a farmer going about his daily business either. I see the thing *posing* as an old farmer going about his business. He's back out on the sidewalk, no purchases in his arms, but strolling along in that ugly ass jacket with layers of flannel and thermals underneath, heading somewhere with, no doubt, horrific intent.

I knock over a display of WD-40 cans as I rush for the front of the store and the exit. The cans bonk and rattle and roll against the cracked tile floor. The kid behind the counter, when he sees me running the way I am, backs up and crashes into the racks of candy bars and gum in front of the next checkout. More things are falling to the floor as I hit the exit door, leading with my shoulder.

The thing posing as a huge man in a seed jack is already a block away. Further than his steady strides could have carried him in the time it took me to leave the store. It was as if it slipped through time to cover a hundred feet in a single second. He is heading for a newer model SUV crossover, a modern vehicle that doesn't match the man at its door. The demon wearing a man's skin rips off the handle when it opens the door. Metal pieces fall to the snow as he climbs inside. If he gets in and drives off, I'll lose him for sure. My car is too far away. Either I'll catch him now, on foot, or he'll be gone.

I scream as I run. Rather than holding the ax like a charging World War I soldier clutching a rifle, I hold the end of the shaft over my head and let the blade hang behind my back, ready for the over-the-head swing I'll use to bury it in the thing's head. But it's already climbing behind the steering wheel. When I try to run faster, I slip and almost drop the ax. As the crossover backs out of its spot, I regain my footing and storm through the snow and ice and slush. By the time I reach where the SUV had been parked, it's already in the street. The thing behind the wheel shifts into drive and pulls away.

I stand, panting, legs spread wide to keep my footing, the head of the ax resting in the street slush. A few blocks down, the truck turns onto Hill Road, and I know there is no chasing it down.

Chapter Eleven
The Man Himself

I return to work without a book and feeling like I've just finished Woodduck's Annual Thanksgiving Day Turkey Trot 5k. The ax thumps against the floor and the handle clanks against my workstation. I say nothing. If I'm late coming back from my lunch break, or if I'm early, I don't know, and Lilith doesn't say. Hank, as is his way, reacts with the same passion as a carrot responds to being cut into slices.

I know I'm supposed to sit back down and go through emails and be ready to help customers, but when I try to do those things, I'm only pretending. I want to keep watch of the stairwell behind me. I want to get back into town and hunt down the thing in the seed jacket. I want to plant my ax in the fake head of the fake version of my sister. But instead, I sit at my desk and click away with my mouse on things of infinite unimportance.

An email comes in that catches my attention. It's from the library. The body is short and to the point.

> "Regarding your application for the position of ASSISTANT HEAD LIBRARIAN. All applications have been received and the position is now closed. Due to the low number of candidates, we won't be conducting in-person interviews. We will review the applications and resumes of all candidates and make

our hiring decision in the next few days. Thanks for your interest in working for the Woodduck Public Library."

No interviews? Is that good? They probably already know who they are going to hire. Probably knew even before the applications came in. I think I've built up a good reputation with all of the ladies at the library. After all, I've known them for years and have always been friendly and returned my books on time and volunteered to read to kids during their summer reading program. They know me. And Lilith wrote me a glowing letter of recommendation, and they know Lilith. Is that enough, especially in such a small pool of potential hires?

What about Jason?

But what does it matter? It's best if I'm not selected. Let the kid have the job. I'm sure he needs the money, and he told me himself there's no basement at the library. Even with three demons roaming through Woodduck, I have no reason to believe that Hell is empty. I still need to maintain my post before the stairwells.

But, God, how I wish I could surround myself with all those books and characters and worlds and far-flung adventures. Inside a book, I don't have to worry about things like fees and fines and building permits, or basements and demons and the sight of my dad after a bullet went into his mouth and out of his skull. I stew for longer than I should.

Sometime after lunch, the one person I've been dreading all day strolls up to my desk. Eric.

He isn't wearing his patented aw-shucks smile. He's aloof. Unsure. Cold. Seeing him that way, distant and apprehensive, sticks a skewer in my heart. Of course, I know why he's feeling awkward. I bailed on him and then sent him that cryptic text without any sort of explanation. And I'm about to tell him the same thing I told him in that text. That he can't work in the tunnels. That it's not safe. Never mind all the equipment he's lugging into the courthouse along with him.

"Oh. Hi, Eric," I say, painting a smile on my face I can only wish is as natural and ready as his usual disposition.

"Abby. Good to see ya," Eric says. A smile sneaks to the corner of his lips and a reserved version of his normal mood returns, as if he can't stay unhappy for long. "Is everything okay? You left in such a rush last night, you made me a bit worried."

"Oh, yeah. Just, you know, family stuff," I tell him. If I stretch the definition of "family stuff" to include seeing a demon wearing my sister's skin, I'm not lying. Still, I feel a familiar pressure wrap itself around my lower back.

"Well, I hope everything is okay," Eric says, always polite.

His light-heartedness gives me the courage to believe that perhaps everything will be okay. My first taste of optimism today. "Can we reschedule our date?" I ask. "I really was having a good time, and I'm sorry I had to run out on you like that."

"Um. Yeah. Okay," Eric says, and then cheering up a bit more, "Tomorrow is Friday. We missed out on the meat raffle and the two fer ones, but should we meet up at Woody's again tomorrow night?"

"That'd be great. And I promise, no running out this time," I say but the squeeze on my back is increasing. Soon, something might start working its way up the steps.

"Yeah. Great. I'll put it on my calendar. Say, I really do need to get to work downstairs this afternoon. I'll never finish if I don't get started," he says as if the things from below aren't calling his name.

So my strange text wasn't enough to deter him. I don't have any ready stories to tell him that might be any more convincing. What am I going to say? There are rats? There's a gas leak? There's an earthquake coming that will cause a cave-in? That right now, murderous hell fiends are creeping closer, and I know this because I can feel invisible hands gripping and twisting away at my spine?

"I can't let you down there," I say, figuring a trickle of truth is better than a deluge of lies. "There are things down there. Bad things."

Eric sort of screws up his face a little bit, unsure of what I mean. "Bad things like those old fuses I suppose, but–"

"No," I say and stop him cold. I want to tell him more, but the truth is so strange, I have to hold it close, keep it just between him and I. Lilith is still in her office. Hank isn't looking our way. I clamp my hands together to keep them from shaking. I do my best to suppress the quiver in my voice as I let that trickle of honesty seep through the dam. "There are things down there that aren't... They're not from here. From this plane."

"'This plane'? What are we at the airport? What the criminy are you talking about, Abby?" he says and he's still smiling, but in a different way. A somehow *cruel* way.

"Look. Don't make fun of me. Just believe me when I tell you that there are things down in those tunnels that none of us understand. They're evil, and they're dangerous, and I can't possibly let you down there. Not today. Not while I'm not around to make sure it's safe. Okay?"

"Abby, the county hired me to do a—"

"Just not today," I plead with him, hoping against hope that he'll listen. "I took some PTO and I promised myself I'd make it over to The Book Bazaar so I could get Eventide to sign my book. Tomorrow and all the rest of the weekdays I'll be right here, and I can make sure... I can make sure it's safe. Just wait until tomorrow when I'll be here all day. Then I can let you down there and everything will be okay."

Eric seems to pace inside his skin, uncomfortably looking for a way to make me happy but also be an honest contractor and businessman. Nonverbally humming and ha'ing. Looking to his left and right as if the Better Business Bureau is lurking around every corner.

"I mean... I guess I can say I had another customer call me with another furnace issue," he whispers to me. "But you have to promise to let me down there tomorrow and all the days going forward. And..." He holds out, piling suspense onto this last part. "...You have to promise me a full date tomorrow night. And I promise I'll do my best not to bore you by telling you the same joke twice."

For the first time that day, I match his smile. Maybe he doesn't believe me, but he's not ridiculing me and he's not going into the tunnels. And he still wants to go out with me.

"Deal," I say and even stick out my hand to shake on it. My smile doesn't waiver, even as the clench around my spine tightens ever so slightly.

Before I leave for the day, I creep to the door in the back of the room. No compression in the small of my back. That has eased with time. When I open the door, I find the staircase empty. All the same, I clutch my ax in one hand and flip on the flashlight app on my phone with the other. Each footfall against the steel steps echoes against the narrow walls. When

I reach the bottom, the beam from my phone doesn't travel far. Nothing to see but cinder block walls and the dust-covered floor.

I wouldn't call it wind, but something like a breeze or a draft moves through the tunnels. It's impossible to notice outside of still moments like this, but I feel it now as it brushes past my ears. A push and a pull, like waves against the shore. Or an inhale and exhale like some giant beast that's bigger than anything I've seen yet. Something bigger than the tunnels themselves. Something that could swallow all of Woodduck if it chose. Something older than time. Something that could drive me insane from a single encounter.

But the ache is gone from my back. My consciousness is clean. Nothing stirs. All things being the same, I climb up the steps backward, never letting my eyes or the beam of flashlight break from the blackness until I'm back in the office and the door is sealed shut.

With things settled with Eric, with the tunnels empty, and with my PTO starting at two, I say bye to Lilith and Hank and take my ax and my library copy of "A Black Heart Unbroken" out the door.

I still haven't gotten my own copy of the book. Not after the fiasco this morning. And I'm almost certain that by now, Jane's sold out of her inventory. All the parking spots along Main Street are full, and people are already flooding into the bookstore. But I have a plan. The library copy is covered in extra barcodes and stickers labeling it as property of the Woodduck Public Library, but only on the thin plastic jacket that covers the actual dust jacket that came from the publisher. The plastic jacket is taped onto the real jacket, but as glossy as the real jacket is, I can peel the tape off of it. So after I park in front of the Paramount, I take a minute to scrape a corner of the tape up with my fingernail until I can safely remove the plastic jacket. I'm left with what looks like a regular, purchased copy of HHR Eventide's latest masterpiece. It's a temporary fix. As soon as I can get another copy, I'll put the plastic jacket back on the unsigned copy and return that to Jason at the library, and no one will be the wiser. Maybe it's something related to theft or lying or deceit, but only distantly related, like a great aunt whose funeral you make excuses not to attend. But as I free the book from the library's jacket, I feel the return of that pressure snaking its way up my vertebrae. I ignore it. This is only a small incursion of my morality. Like sending a sympathy card to the children of that passed-on great aunt whose funeral you choose not to attend even when you have no real excuse. Nothing I can't handle. I'm a good person and wouldn't normally deface library property. Even if I do have to return this copy with Eventide's signature on the inside, they can hardly call that "damage."

But I have to leave my ax in the car. No amount of storytelling can explain why I feel the need to bring that into a bookstore. I mean, what would I tell Eventide?

Despite all the events of the past few days, despite killing the wolf demon while the hockey kid stood on my front door, despite staring down the three-headed beast while I was at work, despite Eric intruding on the most dangerous place in all of Woodduck, and despite seeing demons mimicking humans all across town, I'm still excited for this day. I have never met HHR Eventide. Never even seen him about town. I've read his books since I was a kid and some of my fondest memories are of my dad and I gushing over Eventide's greatest works.

Dad swore his earlier books, the two he wrote before he got big, were his best stuff and that "Storming Sea of Souls," was the scariest thing ever put into print. Dad always said Eventide was at his best and most relatable prior to hitting it big with his third book, "The Towers of Silence and Sand." But if you ask me, Eventide has only gotten better with each book he writes. Last year's "Apothecary of Agony" looked deep into my soul and thrilled me with every sentence and paragraph. How "A Black Heart Unbroken" can top it, I have no idea, but I'm eager to find out.

I wish Dad were here. If he was still alive, I know he would be right next to me. Even at his lowest, even at his worst, I know he would have made time for me and Eventide. More than anything else, more than the library job, more than a date that ends well with Eric, I wish Dad was here with me so we could rekindle some of those good times and make more memories together. But after losing someone, you're left with the memories you have in the bank. No creating more. So the finite memories you have become all the more precious. But what I wouldn't give for just one more chance to tell Dad that I love him, that he matters, that no matter what is whispered into his ear, he should stay here, on this Earth, with me. That we can make more memories. Good memories that will make it easier to ignore the demons and embrace the people we love. Great memories even, the kind that might banish them forever.

I walk across Main Street to The Book Bazaar knowing that the reason he isn't here with me is because I couldn't stand watch when his demon came up from Hell. That knowledge sours my otherwise good mood. But, if I was being fair with myself, I have to admit that if Dad were still alive, he'd be here with me, excited to meet our hero and get his autograph. And if his spirit has carried on, I know he wants me to enjoy this moment, not despite his untimely death, but because of the good times we shared when he was alive.

I clutch my liberated copy of "A Black Heart Unbroken" and march into The Book Bazaar.

Inside the door, it's bedlam. I've never seen the place so full of people. Clatter and rabble fill the air. Oy, the giant Maine Coon who normally sleeps on shelves and perches next to the register and purrs like a two-cycle engine on a sleepy Sunday morning is nowhere to be found. Near the back of the store, Jane has pushed aside the tables and displays that normally occupy the space and set up rows of chairs facing a lone stool in front of a door leading to the backroom. She's doing her best to corral people into those chairs, but there clearly aren't enough. The rest of the crowd, mostly middle-aged mousey women like me, has to stand around the edges and crane their necks over each other's shoulders for a look at the lone wooden stool. We all know who will be sitting there in a few minutes.

As far as buying my copy of the book before Eventide comes out, I don't even bother. Jane isn't behind the counter and has her hands full with the event. I don't see any copies left for purchase anyway. Surely with as many people crammed into this small space, all the available copies are gone. Looking around the room, I see some women don't have a copy of his latest book but instead cling to some of his earlier works. The man across from me has a copy of "Storming Sea of Souls." Dad's favorite.

We all know what's coming. We all know when the man of the hour is scheduled to appear, and we're all checking our phones and watches as the time draws near.

When the top of the hour strikes, no bells toll, but a few phone alarms chirp and buzz. Members of the crowd kill them, and others are reminded to turn their own phones to silent. A minute after the hour ticks by. At two minutes after, the bells in the steeple over at St. Augustine's chime the first notes of What a Friend We Have in Jesus. At three after the hour, Jane slips through the door behind the lone, empty chair, and we're all beginning to wonder if something has gone wrong. Did Eventide not show up? Did Jane promise something she couldn't deliver? Are we ever going to see him?

Meanwhile, I feel a slight sensation of evil things drawing closer. But it's faint and I ignore it. I deserve this. I can't possibly be expected to stare down an empty stairwell my entire life. I'm not doing anything wrong by being here. The demons can, for just one afternoon, sit in a corner, look down their pants, and play with whatever they find.

"Okay everyone," Jane says, and the people all go quiet. "Thanks for coming out this afternoon on such a beautiful January day. At least the sun is shining, right?"

We all kind of laugh and agree with that. Like friends made in foxholes, we bond over living in such an inhospitable climate.

"As some of you already noticed, I am, unfortunately, already sold out of my first delivery of 'A Black Heart Unbroken.' But don't worry. I have another shipment coming next week. In the meantime, Mr. Eventide has agreed to sign any of his books you have. So, if any of you have a first edition of 'The Coffin Nail Also Turns," today is your lucky day. Okay. Without further ado…" Jane says and then unfolds a sheet with a printed-off official introduction. "HHR Eventide was born in Duluth Minnesota in 1989. He published his first novel, 'The Coffin Nail Also Turns,' in 2012 and released his sophomore title, "The Storming Sea of Souls" the same year. But it wasn't until his third work "The Towers of Silence and Sand," that he earned his first Bram Stoker Award and became a household name. He has gone on to publish twelve novels and three short story collections. His latest work, 'A Black Heart Unbroken," has already reached Number One on the New York Times Best Seller List, and according to the Minneapolis Star Tribune, is 'A tour de force that leaves an indelible mark on the landscape of gothic literature.' Ladies and gentlemen, please welcome…" Jane takes a breath. "Mister HHR Eventide."

And then the man himself steps through the door.

He's tall, taller than I imagined him to be. Larger than the cardboard cutout of him in the window in every way. He's older than me but not by much. The creases near his eyes only make him more impressive rather than weathered or tired. As for his eyes, they're intense and mysterious. His black suit is meticulously tailored and pressed. His hair is jet black. Every lock is set in place. His face is slender and keenly aware of his surroundings, but his expression is by no means unpleasant. It's a relief and a pleasure to see that he's happy with our little flock of barnyard hens here in Woodduck. His movements are slow and purposeful. He glances up at us all as we applaud and gives us a few short waves, as much signaling us to relax and quiet down as to greet us. His smile is reserved and calm. This tiny amount of fanfare means nothing to him. He's spoken at colleges and universities to entire theaters packed full of fans. All of his book releases he's hosted in prestigious, metropolitan locations. I suspect he's doing this here in Woodduck as a favor to his new hometown. He just came off a whirlwind two-day blitzkrieg with stops in Boston, New York, Philadelphia, and Chicago. Next week, he'll be on a jet for his European invasion with appearances in Vienna, Zurich, Paris, Munich, Berlin, Amsterdam, and London. Places half a world away that I'll *never* see. But for now, he's here, just fifteen feet from me, waiting for us all to stop clapping so he can sit down on the stool and have a word with us. I ease the grip on my copy of his book so I don't dig my nails into the cover.

"Thank you, everyone," he says in a smooth, cordial voice. The clamor in the store goes dead as quickly as if he twisted a volume knob down to zero. He sits down. The people who came early enough to get a chair sit down as well, granting me and the people around me a slightly better view. "Thanks so much. Thanks, Jane, for having me here today."

"Thank you, Mister Eventide," Janes says. Then, to us, "Here's what we have in store for all of you today: Mister Eventide will give a short reading from his latest work. We'll have a few minutes for questions and answers, and then we'll all form an orderly line and Mister Eventide will be glad to sign each of your books for you."

"Thank you, Jane," he says again, and I'm still mesmerized by his presence. I've never seen him in real life before. I've never heard him talk.

His voice is rich and unrushed. Confident. Compelling. This man's words have run across countless pages and through my mind my whole life. Only now am I hearing him speak. "I'm going to read to you an excerpt from the fourth chapter of 'A Black Heart Unbroken.' In this scene, our two protagonists, a young couple by the names of Sam and Jen have broken into an abandoned mansion on the edge of town."

He then cleared his throat and turned his eyes to an open copy of his book.

"Sam didn't look like much. His face was slender and pocked with spurts of hair growth. He was rude and swore and wasn't always kind, but she recognized something feral in him that reflected her sovereign spirit. They shared a kinship of coming from nothing, having nothing, having little means to attain more, but remaining undaunted in achieving their goals all the same. Her eyes tracked him closely as he navigated through the empty mansion by flashlight. The way he walked. The way he opened and closed doors. The way he thoroughly searched every nook and cranny of the sprawling estate. He had an objective and was honed to it like a compass needle drawn to a lodestone. Nothing would divert him from his aims. His will was an ice-breaking frigate, keeping clear their trade route through the Arctic. This would only end when he reached his destination or sank in the attempt. Jen's only real question was whether his ambitions were as grandiose as hers.

"They took their time searching through the mansion. After all, it was the largest and most labyrinthian home either of them had set foot in. Over an hour passed while they hunted for any signs of occupation, during which, both of them checked out the window to the front courtyard for any signs of the homeowner's return. All that moved outside were a pair of black-capped Chickadees, a male and female, chasing and courting each other in short, fitful flights over the brick pavers. Currently, Jen looked down on them from the highest room in the mansion, the master bedroom.

"'That settles it. We're all alone,' Sam said.

"'But that's…' Jen began the sentence while still watching the songbirds outside, but before she finished her thought, she turned around and saw this young man she hardly knew. He stood next to a bed larger and taller and more finely dressed than any she'd ever laid her head on. The bed was dressed. Sam on the other hand pulled the tail of his shirt over his head and tossed the garment to the floor. As he unbuckled his belt, her last unspoken word, 'impossible,' echoed in all its permutations and left her contemplating not what was impossible, but all of the possibilities fate was presenting her.

"By the eager shine in his eyes and the patient stillness of his feet, she again saw something in him that also existed in her. A hunger. A passion. A refusal to let good enough be good enough. It was a thrill to disassemble and discard all the impossibilities. With Sam, it was as easy as ripping out of their clothes and letting the fabric fall to the floor like dying leaves in autumn. Their nudity revealed endless potential."

Oh my god. Is this a sex scene? Is Eventide reading us a sex scene, here, in a place as public and reserved as a bookstore? In earshot of the bells of St. Augustine's?

"Upon collision, her breasts compressed into his bulwark chest. His rigid member probed her soft stomach. Their lips intertwined, no more of their words demanding to be spoken."

Jesus Christ, he is, and I can't say I'm upset.

"When he lifted Jen and lowered her onto the bed in the dimly lit master suite, her heart accelerated and her nerves fine-tuned to every touch," Eventide continued unabashed. "Sam was powerful but never hurtful. Firm but measured. He knew his strength and used it every way he should and none of the ways he shouldn't. He climbed on top of her, and she gripped his solid biceps like handlebars on a motorbike. Her world existed inside that small space between them. They kissed and all the worries and uncertainties in the world beyond them were gone.

"Were they safe here? Would they uncover the secrets of the mansion? Might they find things in this place that would grant them even a meager portion of the things they dreamed of? Would this relationship last, or would it burn out as quickly as it sparked? For a time, none of that mattered to them. It was just Sam and Jen, existing as one."

I'm swept away in the scene. I am no longer an unmarried, unclaimed woman living alone in an old house, working a boring job in her hometown she can't escape. I am trespassing in a mysterious mansion and having sex while sex is young and thrilling and dangerous. I am Jen. And who is my Sam? As I look into the cool poignant eyes of HHR Eventide, I admit, it isn't Eric.

"Sam put Jen on her hands and knees and got behind her. She looked up as he went inside, and she saw the dead body reclined in the lounge chair, watching over both of them.

"Jen didn't scream but scrambled off the bed like she'd touched fire. A series of profanities spilled from her mouth as she scurried to the floor opposite the body.

"'What? What happened? Did I hurt you?' Sam said.

"From her spot on the carpet, Jen stabbed a pointed finger across the mattress. 'Look! Look, you fucking jackass!'

"Why they didn't smell the man when they first came into the master bedroom, Jen never knew. But what changed the man from a man into a dead body was obvious. A Smith and Wesson forty five caliber revolver hung precipitously from the half-curled fingers of his right hand. Black and dried blood coated his neck, chin, and lower lip and hinted at the entrance wound inside his open mouth. The volcano-like splatter art on the ceiling, punctuated by a bullet hole in the paneling, made the path of the bullet clear."

The horrific memories of the night Dad died catapult back to the forefront of my mind. They're not welcome. I've done everything I can to forget what I saw that awful night of the first snowfall, but like an uninvited houseguest, once that image is in my consciousness, it won't leave.

Eventide doesn't know. How could he? It isn't like he knows me or knew my father or has any interest in the tragic but all too common ending of another tortured veteran who never found his way back from the terrible places he was sent. I remind myself of this while I wrestle with the memory of that night and do everything I can to shove it back into the depths of my mind where I wish it would stay. I shouldn't hold it against the man who wrote a scene so close to my reality. He couldn't have known. He most likely wrote this scene months or even years before the night my father died. He writes horror and horrible things happen in his books all the time. It's my fault that this scene has struck a chord so familiar to the worst night of my life. And I remind myself that this was only one scene in a very thick book. That I should be able to deal with things like this. That I should grow up.

Eventide slowly closes the book and lifts his eyes. For a moment, his eyes meet mine, and when they collide, fear and exhilaration explode from the connection. The trauma of my memories transforms into the adrenaline of my present. It's only momentary. Those deep-set eyes are soon scanning over the rest of his dedicated readers crammed into the tiny space that is The Book Bazaar. We're all quiet, none of us brave enough to break the still. It's scandalous, what he's read here to this room of normally conservative folks in rural Woodduck, Minnesota. Not for the violence. Never that. But for the sex. He's entranced us, a trick he's performed countless times before made all the more effective by his deft, practiced, magician's hands. I'm enthralled. I'm afraid. I'm aroused. I know I've been through the worst part, and now I'm greedy for more of that scene to spill from his lips. Having not a minute to read "A Black Heart Unbroken," I have no idea who Sam and Jen are. I have no idea why they snuck into this mansion. I don't know what drives their love. I don't have a clue who the dead man sitting in the corner is, but now I need to know. I want to be there in that master bedroom with them, hearts racing from the thrill of sex and the threat of death. Because I may not know any of the details, but I know from reading all of Eventide's previous works, that the dead don't stay dead for long, and there is never a moment when the main characters should relax.

During the Q&A session, I'm too intimidated to make a peep. Eventide, ever the gentleman, takes each query into careful consideration regardless of how pointless it might be. He finds a way to respond to even the dullest questions with a funny, intriguing, or insightful answer.

A woman mentions that male and female Chickadees are identical, unlike, say Cardinals, in which the male has a brilliant red plumage, but the female is rather dull brown in color. And since there's no telling between male and female Chickadees, how could Jen be so certain about what she was seeing from the master bedroom window?

Eventide hides a smile by looking down at the text. Has this old birdwatcher caught him in a faux pas? "Well, my dear, I'll admit, when writing this passage, my focus was not on the plumage of the Chickadees. Perhaps Jen saw something in the songbirds that she recognized in the energy between her and Sam. A feral magnetism. Perhaps, you yourself could use more practice in recognizing that energy?"

If the old woman intended to embarrass the one and only HHR Eventide, her attempt has horribly backfired. The man is a genius. I was convinced of that prior to today, but I'm doubly convinced of it now.

Eventually, Jane closes the Q&A session and directs us to form a line starting with those seated, trailing back toward the front door. We have to snake through the aisles to make room, and when I find my place, I'm so far back I can't even see the front of the line. The people around me babble with conversation and discussion about the reading and the questions and answers. I try to shut them out to avoid any spoilers. Most of the people here have read beyond the sex scene in the mansion's master suite when Sam and Jen find the body. Some have even finished the whole book already. But I don't want to hear a word about it from any of them. I want to read it for myself. Actually, that's not entirely accurate. I want Eventide to read the whole thing to me in that rich, smooth, unrushed voice. And in the process, I want him to transport me into that mansion. I want to peel off his black suit and white shirt. I want to fall into that massive four-poster bed. I want him to climb on top of me and I want to only exist in the space between his arms. I want... oh the things I want.

As I approach the front of the line, Eventide once again comes into view. I watch him closely. With each person, he's gracious and patient. For some people, they take this as an opportunity for their own personal question-and-answer session. I eavesdrop, cautiously, leery of spoilers, but still hungry to hear more of Eventide's silky voice.

"So, when Sam and Jen find the body in the master bedroom," the woman in front of me is saying to Eventide while he takes her copy of the book. "I feel like they've only just begun to face the dark things that are coming their way."

Eventide turns the book around, opens it to the title page, and signs it with a big, black Sharpie. "Have you read beyond that scene yet?" he asks the woman.

"No, not yet," she says and when he hands her back the book, she holds it tight against her chest. "But when I get home…"

"You have no idea of the darkness they're about to face," Eventide says. "But as they say in Rome, 'Verba volant, scripta manent.'"

Jane is there to keep the line moving along. With a touch to the elbow, she ushers the woman away with her signed book. It's my turn. I shuffle in front of Eventide and there's nothing between us but a narrow table. My lungs are tight and strained. I can hardly breathe, let alone ask him anything intelligent. Failing to utter a word, I set down my borrowed copy of "A Black Heart Unbroken." With hands grown agile from repetition, he brings the book in front of him, spins it around, flops open the cover to a blank interior page, and readies his marker.

"And you, my dear, how are you doing on this beautiful winter's day?" he asks me.

He... HHR Eventide, author of a dozen novels, many of which have landed him on the New York Times Best Seller List and won him numerous awards... asks me... Abigail Hendrix, the boring, homely gal who works for Accounts Receivable at the county courthouse... how I'm doing. His eyelashes are thick, so thick it almost looks like he's wearing eyeliner, and I didn't know before this very moment that I would find that attractive, but now? Oh my god.

"I've seen some darkness myself," I manage to say, my mind still lingering on his answer to the previous woman's question. His patient, deep eyes have me transfixed, but a thought intrudes. "Could you–"

He pauses, the tip of the Sharpie an onion's skin above the title page. Those eyes like water wells look to me.

"Could you sign it to both my father and me?" I say. "He and I, both of us have seen some dark things."

He finishes signing the library's book, spins it back around, and slides it to the edge of the table with his longer fingers forming a teepee over the cover. "Well, I think there are things in the darkness we should embrace. Just like it says on the back of the book, 'Demons are meant to be played with.'"

Then Jane touches my elbow, and although I'm hardly aware of anything besides the man in front of me, I know it means my turn is over. I surrender Eventide's attention to the next person waiting in line. I don't resist but I don't turn away either. My heels lead the path away from Eventide until Jane is in front of me, handing me the book he signed for me.

"Isn't he something?" she asks.

"I... I have to get home," I tell her.

Chapter Twelve
Under the Moonlight

If the form the demon has taken is supposed to garnish it any sympathy, it's not getting it from me.

All the way home, I feel it coming up, no different than how Zoey felt before vomiting in my toilet. When I pull into my garage, I grab both my newly signed copy of "A Black Heart Unbroken" and my ax, and storm into the house. The book I set on my kitchen counter, careful not to place it down on top of any stains or dried-up old food. The ax, however, stays with me. Before I even open the door leading to the basement, I know I'm about to swing. The door screams on its hinges. The demon is two steps away.

It's an unholy amalgamation of a dozen or more human infants. The demon's limbs, its torso, its head, if you could call any one of its appendages a head versus another arm, are all made of naked, crying babies. If I'm supposed to hesitate and slow my ax due to some maternal instinct, I don't. I go to work slaughtering all of those wet, writhing, whining things like I was born to do it. My ax sings through the air and cleaves into the soft, pudgy skin. Blood as black as Indian ink spits out and splatters hot and sticky on my face. It paints the walls and stains my clothes. I rip loose the ax head and take another swing, landing it into another one of these sewn-together babies. Sometimes I chop whole infants loose from the amalgamation, other times I just cleave off the limbs of the babies. Little arms or legs or heads or whole bodies go tumbling back down the stairs and into the dark. I blink away the black bile that burns my eyes and wail louder than the dozen mouths attached to the hell-thing in my stairwell. But I don't stop until it's in so many pieces the demon can't climb another step. Even as it slips and falls down the stairs, I pursue it and render it into smaller and smaller chunks. I only stop at the furthest edge of the light from my kitchen. My basement, a floor below my main floor, should only be a step or two deeper into the dark. But when I sever an infant head from the demon's central wad of baby parts, it thumps down and down and down as if the stairwell has no end. Then the entirety of the demon spills backward into the abyss from which it came.

Maybe the other three demons got away. Maybe things that look like a creature from the bottom of the ocean, or my sister, or a giant repulsive slug covered in short ambulatory hairs, or an old farmer, or a naked man covered in tar with the horns of a goat, or an as-of-yet anonymous thing posing as a human are somewhere out in the cold, darkening night of Woodduck. But this one? This one I put back to bed.

And so, I close the door to the basement and rest my ax against the end of my couch. I scrub my hands and face with the hottest water I can get from the kitchen sink until my skin is red but clean. I recover my copy of "A Black Heart Unbroken" from the counter and place it on the end table next to the ax. I change out of my work clothes and into pajamas. I warm up a leftover plastic dish of chicken soup and I find the bottle of whiskey Zoey had left behind next to my microwave. I pour myself a glass, mixing it with store-brand cola from a big plastic bottle in my fridge. It went down well enough the night she was here. I wasn't the one hugging the toilet, was I? And the beer I had with Eric at Woody's? That was nice too, for the short time I was able to enjoy it along with his company.

See, the thing is, I wasn't always the way I am now. I wasn't always so restricted to my house and my work. Wasn't always so paranoid of violating some rule or creed or commandment or article of faith. It wasn't that long ago when, sure, I wasn't Miss Sorority Sister Party Girl, but I was familiar with the inside of Woody's and could down a tequila shot without the training wheels. I had boyfriends and had sex and drank and drove too fast and chased my wants and desires. Sure, Zoey turned those things into an art form, but I wasn't always so innocent either.

It was only after Dad's death, after seeing that first demon climbing up the steps, and realizing that those two things weren't unrelated, that I became such a reclusive, tea-totaling celibate. And I don't like it. So if the wages of sin are staring down some bastard creation of Hell in my stairwell and chopping it to pieces every so often so I can enjoy a night at home with a drink and a book and fantasize about who might love me, then so be it.

I gather my drink, my reheated soup, my book, and my blankets, and I dive headlong into "A Black Heart Unbroken."

A minute doesn't pass by before I'm engrossed, lost in the words, hearing them in the author's own voice now that I've captured it in my ears. That smooth and steady tone speaks each of the narrator's lines. He is Sam, and when he introduces Jen, a young woman who is alone and down on her luck, she speaks with my voice. And I know that there will never be a book that is so personal to me. I'm not even a chapter in, and I know I'm holding my new favorite book.

The plot, I'm beginning to surmise as soon as I'm into the second chapter, is straightforward and easy to embrace. Sam is a delivery driver. Jen cleans houses, not because she wants to, but because she needs the money. Of course, they're sent to the strange old Tudor mansion hidden deep into the woods on the outskirts of town. A home not identical to Eventide's residence. He lives in a Renaissance Revival manor on top of a hill. But I can see he's drawn inspiration from his home here in Woodduck, and I can't wait to read if he's woven any stories of suicidal mayors into the backstory. When Jen is first contacted by an anonymous person from the mansion, she's given instructions on where to find a key and to lock the door again when she leaves. Once inside, she finds the mansion is well-maintained but completely empty. There are no signs of anyone living there. No laundry in the hampers. No dirty dishes in the sink. But there are clothes in the closets. There is food in the refrigerator, freezer, and pantry. The lights work. Hot water runs from the taps. The giant and modern TV in the living room even gets all the cable channels and streaming services. But something bothers her about the place, so she does her job, does it well, and quickly leaves. Things don't get too strange until someone rings the doorbell one day while she's cleaning. She answers the door to find Sam at the front step, delivering a warm meal from a local restaurant. He tells her this isn't the first time he's delivered here, that no one ever answers the door, that he's always paid and tipped well, electronically, and that by the time he delivers another meal, the previous delivery is gone.

I can already see how they end up together, in the master suite, on that big four-poster bed. It's not a spoiler. More of a teaser that has me eager to flip to the next page. But with Eventide, it's always a slow burn.

First, they agree to meet up at a local dive bar. There, amongst the bustle of waitresses and the banter of drunks, they devise a plan. When Sam gets his next order to the mansion, they'll arrive together. Jen will inevitably need to stay and clean long enough for the food on the front step to grow cold and inedible. Perhaps then the yet unseen resident will come out of hiding to fetch the meal. Sam waits. Jen cleans and checks through every room and behind every door, but no resident appears. Defeated but undaunted, (unbroken perhaps) they leave the mansion together. The food on the front steps remains untouched.

By Chapter Three, Jen and Sam are forming a quick bond. Sam is funny. Jen is sexy. They fill the gaps that exist in each other's lives. They flirt with the growing attraction but don't commit. Obviously, that can't happen until they're back in the mansion in Chapter Four. But I want them to give in to their desires. I'm urging them on, feeling the attraction myself perhaps more than they do. After all, I'm a real woman who might recognize a male and female Chickadee when they land on a branch outside my window, and I have very real desires that I've left unsatisfied for far too long. Eventide has tapped into that and is playing me like a fiddle, and I'm enjoying every note.

So much so, I don't notice the slow-paced scrapes of something coming up the stairs. The wind whistling over my eaves covers them. The whiskey numbs the sensation of the compression around my spine. My mood smooths any tension in my nerves. A demon is coming up, but as enthralled in my book as I am, I can't even tell. Not until the latch of the door clicks open and the whine of the hinges pulls me out of my dream state.

I twist around on the couch. My bowl of half-finished soup and spoon make a racket when they tumble from my lap. The cold chicken broth leaks through my blanket. The bowl lands upside down on the carpet.

My eyes land on the demon who still has a hold of the doorknob but is now standing almost upright in my kitchen.

It is a towering thing, scrawny like a skeleton, so tall it has to curve its spiked hunchback in an arch to fit under my ceiling. It is layered in what might be tatters of old clothes or shreds of blackened, rotten skin; I can't tell and it doesn't matter. What matters is the thing is glaring at me with the burning embers it has for eyes. And for the first time since meeting these demons, I feel like it has the upper hand. I haven't cornered it. I haven't trapped it where I have the high ground. I haven't even chased it through the corridors of the courthouse with my ax at the ready. No. I'm wrapped in blankets, soaked in chicken soup, with a book in one hand and a half-finished whiskey cola in the other hand. My ax might as well be a mile away, even though it's only at the end of my couch. The skeletal monstrosity in my kitchen freezes, but if I make a move, I'm certain it will be chewing the flesh from my throat long before I reach my ax.

A moment passes during which I'm almost able to fool myself into believing that the infernal thing in my kitchen is immobile, like some kind of giant, hyper-realistic Halloween decoration. Its eyes lock with mine and I know we're both waiting for the other to make a move, to draw a six-shooter, to blink. Then slowly, its jaw creeks open as if pulled down by the weight of gravity. Thick, burning, tar dribbles from its maw onto the linoleum.

The thought of that bile pouring out of the demon's mouth and onto my bare neck as it closes in to devour me breaks my paralysis. I fling the blanket off of me in a flurry so I can use my arms. The whiskey and the book are forgotten and tumble to the floor. I grab my ax.

My sudden motion shocks the demon to life as well. It howls, loud and horrible, and more of that burning tar dumps from its mouth and onto my kitchen floor. Then it clambers, quick, too fast for me to intercede, across the linoleum to the garage door. It throws the door open and, too late, I realize it's trying to escape, just like the others.

"Get back here!" I call after it while unraveling my ankles from the blanket and grabbing my ax.

But the beast slips through the door and into my garage. The churn of the motor and chain of the opener tells me it found its escape route, and if I don't stop it, it will blend in with the unsuspecting populace of my nice quiet town. By the time I get to my garage, the giant skeletal creature is on all fours and slipping underneath the still-opening door.

I need to chase it outside, through the snow. Can't let it out of my sight. And I know better than trying to do that barefoot. My thick Red Wings are standing on the mat next to me. I stab my feet into them and don't bother with the laces. When I look up, what I see freezes me deeper than the subzero air pouring into the garage. As the demon made of giant bones and tatters of flesh and rags pulls its last remaining leg from the garage, it shapeshifts into something much smaller and unassuming. I can't see any of the finer features in the darkness, but in the red and green glow of my still-up Christmas lights, I see a woman. A dainty woman at that. Then, it's gone, fleeing around the corner of my house.

I can't let it get away. I can't lose this demon like I did the others. I didn't see the thing's new face, but I saw its size and shape. No longer a massive towering skeletal ghost, but something my own proportions. And if I can look it even in the eyes, then that will make it all the easier for me to chop it down to the height of my ankles.

The snow is deep around the side of my house. That's where I spot it, not running down the driveway or along the sidewalk, but headed for my backyard. It can't move fast, but neither can I. Its motions are rushed and frustrated. It's unaccustomed to dealing with so much snow slowing it down. Meanwhile, I'm stomping through the two-foot-deep drifts. My untied Red Wings fill with snow quickly, freezing my sockless feet and ankles, but I don't let it slow me down. I'm wearing fluffy cotton pajama pants and an old T-shirt. Not what I would have pulled from my closet if I had known this is where the night would take me. The ax is tight in my fists and I'm swinging it as if I'm in a canoe and it's a paddle. Maybe that does some good. Maybe not, but I don't stop.

I chase the demon around the corner of my house and into the backyard. During the winter, I don't go outside to build snowmen or anything else of the sort, so my backyard is an undisturbed cake of two-foot-deep snow. The repeated process of fresh snow falling, melting, refreezing, and being covered in additional snow has left a thin crunchy layer of ice on top, so when the demon stomps through, it leaves a boot-sized hole with each step. I'm able to follow these holes punched through the snow, which means each step takes me less energy. I'm faster. I'm catching up to it. Slowly.

Still, it reaches the end of my yard where the smooth, pristine field gives way to a forest of pines and leafless birch and oak. When its hand grabs the first trunk of the woods for support, it turns its human and feminine face my way. The only features I can make out are its eyes, still burning with some internal fire. It hisses at me like a fire doused with water and I can hear in its tortured voice that it knows in its morphed, human form, it has no advantage over me. And that it is not the first of its kind I've rendered to pieces. It's angry at me. It's afraid.

It pulls itself into the woods by grasping tree trunks, almost like it's swimming. The branches and twigs are no doubt lashing its skin and leaving its human face striped with welts, but why should it care about a thing like that? When I reach the woods, only a dozen steps behind it, I let the leafless branches lash my arms and face as well. I'm going to catch this bitch, and I don't care what it costs me.

Out here, away from the streetlights and Christmas lights and glow of TVs in neighboring houses, I'm only able to see by the pale blue moonlight filtering through the trees. Everything is irregular lines of black and pale blue. If the demon chooses, if it's able to choose to turn back into its previous, spindly, skeletal form, I don't know if I could spot it out here amongst the trees and shadows. The woods would be perfect camouflage. For a moment, I'm certain I've lost sight of it. But human weakness and frailties must come along with its human form. When I catch movement between two thick oaks, it's clear its strength is waning. It's moving slower now, even as it pulls itself along by trunks and branches.

There are wetlands ahead. In summer months, weeds and cattails rim the shallow pond, and leeches, leopard frogs, and ducks fill it with life. Now, it's buried in the same deep blanket of snow as the rest of Woodduck. If you didn't know better, you could mistake it for a smooth, dry depression in a large clearing. But there's no worry of falling through the ice. As shallow as the pond is, it's frozen solid all the way down. What matters most is that the demon has no more trees with which to pull itself along or hide behind.

When it reaches the wetland, a thick cloud blows over the moon and cloaks the night in a blacker pall. The demon turns around, still retreating but doing so backward now. The only light is those coals burning where its eyeballs should be.

I stomp through the snow and onto the pond. The demon is backing away from me, but that's not easy to do in the snow. The way it's leaving a path for me to follow, I know I can reach it in just a few seconds. I'm walking now, doing what I can to catch my breath so I have air in my lungs when it comes time to dismember the thing before me.

"No use running," I tell it as I steadily close the distance between us. "I know what you are."

"And I know who you are, Abigail," the demon says in a familiar female voice that could fool anyone but me. Even so, the familiarity of the voice sends a chill through my already freezing body. When the blowing wind peels the cloud away from the moon, that cold blue light shines on the demon's face, and I see whose skin it has decided to wear.

A woman. Unassuming. Plain faced. No makeup. Hair undone. Nothing but a thin t-shirt covering her chest. No bra. St. Patrick's Day pajama pants patterned with four-leaf clovers and rainbows and pots of gold trail down into the deep snow. All of it is beyond familiar. The demon is me.

"I know what you saw," the demon says, and I know exactly what it means. I hear my own disgust for my inactions in my voice, spoken by the demon. "I know what you didn't do. I know how you ran. We all know. You let him die."

I'm lost for words, but not for screams. I bellow like a wild animal as I heave the ax head toward the moon and don't stop when it lands thick and wet in what looks like my own chest, wearing my old t-shirt. Black blood gushes from the hole ripped through the fabric. When I rip the ax free, an arc of burning tar sprays across the unblemished snow. The demon crumples but isn't down. My ax slices through the night air and into the demon's shoulder and neck. More brackish blood. More howling at the moon, both from the demon and me. We're twins in that way, sharing the purest form of sororicide. I swing again and again. With each hit, the thing that looks so much like me is broken down and buried in the snow. Too soon. Too soon because no amount of swinging can sate my rage. It's easy to tap tonight. Easy to deliver even while I send the ax head into my own body, sectioning it apart until our likenesses no longer match. Soon, there's only one set of lungs crying in the night. The thing that took my face and my form is now a mass of sludge and flesh, pooled in a depression in the snow.

Finally, my lungs run out of air and my screams die. I'm sucking the cold down my throat and panting out puffs of steam. Ice is building on my eyelashes. All around me are splatters of black blood. It's hot and melts through the top layer of snow and sinks to the ice past my cold, numb feet, perhaps even through the ice to the dead leeches and hibernating frogs. Across the surface of the pond, ice crystals of snow twinkle and glitter in the moonlight.

Chapter Thirteen
A Sleepless Night and an Email

I can't sleep, not after seeing what I've seen, hearing what I've heard, and doing what I've done. I'm exhausted, I can't get the chill out of my feet, and the furnace can't seem to keep up with the drafts in this old house. Wind whistles as its icy fingers find paths through the window sills. I want peace, but I know it won't come, and the words of the skeletal demon that wore my clothes, covered itself in my skin, and stole my voice keep ringing in my ears.

"I know what you saw. I know what you didn't do. I know how you ran. We all know!" It finishes with the words I've said to myself a thousand times before. "You let him die."

There's no sleeping, so I spend the rest of the night with my butt on my kitchen floor and my feet on the second step leading to my basement. My ax is next to me. "A Black Heart Unbroken" sits on my lap. It takes me a while to leave this world behind, comfortable knowing no demon can sneak past me here. But eventually, Eventide's words and world sweep me away.

By dawn, Sam and Jen have made their way back into the old Tudor mansion buried deep in the woods. They've consummated their relationship on the king-sized four-poster bed in the master bedroom and discovered the corpse that had watched them as they did, just as Eventide read to me. They've gone on to discover some of the house's darker history and more threatening features, like the appearing and disappearing corpses of all the people who have previously died inside its wall. But they've also realized that all the wealth and opulence the mansion offers could be theirs, that they could live a life of luxury if they can come to terms with the previous occupants.

No part of the town's mayor dangling from a chimney yet, but I feel like that might come with the turn of any page.

Through the night, no more demons come up from the basement. With each page turn, I look up from the book and down the steps just in case the sounds of scraping slip past my ears and the pressure squeezing my spine goes unfelt. Nothing. Come morning, light filters through my windows and reveals my basement's entirely normal and unthreatening concrete floor.

I don't know if these demons ever set foot in my basement, or if in the darkness the stairs descend deeper than the house's foundation, all the way to Hell. But now, in the daylight, I know I can go down there and find my water heater, the oil furnace, and the plastic tubs in which I store decorations for Halloween, Thanksgiving, and Christmas. One tub down there is still open and waiting for me to take down the red and green lights from my front eaves, but all that concerns me now is keeping what comes from down there down there. That, and the fate of Sam and Jen.

But there is something else that should be bothering me. It takes me too long to realize that the daylight means I should be dealing with all of life's usual problems. Like getting to work and keeping my job. Like the date I have scheduled tonight with Eric. Like how he said that since he hadn't gotten anything done yesterday, he absolutely has to get to work today.

Oh my god. Eric.

I look at the time glowing in green LED above my stove. I'm already late for work.

I slam the door to the basement shut and leave my signed book, the library's signed book if I'm being truthful, on the floor. And I should be truthful because I know what my lies can summon. I've relied on the theory that the demons rise up somewhere near where I am and that I can funnel them toward me by going to the top of a stairwell. But that's just a theory. Perhaps the other night when I rushed to the courthouse to cut off their escape route, other demons were climbing out of other basements. Perhaps here in my home and perhaps from other homes. If that's the case, if they're not restricted to rising up from wherever I am at the time, then they could be closing in around Eric as I speak.

While I run a brush through my hair and scrub my teeth and find clothes that are work appropriate, I remind myself that I can keep these things at bay the same way I have for all the days and weeks prior: by being pure of mind and soul. No jealous thoughts. No lustful desires. No rage or wrath. Patience. Kindness. Goodness. Self-control. I can rattle off the Fruits of the Spirit, the Ten Commandments, the Seven Heavenly Virtues, the Five Pillars of Islam, the Five Precepts of the Buddhists, the Twelve Steps of Alcoholics Anonymous, the rules on the chalkboard in my Kindergarten classroom, the regulations in the Minnesota Driver's Education manual, but none of them will do me a bit of good if I don't abide by them. As I grab my purse, my phone, my ax, and my car keys, I coach myself to calm down, breathe deep, have faith, be patient, trust in a higher power, don't give in to fear, don't give in to hate… By the time I get to my car, it feels like Yoda is telling me how to be a good Jedi Knight.

"Just get there, Abby," I say as I back out of my driveway.

Reciting the articles of a dozen different faiths keeps my mind busy during the short drive from my house to the courthouse. By the time I'm in the parking lot, the act of repeating these mores and ethos over and over again like a mantra calms and reassures me. It feels like a child's game, as effective as chanting, "I hate white rabbits" to make the smoke from a campfire blow in a different direction, but it works. I push open the doors to the courthouse and let loose a sigh of relief.

Eric's work truck wasn't in the parking lot, and I don't see him in Accounts Receivable when I walk to my desk. No toolbox or bucket of parts or anything to indicate that he'd arrived at the office. I don't see Lilith either, even though I've arrived at work a solid fifteen minutes late. That's odd but not unheard of. Hank is at his workstation, as engaged with the world around him as he ever is. The door at the back of the room leading down into the tunnels is closed and quiet. I keep my cool, rest my ax against the far corner of my desk, out of sight of any customers, and hang my coat on the back of my chair.

"Morning, Hank," I say.

"Morning," he says but doesn't move his eyes from his computer monitor. If he's noticed my tardiness, he makes no mention of it.

"Where's Lilith?" I ask.

"Director's meeting," he says and no more.

That's right. It's Friday, which means Lilith will be upstairs in the conference room for at least an hour. Since the meeting starts at the same time as my workday, usually I'm at my desk when it's time for her to rush into her office, grab a few things, and then run upstairs. So it's possible she didn't realize I wasn't here yet and certainly doesn't know just how late I arrived. That's good, especially since I'm positioning myself for the job over at the library, and all the county directors keep a tight circle. But I don't like the deception it creates.

When Lilith comes down from the meeting, should I confess my tardiness? Would it be weird of me to bring it up? How would it impact my chances at the library if I did? Are the directors upstairs right now discussing who should be selected as the next Assistant Head Librarian? I rub the grit from my already tired eyes. Moral dilemmas are exactly what I *don't* need this morning.

As these thoughts tumble through my brain, I log onto my computer and fire up my emails. I'm groggy. My muscles are tired and sore after chasing myself down through the snow and the woods and across the frozen pond. I could use a slow Friday workday. I could use a calm, stress-free weekend too, but that feels like too much to ask for. The hands of the clock on the wall opposite my desk can't move fast enough, yet they trudge along with a sluggish speed as if moving through deep snow.

Maybe the demons will stay below for the day, but work is hell, and the first pitchfork comes in the form of an email. Its tines are sharper than I ever thought possible.

"Miss Hendrix,

Thank you for your interest in the position of Assistant Head Librarian at the Woodduck Public Library. After careful review of all the applicants' resumes, we decided to go in a different direction. Please continue to apply for future vacancies as we believe you might be a valuable member of our team in the future. Have a blessed day,

The Staff of Woodduck Public Library."

So that's that. I wasn't selected for the position. I'll stay here at Accounts Receivable, at my post by the door to the underworld, just as I planned all along. I should be relieved. I should let it go. I should disregard and delete this email the same as if it were spam. But its words trap my gaze. The passive-aggressive euphemisms. The false pleasantry. The lies of what might come "in the future." A blessed day, they say, and ram the pitchfork deeper with every word of their patronizing, bullshit, form email.

They didn't even have the guts to hold interviews so I could look them in the eye and tell them why I'm the best fit, nor the decency to look me in the eyes and tell me why I'm not. Not even a phone call. Nope. They sent me a... They sent me an *email!* And who did they think was a better pick than me? Of course it's that stupid child of a man, Jason. He's there every day to butter them up and show them how nice and sweet and friendly and smart he is. Never mind he's barely an infant slipped from his mother's crotch, and he doesn't know... He doesn't know his head from a hole in the ground and will most likely leave them for another one of his fickle, life adventures that come as often as the wind changes direction. Those gullible, stupid, old maids! How could they pick him over me? Haven't I spent years with the county, showing up each day, on time, ready to work, proving my worth with everything I do? Did they call my references? Did they even talk to Lilith before they made their decision? Didn't she speak well of me? Or was it all predetermined and the hiring process just a sham formality so they could hire their golden child? God, I want to go there right now and demand some answers. I want to go right upstairs into that conference room and insist they tell me just what was going through their thick skulls when they decided I didn't even deserve a shot. And god damn it, I want to bring my ax with me.

My hand is clenched hard around my mouse, so tight, I don't know if I can't let it go. My vision is blurred with tears. My mind swims in all the unfairness of it all. Why is my sister allowed to leave this town and find her dream job and climb up the ladder and get promotions and buy a fancy car and have sexy boyfriends just to leave them for the next good-looking guy that catches her eye? Why am I forced to stay here in the town that's given me nothing but heartache, in the house where I found my dad's dead body? Why are all of these demons after me? What was my original sin, or my dad's original sin that planted them under this house that is as old as Woodduck itself? It's unfair. It's bullshit! It doesn't make any sense that Zoey is allowed to live her life however she sees fit but I'm stuck here, condemned to a boring job and the eternal task of guarding a *fucking staircase.*

I push away from my desk. I can no longer sit in front of that email. As I pace and wish away the world around me, my tears splat against the tile. When I open my eyes, my vision is clear for just a moment before they refill. I'm standing in front of the door leading down below, and in that moment of clear vision, I notice a sticky note plastered over the condemned notice. I pluck it off and bring it in front of my nose. The back of my hand wipes tears and snot from my face. I read the note.

"Abby, Got an early start this morning. Looking forward to our date tonight. Woody's 7 pm. Same time, same place. Sound good? - E"

"Hank?" I call across the office.

"Huh?" he says.

"Hank, was Eric here earlier this morning?" I ask, trying to compose myself as best as I can. My fist crumples the sticky note into a tighter and tighter ball.

"Eric who?"

"The electrician," I say, baffled by his lack of awareness. "The man who was here the other day. The guy I brought downstairs. The guy who's going to rewire the whole building. Was he here?"

Only now, after hearing the poorly repressed fear and frustration in my voice, does Hank look up from his screens. Our eyes meet. He's confused. Maybe alarmed even. Not that I care. He's doing this thing where he's lifting his shoulders as if to say he doesn't know while simultaneously shaking his head from side to side, saying "no."

"Did he go downstairs?" I say, maybe yell. Now's not the time for polite office whispers. "Hank. I need to know. Did Eric come here this morning and go downstairs?"

"I... I don't know," he finally manages to spit out. "Maybe. I wasn't paying attention. It's your job to man the front desk. I just... My job is just to..."

I don't wait for him to justify his salary. I grab my ax, move across the office, and rip open the door leading down into the tunnels. It's dark down there. It's always dark down there. But upon a second glance, I detect a dull glow. That burnt-sunset orange could be a trick played on my eyes. I wish it was, but the truth is that shine is coming from dusty lightbulbs dangling from cords in the tunnels deep below Woodduck. And they weren't on yesterday.

Chapter Fourteen
Into the Tunnels

I pour down the stairs, my rage a river. I'm cursing Hank as I go, but also forgetting him and cursing myself. How long did I sit there on the steps, guarding the wrong stairwell while Eric was here in the tunnels? Most of my thoughts were pure, clean, safe... until I came here and got that email about the library position.

Why didn't he listen to me? Why can't he understand that not everything in this world is so peachy-keen? Why didn't he believe me when I told him it was dangerous down here? And Hank. That lazy, inattentive idiot. He should have known better than to let Eric down here. He should have stopped him. He could have at least *told me* when I came into the office. If he had, well, I wouldn't have wasted my time wondering about Lilith or reading emails.

The email, Hank, Eric... they've ripped off my mask of politeness and niceties to reveal the real woman underneath, a short-tempered woman so much meaner than the nice girl I pretend to be, a woman who is tired of being cheated and ignored and put upon, a woman not pure enough to stand watch, a woman who has no other defenses left except her fury.

But if the demons already found Eric... if he's hurt... I'll only have one person to blame. As I sprint through these too-small islands of dim light, deeper into the tunnels, further from the surface, I know who's at fault. The demons crawl up from their abyss at my behest. I alone summon them. No one else. I don't understand why, but I'm the only one who can wake them up, and I'm the only one who can put them back to rest.

When I reach the T intersection, where we turned left to find the electrical panels, my eyes follow the path of those lightbulbs, a trail of glowing breadcrumbs left by Eric. But I don't see him. I see the electrical panel, the old antique that he needed to replace so badly he came down here by himself even after I told him not to, but he's not there. The bulb dangling from the cord above the panels is slowly revolving in circles, but nothing occupies its shifting pool of light on the concrete floor. God dammit, Eric, why didn't you listen?

A closer examination reveals no more information. The panels are open as if Eric had just been here, working away. His multimeter is dangling from the box by alligator clips and black and red wires, swaying like a lazy metronome with a drop of inertia still left in its pendulum, but there's no sign of its owner.

"Eric!" I call out his name in the darker direction of the tunnel. The sound is swallowed by the rough, porous surfaces of the concrete floor and cinder block walls. No echo. My voice doesn't carry. I turn back the way I came and try again. "Eric!"

A cool fifty-degree draft whispers through the tunnels. Nothing else.

I brought my cell phone along this time. Down here it's worthless for sending or receiving calls and messages, but it has a flashlight. I'd rather keep both hands on my ax and ready to swing it if something is waiting between any of these pools of light, but I need to see. I flip on the flashlight app and a cold, white beam of LED light illuminates the immediate area around me. Like the gray walls absorb my voice, they consume the light from my phone as well. But I can see another twenty feet down the tunnel, and I can see the pull string of the next lightbulb. I run to it and tug the light on. The dusty, sixty-watt bulb doesn't reach any further than my phone light, but it will stay on and shine in all directions. Leaving its island of light, even with the beam from my phone leading the way feels like sticking my hand into a kennel full of rabid dogs. Anything could come out of the gloom and sink its teeth into me before I have a chance to put both hands on my ax, but I go forward anyway. I find the next string and tug the next bulb alive.

"Eric!" I try again.

I'm not worried about drawing the demons to me. It's what I want. One or two hands on my ax doesn't matter. I'm more ready for them than Eric, who only has the vaguest gut feeling of the evil things living down here. Where the hell is he? Why would he go beyond the electrical panel, deeper into the tunnels?

"Eric!" Again, the sound of my voice dies as soon as it leaves my mouth.

Calling for him isn't working, and searching for pull string after pull string so I can move from one island of light to another is slowing me down. Behind me, the intermittent series of bulbs slowly dim in the oppressive gloom, and I feel like a sailor at night, looking back to the harbor before setting out into the open sea. It's a safety line I can no longer afford to cling to. I let the next pull string brush against my face and slip over my shoulder. With my phone and my ax, I plunge forward, deeper into the tunnels than I've ever gone before.

This far from an exit, the tunnels become less hospitable. The concrete floor is uneven. The walls are cracked. Sand and pest droppings cover the floor. Spiderwebs stretch between corners. A dead salamander lies in the middle of my path. I'm beginning to understand why these tunnels were condemned years ago. Maybe maintenance workers like Eric have come down to change out the fuses or a lightbulb, but I can tell it's been a long time since anyone came this far.

There's an intersection ahead. A four-way split. As I approach, pain radiates from my spine. My stomach cinches into a knot. My whole body feels compressed. Something is up ahead.

My light only pierces the path going forward. It touches nothing to the left or the right. If something lurks on either side, it knows I'm coming. I slow to a trot and when I reach the intersection. I whip the light around the corner to the right, then the left.

Two grimy but empty hallways, unoccupied, no different or discernible from the rest. I'm taking my time now, searching as far as I can see down the left branch, looking for any signs Eric came this way. Footprints in the dust and sand. Tools dropped and abandoned. The sticky, oily blood of a demon. Nothing. Still, that sensation of my backbone being wrung out like a dishrag is swelling. But besides the ache, there's nothing. I pan my light a hundred and eighty degrees to give the hallway at my back another thorough examination. Mid-pan, it flashes across something in the hallway between the two. Something huge. Something monstrous. Something demonic.

I cry out and find myself backpedaling down one of the hallways. The demon steps into the intersection and turns to face me.

It's something like a deer. A buck or many bucks. Brown fur has peeled away from its skull to reveal dry white bone, empty eye sockets, and deep nasal passages webbed with brittle cartilage. Long rows of teeth too canine for any earthly deer gnash the air. An entire forest of antlers rises from its head, forming a rack bigger than any trophy hunter ever dreamed of. Some tines twist downward. Some sideways. Some intertwine and fuse back together. And the antlers on its head are only a fraction of the total. Tines protrude from its chest and shoulders and back. The thing walks on hind legs and has arms like a bear, but its paws… what should be hooves or paws or hands are more antlers.

The demons I've faced before seemed biblical in origin. Goat heads and raven's feet and such. This thing… It seems primordial, a creation of oral tradition and folklore rather than any established and codified religion. As if plunging deeper into the abyss has generated neolithic, forgotten demons no longer understood by modern man.

I strangle my screams silent as I back into the darkness and aim my light at the primeval thing in front of me. Its antler hands rake the corners of the intersection, cutting me off from any escape route to the surface. I try to choke up on my ax and swing it once, twice, to test if I can fight one-handed and ward the demon off. The answer is a definitive "No." The ax is too ungainly. The beast before me is too big. The antlers are too many. The ones above its skull scrape the conduit lining the ceiling. One of its antler hands stretches toward me. I have to lose the phone, but I can't lose its light.

The solution is obvious. If I want to be able to see and swing my ax, I have to throw the phone. Turning it in my hand, screen down but LED light up, I get low and get ready to toss. If the screen cracks… well, I can only hope my problems will be so minimal. But if it bounces and lands

LED down, I'll be in total blackness and the demon will have its way with me. It takes another step, and I know I can't wait any longer before putting both my hands on my ax. I toss my phone, spinning it like a skipping stone. It bounces once off the concrete but stays screen-side down and comes to rest directly in front of the demon. Its cold shine bottom lights the hellspawn. I stifle a cheer. Both my hands grip the shaft of my ax.

"Come and get me," I say and let the grin spread across my face.

The demon steps forward. The rack of tines at the end of its right arm comes for me. I swing as hard as I can. The weight of the ax smashes into the nest of antlers. Tines crack and rattle to the concrete. The demon wails but takes another step forward. It's backlit now. A silhouette before the shine of my phone. I feign retreat then launch my attack. The ax head slices through the dark until it plows into something hard and wet. The demon cries. Its hot blood splatters on my hands.

It's backing up, my phone directly underneath it for just a moment. I attack again, sinking the ax into its chest. It recoils. Something cracks and suddenly, all the light is gone. Hopefully, its foot is just blocking the light, but for now, I'm left to swing my ax blindly. So I do. As dark as it is, there's no sense in trying to win the fight with well-placed and well-timed strikes. This isn't fencing. This is slaughtering. I scream and swing the ax like the mad woman I am. Fast strikes. Hard strikes. Repeated strikes. That's the only way. And the ax blade lands into flesh. Again and again. I'm getting it. I'm winning.

By the sense of motion and sound, I can tell it's reeling back. Still, the light from my flashlight hasn't returned. Nothing to do about that now. All I can do is swing as hard and as fast as I can. Just when I think I have it, when my next blow will be the killing blow, my ax hits nothing but air. The handle almost slips from my blood-wet hands. I'm off balance. A full rack of tines cuts through the air and rakes across my head, shoulder, and left arm. My body smacks against the unforgiving cinder block wall. Stars explode in my head. All the air is vacant from my lungs. Any sense of direction is gone. The clench around my spine is so painful, any second it might split in two.

The demon is wheezing close by. A moment of inaction lingers, kept time by the rhythmic splats of blood falling from the demon's wounds. It stinks, hot and putrid. Or maybe, some of that acidic, metallic stench is my own fear and blood. No time to dwell and find out.

My feet find uneven but solid ground. My ears lock onto the demon's breathing. I launch myself toward it. The ax hits something solid but not immobile. Bones crack and tinker to the floor. When I try to land another blow, I'm off balance, falling into the gap where it had stood. My face sinks into its stinking, rotting fur. But we're falling together. When it collides with the floor and I collapse deeper into it, it lands with such permanence, I know it's dead.

Climbing off of it, distancing myself from the awful, stinking, mass of downed beast, I'm thankful for the cold, hard concrete. Staying on my hands and knees, I'm just as eager to find my phone, my one source of light, and give my eyes something to see again. Eventually, my hands land on the case. My fingers turn it over and I can already feel the sharp edges of the cracked screen. Hitting all the buttons, swiping and tapping and smacking it, I know it's as dead as the demon I just killed.

My phone clatters to its concrete grave. The corpse of the deer demon, covered in blood and stink and all those antlers rests in the middle of the four-way intersection. Dead, but a thing that seemed dead from conception has no obligation to be more dead now. Rather than climb over it, I go the only direction left to me. I'm completely turned around and have no idea which direction I came from, so there's no way of knowing if this is the right way, or if there is a right way. But Eric, dead or alive, is down here somewhere. I have to find him.

"Eric!" I call out again.

When the primordial deer thing died, the tension eased but didn't release. There are more demons down here. They weigh heavy on me, compressing my ribs and vertebrae. As I move through the dark, I use that sensation to guide me. Occasionally, a lightbulb pull string grazes my face and I brush it aside. By the time any pool of light would do me any good, I'm beyond its reach. I navigate by the pressure. By the squeeze. By the dread of what is ahead. Feeling for corners along the rough, unpainted, cinder block walls, I turn left, turn right, and pass straight through intersections. My fear guides me through the labyrinth, but unlike Theseus, my thread pulls me closer and closer to the Minotaur rather than further away. And when I reach the thread's end, will I find that cursed offspring of bull and queen, or something worse?

Everything is less refined down here. Less civilized. More unearthly. Sometimes the floor is covered in sand. Other times it's wet where water has leaked in. The tunnel is so cracked and uneven, I'm afraid it will drop off into a bottomless chasm any moment. A path straight to Hell where all of these abominations have climbed up. But that pit never comes. Just broken concrete through which snakes and salamanders can gain interest during summer months. I drag a palm against a filthy, rough wall. My boot steps on something hollow and fragile. It cracks under my weight. Bending down, still completely blind, I pick up a shard and use my fingers to examine it. Something old and made of clay. Touching it raises all the hairs on my arms. As black as it is, holding the shard two inches from my eyes doesn't help. I toss it aside and keep moving.

I still have my ax. It drips blood as black as the night. The splats mark time like the ticking of a clock, and I know, if I intend to find Eric alive, every drop counts.

I'm moving. I'm calling. I'm counting drops of blood that fall less and less frequently as my ax dries. I'm searching the all-black of the unlit tunnels for the faintest glimmer of light while my eyes play tricks on me. Kaleidoscope phosphenes dance in the darkness. Another pull-string of a lightbulb brushes across my face, but by now I'd be more blinded than sighted by the shine of the bulb. There is light ahead, impossibly faint, maybe two turns of the tunnels away, but I see it. And that draw of dread and pressure are coming from the same direction.

Another turn of the tunnel and another strand crosses my face. I take a hand from my ax only long enough to peel it off my sweat-wet skin. The tunnels remain their eternal fifty degrees, but that's not enough to keep me cool. Another string drags horizontally across my brow, and I realize this time it's not the pull string of a light. There's another. Then a third. A whole spiderweb. I hold a palm out in front of my face to ward off more sticky threads of silk. That dim light is growing stronger. Sounds come from that direction. Scratching, scraping sounds. Demon noises. The light is growing bright. The squeeze of my spine is growing tight. I turn a corner.

The pure white shine of an LED flashlight is filtered by a thousand strands of a spider's web and by things moving like characters in a shadow theater. Hundreds of teeth click against each other. A man grunts and whimpers. Eric. I swing my ax side to side, clearing away the webs like a reaper in a field of wheat. A whole wall of webs opens as if I'm pulling away a shower curtain.

Shelob's bastard son waits for me on the other side. The demon takes up the full width of the tunnel. It is spider-like in shape only. The legs, which should be black, hair-covered, exoskeletal bones, are instead a collection of additional species. One limb is a millipede with a thousand subordinate legs and tipped with a round mouth full of concentric rings of fangs. Another is an albino python with beady red eyes. Another is a human arm, ending in a calloused and dirty hand with too many fingers. Another is a tail, scaled and spiked at the end like a flail. Where they all connect at its thorax or torso or central hub, there are mouths of just as many varieties. If the thing has any eyes, they're not turned toward me yet.

Beyond the demon, Eric is on the ground, his back against the flat wall of a T intersection, a flashlight in one hand and the pipe wrench from his tool belt in the other. The flashlight is our only light source. His clothes are ripped, his blood leaking from slashes and abrasions, but he is alive. His expression is the only one that can be expected of him: abject terror and quickly slipping sanity. Four of those various limbs of the demon loom over him, waiting for whatever central nervous system commands them to give the killing order. How Eric survived for any length of time against this thing while armed only with a pipe wrench, I don't know. But it's clear by the look in his eyes, he won't last much longer.

I come in hard and fast. My ax is coated in webbing, but that doesn't slow it down. The blade slices through the carapace of a limb before I recock and plant it into that hub where all the appendages meet. The thing screeches. I swing again and the white head of the python flops to the concrete and writhes. The demon rotates on its remaining limbs and turns a horde of segmented eyes my way. If it wasn't for their internal fire, I wouldn't see them. But now that I can, I focus on the middle of the nest. My ax lands dead center, but not before the mouth of the millipede limb sinks its rings of teeth into my ribs and rips out a chunk of flesh. Another appendage knocks me against the wall.

That's okay. I have some distance now. A moment to set my feet and take a breath.

Eric is back on his feet. His pipe wrench is inked in demon's blood. He has it wound up for a strike. But that hunk of cast iron has no edge, and the exoskeleton of this demon is too hard to bludgeon with any effect. An attack on his part is suicide. Meanwhile, half of the demon's burning eyes are veiled in its blood. The rest are focused on me. For now.

I launch myself back into the fight. My ax hits just above its nest of eyes, through its thoracic shell, and deep into its core guts. Eric is committed to his attack as well. He's growling and howling in a way that is so counter to his personality, I hate every sound of it. He's ill-adapted for this. His weapon unfit. His anger too unpracticed. His heart too kind. None of this was meant for him. He earned none of this. I did. This is my fight. These are my demons. So, I do the lion's share of the killing.

My ax is a threshing machine. It churns through the demon's hide, severing limbs and turning its eye-covered hub into pâté. Its branches slack. Its torso sinks. I come down for one final blow with a full, over-the-head swing, the same as if I'm splitting wood. The ax head drops and cleaves through the demon's wet remains all the way through to the floor.

The demon finally crumples to the cold concrete. Eric retreats until his back is against the wall once again. I don't know if he saw me with my ax before the thing fell, or if his vision was consumed by the demon, but he sees me now. And for a moment, I see myself through his eyes.

A woman covered in strands of spiderweb and splatters of black blood clinches an ax like a maniac at bat. She lands a boot on top of the abomination's corpse and walks on top of it. Her head ducks to fit under the low ceiling. Her shoulders are hunched over. Her lungs pump air in and out in big, labored, greedy huffs. Her light-starved eyes now staring into a flashlight are pin-prick pupils with red tributaries cutting through the whites. She's clearly insane, unhinged, dangerous, murderous.

Seeing what my life and my lies and my crimes have done to him, seeing the fear I've instilled in him, I try to soften my face, to let him know I'm not a threat. Not to him. Not ever. I drop my ax and run to him, wrapping him in my arms. My lips are next to his ear and I'm whispering lie after lie. "It's okay. You're safe. It's dead. Everything's going to be fine."

Meanwhile, the giant, invisible fist that's slowly turning my backbone to meal hasn't eased a bit.

Chapter Fifteen
Keeping Warm

As Eric and I make our way through the tunnels, searching for an exit, any exit, the demons keep a firm grip on my spine. Even if it eases, or if I grow completely numb to it, I'm not so naive to think that they're gone for good. And now, someone else knows my secret. I should be happy that it's Eric who found me out and not Lilith or Hank or Zoey, but I'm not.

Eric was the exception to my afflictions. He was a life ring of normality in my sea of sin and shame and grief. With him, everything was new and wholesome and pure. He was everything right with life, keeping me afloat in the tumultuous waves while everything wrong in my life tried to pull me under. But now I've pulled him under the surface with me.

He's quiet for the first few minutes as we hang onto each other and limp our way through the tunnels. He's injured and I suppose he needs time to gather his strength. And to process. That's fair, so I don't say anything either. His flashlight leads the way, bouncing from wall to wall, floor to ceiling, searching for a way out.

Eventually, he says, "Holy mackerel, what the hell was that thing?"

"Nothing," I say. "It's gone now."

"It's nothing? That thing had tube worms for arms! And an elephant trunk with horns! And a plain old human arm!" he says, getting louder and more indignant at the irrationality that has infiltrated his reality. "It had a hundred eyes. A hundred eyes!"

"It's dead now. And the other one too."

"There was *another* one?" he says but doesn't wait for an answer. "Holy Toledo, you killed that thing!"

"We killed it. Together," I say.

"Yeah, but what the hell was it?"

"I told you it was dangerous down here," I remind him.

"Yeah. You said it. Tell your boss I'm going to have to charge 'em extra," he says.

The beam of his flashlight cuts irregular figure eights through the gloom. Along one arch, I catch a glint of reflected light. A pair of eyes? No. It's metal. A ladder. Leading up to where, who knows.

"Look," I say. "A way out."

At the top of the ladder is an ancient, rusted padlock. Eric's pipe wrench takes care of that with a few strikes. The hatch above the lock is equally rusted. When he cracks it open, brown flakes snow onto my head and shoulders. As he forces the hatch up, we're greeted by more darkness, but I can tell by the scent of the fresh air, and the coldness of it, that it's somewhere above ground. Back in the real world. Back in Woodduck. Eric reaches down a hand and helps me up the ladder.

When we emerge, we're in a dark room. Unheated. Drafty. The air is frigid up here and reeking of iron oxide and grease and something akin to manure even though there are no animals or straw. It freezes our sweat immediately. We're in some sort of small utility building, an anteroom to the wider world we're more familiar with. A pale, blue rectangular outline of light marks the doorway. Eric reaches for it.

"Wait," I tell him.

"What is it?" he asks and keeps his hand off the doorknob.

"What are we going to say?" I ask.

"Well, nobody should go back down into those tunnels. I can rewire the electric above ground. I can install the panels in a janitor's closet or hell, anywhere but down there," Eric says. "We should fill that stairwell with concrete."

"That... won't work," I say, and it feels like the start of a confession. Like a leak in a levee that will inevitably tear the whole thing down. Even up here, above the tunnels, that pressure around my spine continues, as if the last demons screwed a vise grip on my bones and there's no handle with which to unwind it.

"Why wouldn't it? We'll concrete this too," he says, gesturing to the hatch we came up. "We'll fill in every opening those tunnels have."

"Because it's not just the tunnels," I say. "Basements. Cellars. I think if it wasn't for the underground places, they'd climb right out of the dirt."

"Not this time of year. You know how deep the frost line is around here?" he says.

"That doesn't matter, Eric. You don't get it. That wasn't just some mutated animal back there. They don't play by the same rules as… gophers and groundhogs. Tunnels and basements and doorways or concrete barriers won't matter. They'll come. When it's their time to come from below, they'll find a way up," I say too much.

"You've seen them before," Eric says.

"Yeah. I have. Too often," I say. "Listen. When we leave here, when we go back out there around other people, you can't say anything about what you saw down there."

"Hell if I can't," he snaps back at me.

"It will be hell if you do," I say. "Listen to what I'm trying to tell you. Nobody can do anything about those things besides me. Okay? They're my problem and I'm handling them."

"What are you, crazy?" Eric says. "I don't know an exterminator on Earth that would take on that job. Why would you think–"

"Because it's my fault," I say. "Those things… I call them up. Not because I want to but because I can't help it. Because I'm weak. Because I'm… I'm a coward. Because I can't control myself and they know it and they use me to try to get to the surface. And some of them have already succeeded."

"You need help," he says flatly and without explanation.

"Screw you," I say. In my case, a shrink would come with a complementary straitjacket.

"You need *my* help," he specifies.

"I didn't want you to get involved in this," I bite back. "I told you not to go down there. I don't expect you or anyone else to understand. And I don't need your or anyone else's help. Just leave me be."

Now I'm the one moving toward that rectangle outline of blue light, and he's grabbing my shoulder, stopping me. I turn on him.

"Let me go," I demand.

"I can't," Eric says. "Abby, I've known you for, what, three days? We've gone out once before and if this is our second date, how in the hell am I supposed to shoot you down for date Number Three? You are, by far, the most interesting person in all of Woodduck County."

I scoff at that. "If you want entertaining, you should meet my sister."

"How glutton for punishment do you think I am? I know who that woman was yelling at the Records Department on the second floor. I could tell you two were sisters from the start. She had the same fire in her eyes you have now," he says. "Only, she doesn't have the honesty in her eyes like you. Or your warm smile. And definitely doesn't have your open heart."

"Eric, I'm trying to tell you, you don't know the whole picture," I do my best to make it clear to him. "There's things in my past. Things I've done. Things I should have done but didn't have the courage to do. All of this is my fault. And as for my heart? You have no idea."

"Show me," he says.

The idiot. I pull away and open the door.

We shield our eyes from daylight as we emerge from an abandoned pump house forgotten on the edge of the forest. We tromp through snow to the icy road, and even there, back in the real world, I have a hard time placing our location. As bright as the day seemed when we first stepped out of the small utility building on the edge of town, the clouds are so thick I can hardly tell where the sun hides behind them. Blown snow blots out anything further than a few hundred yards away. I can see the pump house, the forest, the two-lane blacktop road, and gray.

That is until I complete a full circle and see a tall building standing on top of a hill. It's a nineteenth-century Renaissance Revival manor with a turret, seven gables, and two narrow chimneys that rise above the peaks. The mayor of Woodduck once swung from one of those chimneys.

"Come on. My house is this way," I point in the opposite direction of HHR Eventide's home.

For warmth, we hold hands.

The light of day dies before we reach my house.

Our cars are all the way across town, parked outside of the courthouse, so we have to walk the whole way. As wet as we were with sweat and blood when we climbed out of the tunnels, we are almost hypothermic by the time we reach my place. What was wet is now frozen. The crush of the demons still hasn't left my spine, but the cold seems to have numbed the sensation. Huddled together for warmth, we stagger up my front walk. The head of my ax drags dry across the stoop. I never lock my front door, and we're lucky for that. My purse and my keys are at the courthouse.

If it weren't for leaning and holding one another as we are, I don't think we would have made it to the front door. As soon as we're able to close the door to the cold behind us, we collapse in a heap on the floor. The handle of my ax clatters against the kitchen floor. Minutes tick by while we shiver. There's a drowsiness that consumes me and I can see it in Eric's eyes too. The frost on our clothes is thawing again, rewetting us and providing no relief to the chill.

"Gotta get out of these wet clothes," Eric stammers.

We're toeing off our boots and shucking off damp pants. I spot the mounds of blankets on my couch and crawl on all fours toward it. When I can prop myself up against the couch, I peel off my shirt and bra, because I'm wet all the way down. The discarded clothes smack against the carpet. I'm pulling dry, warm quilts and blankets from the couch. Eric is behind me, still shivering, but down to his skin now. With no words exchanged, we climb onto the couch and into the blankets, naked and entwined with one another. We burrow into the nest together. The shaking cold in our bones begins to ease.

Together, we're warm. Together, we feel safe.

"We'll find a way to fix this. Everything will be okay. None of this could ever be your fault. I'll help you." Eric whispers promises into my ear he has no ability to keep. I don't mind one bit.

There, insulated from the rest of the world, I exchange his lies for my own. "Don't worry. They're gone now. We did it. We killed them all."

Our words won't hold up to the light of day, but here, tonight, inside our haven of blankets, they sound as beautiful as truth. Even the now-constant squeeze of nearby hellspawn blends with our crowded warm embrace. Our skin grows warm against each other. Our strength returns. Our nerves grow eager. When his lips touch mine, they're hot. His kisses warm every part of my body. There is nowhere else I want to exist, nothing else I desire, nothing else I want to think of. Before long, he's on top of me, and I'm guiding him inside of me. I grip his biceps like they are the only things anchoring me to reality. My whole world exists between those arms.

The crush around my spine never dies, but it gives leave to my conscious mind. In the basement of this old house, ancient, evil, and hungry things lust for the surface. All across town, horrible, murderous things salivate for the soft vulnerable delicacies just a frost layer away. And all those stairwells and ladders and hatches and doorways? The gates are thrown open. The watchtowers are abandoned. Outside of my perfect world between Eric's arms, Earth is stripped nude and laid bare on the wedding bed before Hell and all its Legion.

But our love is real. Our communion is whole. And our lies are so strong when morning light pours through the living room window, I still believe them.

Chapter Sixteen
The Next Morning

It's Saturday. No work for either of us for the rest of the weekend. No obligations. No alarms. No outside world pulling us away from each other. Eric and I, we sleep in. When my eyes crack open to the soft shine of morning coming through my living room window, I'm met with a deep sense of fulfillment. Eric is crowded next to me on my narrow couch. He snores as if there's nothing in the world, or below it, to worry about. My wounds from the demons we faced in the tunnels seemed to have healed overnight as if all I ever needed was his touch to overcome their attacks. I climb off the couch, careful to let him keep sleeping. I make coffee. I read. I do the laundry to wash clean the blood and tar and cobwebs and dust from our clothes. He stirs. I make eggs. He rouses to the smell of bacon. We eat together. His bruises and abrasions are also gone as if I've healed him as much as he has healed me. We find ways to joke about the horrors we've endured. As I see the sunrise reflect off of those innocent blue eyes, I know things aren't so bad. In these thin hours, I actually believe that everything will be okay.

The tightness around my back is still there, never wavering now, but I'm used to it. Hardly feel it at all.

Both of our cars are up at the courthouse, and eventually we come to the conclusion that we better go get them. It's bitterly cold out. Of course, it's cold out. After a night spent together, crammed side by side on the couch, sharing all those blankets, everything is cold in comparison. But that chill that sets into my bones in December and usually lasts through March has thawed. My marrow is fluid once again. It's easier to find the courage to step outside. We wear old coats that belonged to Dad, and when Eric holds my hand inside the worn-thin, leather, work glove, it stays warm.

We walk along 7th Avenue to Hill Road. The sky is gray. The light is muted and drab. All the colors are faded and diminished. The sidewalks are poorly cleared, sometimes covered in slush, sometimes ice, sometimes salt. Only rarely is there bare concrete. These are all the reasons it should be a miserable Saturday morning, but that's not how I feel. So I didn't get the job I wanted. So I'll never be as sexy and cool and self-determined as my sister. So maybe all the demons are dead or maybe they're not. I don't care. The heat of another hand is coming through the old leather gloves, and that's plenty enough to keep me warm.

When we reach Hill Road, we look both ways. Not because of traffic. No one is out this morning. First, I gaze south to Eventide's mansion and the way we came from yesterday.

"Maybe they are all gone," I say.

"What's going on up there?" Eric says, looking in the opposite direction.

To the north end of Hill Road, toward the courthouse, there are police lights. Initially, I assume somebody got pulled over, but what doesn't make sense about that is that the sheriff's deputy's car is turned sideways across Hill Road as if to block traffic.

"An accident?" I posit.

We walk toward the police lights because we don't have much of a choice. After all, we have to get to our cars. As we approach, I'm craning my neck, trying to see around the emergency vehicles. Two cop cars and an ambulance cluster around the intersection of 3rd Avenue and Hill Road. There are no other vehicles. No smashed-up wrecks. No tow trucks. Not even broken glass as far as I can tell. We're approaching downtown but still in a neighborhood, so residents are standing on stoops trying to see whatever it is we're also trying to see too. Then I notice the Woodduck Public Library on the corner. It's the only public building on the block, an anomaly of zoning regulation, but it matches the reserved serenity of the old houses and old residents. And somehow, I know it has something to do with what has happened between all of these flashing lights.

"Oh, Jesus," Eric says when we get closer.

He's a few inches taller than me, so he sees it before I do. I get a good look at the crime scene seconds later. And it is a crime scene, complete with yellow tape strung up between stop signs as if the intersection is an impromptu boxing ring. And in the middle? A body lying on the canvas. Or on the iced-over street rather. And just like in a Hollywood crime drama, the body is covered with a white sheet. Under it, someone is dead. Somebody from Woodduck. Somebody I probably know.

Eric must be thinking the same thing. His hand is clamping mine tight. The leather is no cushion. He's hustling to the scene, dragging me along. Although, an awful possibility torments my mind and mine alone. I have a short list of suspects who might have perpetrated this crime, and they were all summoned from Hell by yours truly. Because even if we killed the last two remaining demons that lived in the tunnels, that still leaves at least three above ground unaccounted for. Two who escaped from the courthouse the night of our first date, and the first demon who escaped my house the night Dad was killed. And last night, in the throes of passion, would I have noticed if additional hellspawns crawled up from my basement and slipped out my door?

It's only now that I realize how out of control of myself I'd been last night. How I threw all of my discipline and diligent piety out the window. How I'd sinned. How selfish I'd been. How much sorrow I allowed to seep up to the surface.

We're against the police tape now. Deputy Ruiz is here in her brown Sheriff's Department coat and one of those hats with the ear flaps that makes her look like Snoopy. She's telling us to keep our distance, that this area is restricted, that there's no present danger or cause for alarm, and how they have everything under control. That last bit, it's more like she's telling herself than us. To be honest, I don't hear much of what she's saying. A high-pitched ringing fills my ears. My eyes are fixed on the shape under the bed sheet. I don't have much time to contemplate who might be underneath it before the cold January wind does us a favor and spares us any more speculation. A breeze catches a corner and flips it off the corpse.

It's Jason. From the library. The young kid taking a break from his college anthropology studies and so recently selected for the position of Assistant Head Librarian. His blood is frozen dark but that doesn't make it any less visible on his white Adidas hoodie. I glance at the library's entrance and see there is an X of yellow tape stretched across the front door. It's easy to fill in the gaps from here. Jason went into work this morning, and someone or something lured him out here and murdered him in the street.

It's only when I return my gaze to the crime scene that I see the murder weapon. It's not far from the body, next to a little paper tent with the number 1 written on it. It's an ax.

"We're just passing through," Eric explains to the sheriff's deputy, but his eyes are fixed on the body and the weapon the same as mine.

"Go. Stay out of the tape and go about your business. This is an official crime scene," Deputy Ruiz tells us.

Eric pulls me away, not just from a crime scene, but from a murder scene. Because regardless of my morning's optimism, the truth is, things that kill are stalking through the streets of Woodduck. I invited them here, and I realize for the second time that I'm responsible for someone's death. First Dad. Now Jason.

"Holy cripes. Did you see that?" Eric says as we go on our way toward the courthouse.

I hardly hear him through the combined sensation of cotton stuffed in my ears and a violin playing inside my head. The strangulation of my spine is constant now.

"Do you know who that was? I didn't recognize him, but he looked familiar. I know I've seen him around town. He was young. Do you know him?" Eric is babbling, verbally processing every thought spinning through his brain.

"Yeah," I say. "I do."

"Who was that? Who would do that to him? In Woodduck, no less. Was he, like, a drug dealer or a criminal or something? Maybe somebody come up from the Cities? Who was he?"

"A librarian," I say.

"Shit," Eric says, and the word seems so much more profane coming from his mouth. Any residual beauty from our peaceful morning is carried away by the cold wind like that white sheet stolen from the body, its horrors revealed as they should be, because truth is rarely beautiful.

Eric's work truck is parked around the back of the courthouse, which explains why I didn't see it yesterday when I showed up late. Having not seen it, I assumed he wasn't down in the tunnels, but all I would have had to do was ask around or maybe taken the time to notice the sticky note he left on the door. I was being careless, self-absorbed, and inattentive. That kind of recklessness, I can't afford it anymore. The demons are above ground and they're killing people in Woodduck, and it's all my fault. The guilt grips me as tight as the hands wringing my spine.

When we reach the edge of the courthouse parking lot, we have to split ways.

"Can I call you?" Eric asks.

"Actually... I broke my phone yesterday," I tell him.

"You got a house phone?" he asks.

"Who does?" I say.

"Well, can I stop by later on today? Just to, you know, check in on ya?" he says.

"Yeah. Maybe. I don't know. I got some stuff I need to take care of," I say.

"Like getting a new cell phone?" he says.

"Yeah," I say. That and hunting down demons who look like humans who are framing me for murder.

"We'll have to figure out what to tell them," Eric says. "About the tunnels. Come Monday morning, they're going to expect me to go down there and replace that panel. And if I don't do it, they'll find someone else who will."

"Okay. Yeah," I say, not really communicating with Eric, because my mind is on a million other things. And because I can't help but suspect that what happened this morning is because of what we did together last night. When he steps close to me, close enough to touch my hips, it's like an electric shock.

"Look, if I did something yesterday I shouldn't have..." he starts.

"No. No, it's nothing you did. It's just… I'm just… I'm upset is all. I need some time to figure things out," I say. "Don't come over today. I'll get a new phone and I'll call you when things are better."

"When is that going to be?"

"I don't know. Not today. My keys are inside," I say and gesture to the courthouse. "I'll call you."

"Okay," Eric says.

We don't kiss. We're backing away from each other now. This is the furthest we've been from each other since we were inside the tunnels. With each step that distance grows, but I have to let him go.

"Call as soon as you can, okay?" he says.

"Yeah. Talk later," I say and turn my back to him.

He heads off to his truck and I head into the courthouse. Need to gather my things. Need to get a new phone. And then?

I don't know what to do then, but I have to do something.

Most Saturdays, the courthouse is locked and empty. But today? It's clear as soon as I walk inside that the murder just a few blocks away has woken up more people than just the sheriff's department. The place is busier than any Monday in recent memory. I don't want to talk to anyone. As they shuffle along the main corridor, rushing from one department to another, it doesn't seem anyone wants to talk to me either. I'd prefer it if no one even saw me, but once I get into Accounts Receivable, there's no getting around it. Lilith is here, going from her office to the printer and back, frantic and not her usual demure self. As if accountants are going to somehow solve the ax murder outside of the library. As soon as I walk in the door, she freezes and our eyes lock.

"Abby where were you yesterday?" she asks, sparing any pleasantries.

"I…" I stall for time. "I was down in the tunnels with Eric. The electrician. He needed me to show him the way. Hank should have told you."

No lies so far, which is good. The last thing I need is more sins summoning more hellspawns from below. Or to implicate myself any further.

"All day?" she asks. "I called you and you didn't answer."

"Yeah. All day. There's no reception down there. Sorry. What's going on here?" I ask, even though I already know and I'm already at my desk and gathering up my things.

"Something happened. Something bad. Over at the library." She's going about whatever business she has again, making it clear my absence yesterday isn't her biggest concern. Or, pretending that she doesn't already know I'm the number one suspect and intentionally avoiding conflict with a murderer. "I don't know if I'm allowed to tell you about it."

I ask the next question, not because I want to, but because I'm expected to ask it. Because it would be suspicious and rude if I didn't. I can't afford for her to answer "Yes," but I ask anyway. "Do you need my help?"

"No," she says. "It's okay. I got it."

Whether she says that because she's a good boss and doesn't want to tie up her employee with unnecessary busy work on a Saturday, or if she's truly afraid of me, I can't tell. All the same, her answer is a relief. I grab my things and leave as quickly and as quietly as I can.

I have a motive. I had the opportunity. I had the murder weapon. Sure, now there are two axes around town, but somehow I doubt showing that off will lessen my culpability in the matter. As soon as Sheriff Graham talks to the right people and has time to put two and two together, they'll haul me in and throw away the key. Every resident in Woodduck is a potential witness. My every observable action is evidence.

But I need a new phone. And there's only one place in town where I can get one. I'm left with one, disgusting, and desperate choice:

Walmart.

It's out along the highway. Far away from everything going on in town. It's Saturday morning, so it shouldn't be too busy. And they have those self-checkout lanes. I can be in and out. Quick. Clean. Completely anonymous.

When I pull my Volt into the parking lot, I realize that the place isn't going to be as empty as I thought. Stretched in front of me is an endless field of cars and carts and pedestrians from all around the county. A horde of folks all eager to export their money from the local economy to a corporate headquarters in Arkansas and stockholders in Manhattan. If there's any place above ground in all of Woodduck I'd rather not be, it's here. But I'm only here to get one thing. Nothing else. I find a parking spot near the back and speed walk inside.

I tuck my chin in my chest and make no eye contact along the way to the electronics department. The cheap, push-button-keypad, pay-by-the-minute phones, as affordable as they are, are still behind a glass case, which means I have to wait for an employee to unlock them. Meanwhile, my head is on a swivel, watching for anyone whom I might recognize or who might recognize me. I wipe a puddle of sweat from my brow and as I turn back to the worker, I realize I'm only making myself more conspicuous. After all, don't they call these kinds of phones "burner" phones? Because drug dealers and criminals use them and then throw them away when their misdeeds are done?

Those worries are valid, and I know I should be worried about them, but all of those thoughts evaporate the moment I spot a familiar face over by the book racks.

It's Jason.

The librarian. The new Assistant Head Librarian. Or, it's something that looks like Jason. And somehow, I doubt that was the body of a demon only mimicking Jason lying there in the middle of 3rd Avenue and Hill Road.

He hasn't seen me, or he pretends not to see me. He– Not he. *It*. It is browsing through the books, exactly the sort of thing people might expect a still-living Jason to do. But I know better than to go after it. My ax is back home and rendering a demon to pieces in a Walmart on a Saturday morning isn't exactly my idea of being inconspicuous.

"Ma'am?" the worker says. He has my new phone in its blister pack on the counter between us. "Are you okay?"

"Yeah," I say. The Demon-Jason walks down an aisle, out of sight, which cases my nerves the same way a pebble in the path might slow a boulder rolling down a hill. "Thought I saw a ghost, is all. I'll pay upfront."

I take the burner phone and head in the direction of the bookshelves. I can't let it see me, but I can't let it wander off either. I know the disguises of the two demons who slipped out of the courthouse the night of my first date with Eric: the man in the green seed jacket and my sister. I don't know the disguise of the demon that killed my father, but for reasons I can't articulate, I'm almost certain it's not Jason. No. This, I'm fairly confident, is a new demon. Most likely a demon that found a way up from Hell last night and murdered the real Jason this morning. When I reach the aisle where it disappeared, I peek around the corner. Nothing but books and magazines. And what book is right here on the end cap? Of course Walmart is fully stocked with copies of "A Black Heart Unbroken." For a moment, I think about grabbing a copy. Instead, I head for the front door.

    I poke my head around every aisle, on edge, ready for this Jason fraud to attack me. Or anyone else for that matter. There's no way it's a coincidence that the demon is here in Walmart on the one day of the year I also came to Walmart. Is the thing really going about pretending to be the human it just killed? Is this what demons do in their free time? Shop at Walmart? As ridiculous as that sounds, it makes a lot of sense. In hindsight, if I were to discover that every shopper I've ever seen in a Walmart was an unholy, hell-born, infernal beast, it would answer a lot of questions.

    In the men's department, I spot the old farmer still wearing the ugly, green, Northrup King seed jacket. There is no way to tell the man apart from the monster. As much as I want to grab an ax from the hardware department and bury it between his eyes while he browses for underwear, I'd be as likely to kill an innocent human being as rid the town of a hellspawn. So I break my eyes away from him, from it, from who knows… and head for the self-checkout. Along the way, I'm scanning every aisle and walkway. If the demons know I'm here, if they know who I am, if they know how many of their brethren I've killed, they should either be running for the front door or surrounding me to finish me off.

    I'm almost out of this man-made hellscape when I see another familiar face. Over in the pharmacy department, perusing through pills and band-aids. He doesn't spot me, even though I've stopped right there in one of the big busy walkways. I don't know if I want him to or not. My brain has my body paralyzed while it tries to sort out the chances of the man I'm watching being an actual man, or the demonic replacement of a man.

    It's Eric. He's wearing the same clothes he wore when we parted ways at the courthouse. When my fingers traced the contours of his naked body this morning, the cuts and scrapes were gone. So why is he shopping for band-aids and aspirin? But is that really enough evidence for me to attack him in the middle of a Walmart? On the other hand, if I go up to him and tell him I have a phone now and give him the new number, how can I be sure he won't make me as dead as Jason?

I break my paralysis and aim the cart for the self-checkout. The truth is, I can't trust anyone in Woodduck. Not anymore. Not until I hunt down and kill every one of these things. Of that much, I'm certain. What I don't know is how the hell I'm supposed to manage that all by myself.

Chapter Seventeen
Wanted

Back home, I do something equally disgusting and out of character. I turn on the news. The station is out of Duluth, an hour and twenty minutes away, but they're covering the murder here in Woodduck. It doesn't look like they have any reporters on site, but that won't take long. Meanwhile, the anchors are leaning heavily on words like "shocking" and "grizzly." This is only going to draw more attention and more people into town. More potential victims. More potential faces for demons to hide behind. More law enforcement to inevitably put the pieces together and come knocking on the door of the woman who recently lost a job opening to the victim, was gone the day and night of the murder, and regularly carries around an ax identical to the one the victim was murdered with.

Then it hits me. Zoey. She's down in Minneapolis, not here where all the demons roam. Certainly, she can pull some strings and use her connections to help me out. After all, what are sisters for if not for keeping each other out of federal prison?

It takes me a few minutes to activate my new phone and load it within minutes. It takes longer for me to remember Zoey's phone number. It only rings twice before it goes straight to voicemail. That bitch! She saw the call come in and intentionally sent it to voicemail. I call again. Again, straight to voicemail, after only one ring this time. I call again and this time when it goes to voicemail, I start leaving a message.

"Zoey, I can't explain over the phone, but I need some help. Call me–" I'm saying when the phone makes a weird noise I don't recognize. Looking at the screen, I see there's an incoming call from her number. I end the voice mail and answer the call.

"Who the fuck is this?" my sister says before I have a chance to say anything.

"Zoey, it's me, Abby. Is that how you always answer the phone?"

"It is when caller ID tells me you're a 'Scam Likely.' What are you calling from a burner phone?" Zoey says, smacking gum in my ear.

"Yeah. I can explain. Actually, no, I can't. Are you watching the news?" I ask.

"The day I want my skull drilled open, drained, and topped off with liberal bullshit will be the day I'll watch the news. No. I'm not watching the news. But I bet I know why you're calling. Somebody got unalived in your nice, quiet, little town and now you're scared, and you need big sis to come and tell you everything is going to be okay. Is that about right?"

"I mean, sort of."

"Okay. Sure. I'll get right on that. Just as soon as you pay a twenty eight dollar fee so I'm able to requisition the fuck I'll have to give."

"Zoey–"

"See how it feels?" She says, the gum loud in the earpiece.

"Would you listen to me! There's more to it than that. They're going to think I did this."

"Now why would they think that?" Her voice is coated in impatience and indifference.

"Remember my ax? The one I had leaning against my couch?"

"Oh yeah. Your Paul Bunyan cosplay prop. Yeah, I remember it. Holy shit–" Suddenly, her voice is free of sarcasm. Now, finally, she's interested in what I have to say.

"Yeah. I know," I say.

"Did you kill that motherfucker?" she asks.

"What? No! Why would you think that!"

"You said it was your ax!" she says.

"No I didn't! It wasn't my ax, but it sure looks like my ax. And me and the guy who died were just applying for the same job and he got picked over me and now…"

"Well, okay, so what? I mean, you got an alibi, right? A story you can tell about what you were doing when it happened, preferably a story that involves other people?"

"Not a story I can tell anybody," I say.

"Huh," Zoey says. The gum fills the silence before she concludes, "Yup. You're fucked."

"They haven't said anything to me yet, but…" I'm hiding around the frame of my front window as if an FBI surveillance team might be watching from a van across the street.

"You want my advice?" Zoey says.

"What I want, is for you–"

"Call a lawyer," she cuts me off. "Don't say a fucking word without a lawyer present. And make sure it's a good one. It's going to make you look guilty as all fuck at first but–"

"Zoey! I can't… There's no good lawyers in Woodduck. I need you. Here. Today!" There's not a lawyer in Woodduck or the whole planet Earth who would take my case if I told them everything I'd have to tell them.

"Alright. Fine. You know it's my Saturday off, right?"

"Zoey, this is serious," I say, and just then, a sheriff's car rolls past my house.

"Jesus! Alright already. God dammit, I fucking hate that town," she says and then hangs up.

I throw the burner phone on my couch next to my borrowed and signed copy of "A Black Heart Unbroken." I grab my ax and go to the stairwell. I fling open the door. Nothing. Of course the one time I want one of those things to be climbing up my steps so I can introduce it to my rage, the stairs are empty. The midday light shines down on the dull concrete floor. I slam the door. I pace through the kitchen. I open the door again. Still nothing. Even the pressure that had twisted its way around my spine is gone. Has been gone since…

I shut the door.

It will be at least two hours before Zoey arrives in Woodduck. That's if she leaves immediately and speeds the whole way. I have full faith and trust that when she makes the trip, she'll be doing ten to twenty over the whole way. As for leaving immediately? Not so much faith there.

I have to bide my time. I have to find a way to stay safe. Better yet, I have to come up with a plan. A way to lure the demons far from the general population to a place where I can put my ax to work. But I also have to stay pure of thought and reject anger and impatience. Sinning and summoning more of them up from my basement will do nothing to draw in the demons that are already above ground, out there mingling with the rest of Woodduck's population. What the hell are those things doing out there? Are they really just acting like regular people, going to hockey practice, VFW pancake breakfasts, brunch at Maggie's Cafe, and shopping at Walmart? Or are they surrounding the house and watching me closer than any van full of federal agents ever could? There's no way of knowing and no point in dwelling on things I can't affect. I have to relax. I have to bide my time.

I go back to my couch and toss my ax next to Eventide's book. It kept my mind occupied just two nights ago. Maybe it can settle my nerves for the time it will take Zoey to make it up here from the Cities. Once she gets here, then we can come up with a plan. She'll know what to do. In the meantime, well, it will be better to worry about Sam and Jen's problems than my own. I force myself to sit down and pick up the book. I do some controlled breathing exercises, close my eyes, center my energy, and crack the spine.

For the first time since I was at the bookstore with the author directly in front of me, my eyes fall on the interior cover page. In big, black, permanent marker, there's HHR Eventide's signature. But there's more. He's scrawled a short message above his name. It's hard to read since he wrote it with such a thick-tipped marker, and in cursive no less, but it doesn't take me long to make it out.

"Abigail, I can show you the way through the darkness. I can make your Black Heart Unbroken."

"What the shit is that supposed to mean?" I whisper to my empty house.

I'm swearing. I shouldn't be swearing. Grabbing my ax and abandoning the book, I'm back at the top of the stairs two seconds later. The door is open. The daylight shines down. Nothing on the stairs. No demons. No monsters. There's no squeeze compressing my spine down into narrow pencil lead. But I feel something else. A tingle like an approaching electrical storm or the onset of full-body goosebumps from the first swallow out of a bottle of whiskey. The odd thing, I realize, is that it's not new. I've felt it every time I've looked down these steps, but my mind was so focused on the visuals and the clinching of my spine, I ignored this more subtle sensation.

I shut the door and walk away, telling myself it's all my imagination. I make circles in my kitchen until the sensation goes away and the hairs on my arms lay flat again. When I'm back to normal, as normal as I've ever been anyway, and that static energy buzz is gone, I go right for the door leading downstairs.

The moment I open it, the sensation is back. Still no demon, but there is something else, like a subaudible hum vibrating through the floorboards or a blast of radiation from an x-ray machine, sensed more than felt. Something is down there.

For the first time in months, I make my way down the stairwell.

The light switch is just a few steps down. I flip it as soon as I can reach it. The single lightbulb in the center of my basement snaps to life. As I descend, more and more of the basement reveals itself to me. This house is ancient, so the basement has never been clean and hospitable. Great for spiders and salamanders. Good for storing canned vegetables and Christmas decorations. Not the kind of place a guy would finish and turn into a "man cave." Halfway down, the left wall gives way to a two-by-four hand railing. Beyond that is the bare concrete floor with a drain in the center. Along the far wall, just below an egress window, are the storage boxes for my Christmas decorations. The one where the outside lights go in is on top of the stack and still open. Never mind the step ladder and the snow and ice outside. This basement is the real reason the Christmas lights are still up. Because leaving them hanging on the house meant not coming down here. But now... now that I've gone deep into the tunnels and killed what's there, I think I have just enough courage to keep going, one step at a time. The walls are rough-set bricks, canted and misaligned, evidence of an old, shifted foundation. The hot water heater and oil furnace are on the opposite wall of the storage boxes.

My foot lands on the concrete floor. Then the other. I'm in my basement.

Back up the stairs, the door leading upstairs looks a hundred miles away. From here, my kitchen looks modern, sparkling clean, and welcoming. Still, I don't run back to it. The hum, the buzz, the tingle… whatever that sensation is, it's stronger down here.

There are other items scattered around the basement. Normal things you might find. Discarded things. Forgotten things. Unneeded things. Old garage sale signs. Rusted dumbbells. Moldy camping gear. Stacks of books Dad bought and read and decided to keep. Old furniture covered in drop cloths. The air permeates with mildew. Beyond the Christmas boxes are others. A whole family's lifetime of grown-out kid clothes and shoes and toys. Evidence that we were once whole and happy and hopeful and yet unbroken. Some of Mom's old things none of us had the heart to throw away, turned sacred by death and time. Some of Dad's old Army stuff.

I have a sudden compulsion to throw open the olive drab foot locker and dig through the duffle bags and launch an investigation into why he left us when my right toe kicks an object. It scuttles dry and hollow across the concrete like an empty human skull.

In the dim light of the single bulb, it looks like an old, dusty, cereal bowl or a piece of 70s-style Tupperware. But the gritty noise it makes as it wobbles and swirls, bowl up, against the concrete tells me it's not plastic. Its spinning slows and resettles on the floor. There's writing on the inside. In the bowl so if it was full of cereal or soup or whatever, you couldn't read it. I get on my knees for a closer look. It's not made of plastic. Not modern at all. As a matter of fact, when I pick it up, I touch hairline cracks and porous clay.

An old art project then. The obligatory ashtray either Zoey or I made Dad when we were in the third grade. Or maybe the only artifact from a pottery class Mom took before I could even remember. An amateurish creation that served no purpose and so was relegated down here.

But what the hell was it doing in the middle of the floor?

That buzzing sensation is stronger now. Like there are eight tiny legs of a spider crawling up the collar of my shirt to the base of my skull, positioning its hungry fangs millimeters above my skin.

I turn the bowl in my hand. It's an ugly, unpainted, unglazed, earthy, brown thing. Thin fissures run through the dusty, porous exterior. There are designs on the inside, but nothing me or Zoey could have come up with in third-grade arts and crafts. Runes or letters of a foreign language start around the brim and twist down the sides to the center. No As, Bs, or Cs. This alphabet seems simpler, older, rudimentary. Lines. Slashes. Squared off U's, backward D's, backward N's. Each rune is blocky and relatively the same size. No upper or lowercase. In some ways, the writing looks Arabic. In other ways, it looks like old Viking writing. Maybe a historian or an ancient linguist could name the language, but I can't. But the script that starts on the upper lip and swirls around and down to the bottom isn't the strangest thing about the artifact I have in my hands. At the bottom of the bowl, surrounded by the swirling letters, is a drawing of a person. If it had been Zoey or I who made this, I would guess we had drawn that figure when we were maybe six or seven years old. The figure isn't a stick person, it has width and mass, but the skill is hardly beyond that of a third grader.

Upon closer examination, I realize the figure isn't a person at all. It has arms and legs, but the legs end in hooves. A single brushstroke for a penis juts out between its legs. Fur covers its shoulders. From its head, horns twist outward in either direction. The mouth is stretched open, exposing four long pointed fangs. An emulsion of creatures. Something not of this plane. Something wretched. Something wicked. An abomination. A demon.

And not just any demon. This is a drawing of the monster that killed my father.

Upstairs, the doorbell chimes.

I drop the bowl. It doesn't shatter despite how old and fragile it looks, although I wish it had. The thing is cursed. I know that without a doubt and without being able to read a single one of those characters spiraling downward from the lip to the child-like drawing of the demon in the center. It wobbles along its edge and eventually comes to rest like a dropped quarter.

Upstairs, the doorbell rings again.

I leave the bowl where it lays. I leave the light on. I bring my ax with me upstairs and consider bringing it to the door just in case the demons on the surface have come home to roost. I peek around the frame of my front window.

There, parked along the snowbank, exactly where I'd seen Zoey park her Camaro the other night, is the sheriff's Ford Explorer. I knew they'd come for me inevitably. It isn't like Woodduck harbors a huge population of homeless drifters, meth addicts, escaped psychopaths, or known serial killers for the cops to track down and question before they come for me. As small as this town is, any crime has a short list of suspects, and I knew my name would be at the top of the list for this one as soon as I saw the body. The ax, not my ax but a similar ax, only cinched my fate. An open and shut case, I suppose the deputies on the other side of the door are already thinking. But dammit, why couldn't they have waited just two hours longer? Hasn't my reputation earned me that much hesitation? Are they waiting behind the door with guns drawn and open handcuffs ready for my wrists? Do they have backup surrounding my house in case I make a run for it? No red or blue lights spinning on top of the cruiser competing with my Christmas lights, so apparently, they haven't pinned me as a dangerous maniac. Yet. All the same, I tuck my ax on the backside of my front door, out of sight. I won't fight the officers. Sheriff Graham? Deputy Ruiz? I know these people. They're good people. If they are people, that is.

Ready to face my fate, I open the door.

"Miss Abby Hendrix?" Sheriff Graham asks.

Deputy Ruiz stands a step behind him. Neither of them has guns drawn or cuffs ready. They wear thick brown coats with brass badges pinned to the right breast. Ruiz wears her winter hat with the ear flaps. Graham wears the Smokey the Bear campaign hat as if it's a hot summer day in Texas rather than ten below in northern Minnesota.

"Hi, Sheriff," I say. For a moment, I almost concede to my natural instinct and invite them in and out of the cold, but then my sister's advice rings in my ear. *Get a lawyer. Don't say a word.* They can't come inside my house without a warrant or probable cause unless I invite them in. So I don't offer. It feels like a betrayal. After all, the last time Sheriff Graham was here, he held me and did his best to comfort me while EMS took away my father's body. But I know Zoey is smart about these things. I bear the cold right along with Graham and Ruiz. "How are things?"

"Oh, could be better," he says. "That's how come I'm at your doorstep instead of home and warm with the old lady. Let me cut right to the point. You heard about what happened this morning? Just down the way?"

By now, all of Woodduck has heard about what happened down the way. There's no use denying it. "Yeah. Somebody got hurt, the TV said." It'd be best if I don't lie because no lie told to a cop on a murder investigation is a white lie and my basement is at my back.

"More than just hurt, I'm afraid," Sheriff Graham says. "It was a murder. We have no doubt about that. Victim is dead, and the means by which he died leaves little doubt. How well did you know Mister Jason Jones?"

"From the library? The college kid?" I ask, and I know I haven't told a lie, but I'm not being fully truthful anymore.

"One and the same," Sheriff Graham says. "He was found dead in the middle of Third and Hill Road this morning."

Deputy Ruiz eyes me. She saw Eric and me there just a few hours ago. I confess only what I have to. "I saw the crime scene. This morning. Eric Erickson was with me. We were walking into town."

Graham's eyes squint at that as if he's discovered some new piece of evidence. "Lilith from over in the courthouse where you work says you didn't come in yesterday."

"I did though," I say. "She was in a meeting and didn't see me, but I had to go into the tunnels. See, Eric is doing electrical work down there and he doesn't exactly know his way around."

"You went down there?" Graham interrupts me, uncharacteristically surprised. "I thought those were condemned, caved in. Christ. Folks say they're haunted."

"Well," I fake a laugh. "I don't know about that–" an out-and-out lie, "–but he has work he has to do down there so–"

"And you were down there all day?" he asks.

I nod. Zoey's advice is ringing in my ears, but I can't bring myself to do something as bold as demand a lawyer.

"And yesterday evening?" he asks. "You said you walked into town with Mister Erickson this morning."

"Sheriff... Do I really have to tell you about... you know... private stuff?" I say.

"Hmm," he says. Ruiz is diverting her gaze now as if looking down the street will prevent her from hearing all about my personal business. "Some folks around town say they've seen you carrying an ax with you lately. Care to tell us about that?"

"I..." What lie can I tell to make that go away? Deny that I had, regardless of Lilith and Hank and the server out the back of Woody's and kid in the hardware store and who knows how many others who have seen me doing exactly that? "It was my dad's," I tell him the truth I can as if that makes any sense or makes anything any better.

Graham lowers his gaze at that. Rubs some dirt off the thumb of his glove with the thumb of his other glove. This pause, this is as close as he comes to offering his condolences today.

"And this Jason Jones," Sheriff Graham continues. "You and he applied for the same position over at the library. Were you aware of that?"

"I didn't do it," I say, making sure I sound appalled when I do. "If you think I'd hurt Jason... If I'd hurt anybody–"

"Can we come inside, Miss Hendrix?" Sheriff Graham finally asks.

"What? No. I'm not a suspect," I say, burying my refusal in more indignation. There's a throb radiating from my lower back, distracting me. I twist to try to work it out. "Sheriff, you know me. You were here when... when... We've seen each other around the courthouse for years now. How can you..."

"Ma'am," he says, using an honorific rather than a name, instantly turning me from an acquaintance to a stranger with one word. "We can either discuss this further inside, or we can discuss it down at the sheriff's department."

"Are you arresting me?" I ask, panic flowing over the brim of my brain. Because if I'm arrested, then no one will be on the lookout for the real murderers. No one will be watching for demons wearing friendly faces. If I'm behind bars, the whole town will be defenseless. Helpless. Laid bare like a virgin for a sacrifice. I arch and scrunch my back and try to make the pain go away. "You can't. I didn't do anything wrong. I didn't–"

And then Zoey is strolling up the walk behind them. She came! Maybe because I called or maybe at the behest of the BCA and her work. I don't know and I don't care. I know she can protect me. I know she can stop this questioning and make sure I have a lawyer and make sure I stay out of jail so I can do what I have to do out here in Woodduck.

"Zoey!" I call. "Zoey, you have to help me. They don't understand."

Ruiz glances back, but Sheriff Graham remains focused on me. "This doesn't have to be an ordeal, Miss Hendrix. But we have a murder on our hands, and we need to turn over every rock to make sure–"

"Zoey!" I'm still calling her name while the sheriff goes on.

She shows no reaction. Her eyes watch her feet as she strolls up the sidewalk in her black suit and red blouse. It's not until she gets to the steps that she reaches into her suit jacket. I get a glimpse of the shoulder holster she has under her jacket, standard BCA issue, before she pulls out her automatic. Sheriff Graham and Deputy Ruiz pay her no mind even as she puts the barrel behind the deputy's head.

There's an explosion. Hot red spittle and bits of teeth and skull spray my face and the siding of my house. My ears ring and muffle the next gunshot. I blink away the blood and brain matter just in time to see Zoey turn her gun on Sheriff Graham while he fights with his holster. She fires once, twice, three, four times into his chest before he gets a chance to pull his gun free. He collapses on the ground next to Deputy Ruiz who, I now see, has no head from the nose up.

Sheriff Graham is dying slower. His Smokey the Bear hat lands on its edge and rolls down my steps. He coughs and spits red. One hand is slapping his chest as if angry at the entrance wounds. Tufts of down escaping from those small holes in his brown coat. The exit wounds are more obvious, as are the big splatters of blood decorating my house numbers next to the front door. Zoey takes a moment to sight up the gun at Sheriff Graham's forehead. Before she pulls the trigger, she turns two eyes-set-ablaze on me.

This isn't Zoey.

My front door slams in sync with the gunshot that finishes off Sheriff Graham. Two loud bangs a flam apart. I twist the deadbolt just as the knob begins to turn. The door pulls outward but stops in its frame. I grab my ax.

"Miss Hendrix," Zoey's voice sings from the other side. "Miss Hendrix, I'm Miss Hendrix from the Minnesota–"

She kicks the door, hard, but it doesn't give.

"–Bureau of Criminal–"

Another kick. This one harder yet. The hinges and the deadbolt almost rip through the wood. I back into my kitchen.

"–Apprehension."

Three gunshots punch through my front door. Holes let spears of daylight into my dim home. I don't think I'm hit. I don't feel any wounds anyway. Deep in my kitchen, I slam against my cabinets. The basement door is right next to me.

"Miss Hendrix," my sister's voice is singing again, teasing me just like when we were kids. "You're wanted for the murder of Mister Jason Jones, Deputy Ana Ruiz, and the good Sheriff Marty Graham. Now come out, come out little piggy."

She has a gun. I have an ax. This won't be a fight. It will be an execution.

She fires three more times through the door. I don't know where or how a demon got a gun. Maybe it materialized when the thing turned itself from a giant slug or maybe it had to go to a gun store and buy or steal it. Doesn't much matter to me as my eyes fix on the bullet hole in my cabinet door three inches to the right of my head.

My garage door is across the kitchen. I don't wait for the thing pretending to be my sister to kick open my door or empty the rest of her magazine. Keeping my ax, I bolt for the garage door, grab my keys off the little hook, and race to the driver's door of my ever-so-economical and fuel-efficient Chevy Volt.

Chapter Eighteen
On the Run

To the sound of my shattering front door, I hit two buttons. One opens the big door to my driveway. The other starts the Volt's four-cylinder motor. When I get her out on the street, that's when the electric motor will take over. I don't know which will make me go faster. I never worried about these sorts of things before this very moment.

As soon as the garage door is open enough to drive underneath, I slam on the gas. The Volt lurches forward. In the rearview mirror, I see the massacre spilled over my front steps, and I see a demon that looks like my sister bust into the garage from my kitchen. She runs with a handgun held straight out in front of her and fires two or three more times before I turn onto 7th Avenue. A bullet breaks through the back window of my car. It doesn't shatter the glass but leaves a neat, puckered hole from which a dozen spider cracks lightning-bolt out to the edges.

I crank the wheel, hand over hand, taking a hard left. The short car threatens to go into a spin on the icy street. I counter-steer until it flirts with spinning in the opposite direction and then counter-steer again. I'm not making it very far down the road. While I fight for traction, the Demon-Zoey runs to the sheriff's Ford Explorer with the expensive and mean engine under the hood. If the demon that looks and sounds like Zoey drives like Zoey?

"God damn it," I say, but finally manage to get the Volt aimed straight down the street.

I mash the gas pedal into the floor. The tires spin and spray ice into the air. When they reach a spot of bare asphalt, I'm thrown into the seat back. I don't know where I'm going. I don't know who might help me or where to find them. Going to the police, if I could find one left alive, would only be slightly better than facing off against the thing chasing me. Despite feeling like I've known him forever, I have no idea where Eric lives or if he's home or what he could do to save me. Zoey, the real Zoey, now that I have a moment to do the math, I know is still a long way from Woodduck and…

"Shit!" I swear.

My burner phone is still lying on my couch next to the copy of "A Black Heart Unbroken."

The sheriff's car appears in my rearview mirror. It's small but getting bigger every second. It's not Zoey's red hot Camaro that would beat any cop in the quarter mile, but anything is faster than the little electric Power Wheel I'm struggling to keep on the street.

Hill Road is just ahead. I slam on the brakes and feel all the traction between the tires and the ice melt away. My fate is in the hands of physics now. The push bumper of the Explorer slams into my back bumper. The force pushes me out onto Hill Road, between traffic. I already have the wheel turned before my tires get a grip of the road, and when they catch, they almost send the whole car toppling over sideways. I turn, not so sharp to roll me but not sharp enough to avoid the far side snowbank either. The passenger side slams into the drift, but the ice pack is hard enough to bounce off of and keep me on Hill Road. I shove my foot back on the gas, as hard as I can.

The Volt accelerates north toward the library, downtown, and the courthouse. That's my plan, as ill-formed as it is, because the north side of town is familiar, friendly, and well, equally as infested with demons as any other place in town. As far as the south end of town, the only thing that way is…

Eventide's Mansion.

What were the words he'd written in thick Sharpie just above his signature? Something about showing me a way through the dark. About making my black heart unbroken. Cheesy, quippy things to pacify a gushing fangirl at a book signing. Nothing of any substance or pertinence to the world outside of his books. Nothing I should put any merit into. Then again, he signed it to me, by name, specifically neglecting to sign it to my dad like I'd asked him to. Maybe it was more than just a clever quip. Maybe he knows something. Maybe he really was offering to help me. Preposterous, I know, but who else can I turn to?

The Demon-Zoey in the sheriff's car is closing in on me again. It swerves into view of my right mirror, then into my left mirror as if probing for a way to pull alongside me and take me out. My late turn onto Hill Road that sent me, now I decide, in the wrong direction only kept the demon at bay for a handful of seconds. I'll never outrun the brand-new-from-the-factory modified Ford Explorer with its all-wheel-drive and big, souped-up gas engine. Not with my little go-cart. The only way I might escape is to keep driving long enough for the Explorer to run out of gas. Or get to someplace safe.

To Eventide.

Certainly, there can't be two of *him* wandering around town without being noticed. An old farmer, an electrician, a woman in a cheap suit, a young librarian (even if he is currently a corpse) sure. But a New York Times Best Selling author and this town's only celebrity? There isn't a worse disguise between here and San Diego.

The Volt carries me forward in the wrong direction, past the library, snapping through the yellow tape of the crime scene like a sprinter winning the wrong race. The courthouse and Highway 210 lay straight ahead. Remembering the ice covering the last intersection, I know I'm already late in slowing down. I'm barreling too fast, uncontrollably fast, toward the cross traffic on 210. As soon as I start feathering the brakes, aware that slamming on them will send me into another skid, the grill of the sheriff's SUV shoves me forward.

My foot stays off the gas and on the brake. As it plows me into the intersection, I pull the wheel as hard as I can to the left and press the brakes a little harder. Just enough to send my backside sliding around. The car twists and for a moment, we're side by side, both going north, but the Volt pointing south as we skid into the snowbanks in front of the courthouse. We stop like that, and through my side window, I see a face that looks just like Zoey's. A face I've known since birth. The similarities are uncanny. Unnerving how it conjures a thousand memories, both good and bag, with its thin veneer of familiarity. But I know it's not Zoey. Zoey, for all her misgivings, always has a smart-aleck twist to her lips, a bit of mischief in her eyes, and a passion for fun and adventure in her heart.

The thing wearing her face only shines with hate. We're inches apart. Just two tempered panes of glass keep the demon from reaching through to me and ripping out my throat.

The Ford Explorer stalls out. The Volt sounds equally dead, but I know that's just how it sounds any time it stops. The gas engine shuts off, but all it takes is a tap on the accelerator for it to come back to life. While the demon next to me fights with the shifter and the ignition, I press on the gas and shoot back down Hill Road.

Southbound. For the old mayor's mansion. For Eventide.

All the way down Hill Road, I drive as fast as I can. More than once, I feel the grip of the road loosen underneath me and know that the Volt is going to keep going in the direction it's currently traveling regardless of what I do with the wheel and the pedals. Thankfully, inertia and I are on the same team. It's a straight road and there's little traffic. I don't stop for stop signs. I don't pause at crosswalks. The broken yellow tape at 3rd and Hill Road flutters into the gutter like New Year's Eve confetti left to be cleaned up the morning after. I try not to look back in my rearview mirror because I know, as slick as it was, my little maneuver back there didn't end this chase. The demon in the sheriff's SUV is still behind me and gaining ground every second.

But Woodduck is a small town. It doesn't take long for me to blow through downtown, leave the residential neighborhoods behind, and plunge into the surrounding forests. I see the little pump house where Eric and I emerged from the tunnels just yesterday. Beyond it I see the big wrought iron gates leading up the hill to the mansion. They're wide open, welcoming me through.

The driveway twists and weaves through the forest on its way up the hill, and although the blacktop is impeccably plowed and clear of snow, I slow way down as I cross through the gates. Only then do I check the rearview and see that yes, the demon driving the sheriff's car is still behind me. But for some reason, it hits the brakes and skids sideways to a stop just before the gates.

A few gentle curves lead me up to the manor house. I slow the Volt down to a roll, breathing heavily and almost crying. But I'm able to wrestle some control of my emotions when I check the mirror and confirm that the Explorer isn't following me. I creep to a stop in the middle of the large brick-paved courtyard and put the vehicle in park. The gas engine dies.

My ax rests in the passenger seat. Under normal circumstances, no sane person would bring an ax to the front door of a distinguished and world-renowned author. But these are far from normal circumstances, and I no longer claim sanity. I grab it and exit the car.

Looking back down the hill, I see the gates through the trees. The sheriff's SUV idles there as if guarding against my escape. The demon disguised as my sister stands outside the driver's door. The wind wipes the tails of her suit jacket. It makes no indication of following me up the hill.

So, I got something right in coming here. Those words Eventide scrawled in my book... well, in the library's book... must mean something.

Chapter Nineteen
At the End of Hill Road

My boots grind against the brick pavers. The driveway wraps around to the side of the mansion where I assume there is a garage. Or perhaps in a home this classic and old-fashioned, it's called a carriage stable. The only entrance I see is the front door, centered in the front of the mansion, inside a covered and elevated porch, and flanked by multihued stained-glass windows. The signature red brickwork and ornately carved spires and rain spouts of the Flemish Renaissance Revival architecture style rise to either side. The eaves are lined with those sharp, marble spires, blending the aesthetics of a crenelated castle and a fence topped with razor wire. The seven gables, two chimneys, and single turret loom high above my head. In the saddles of all those gables are valleys of deep snow. Huge, frosted-over windows hide a hundred vantage points.

And certainly, in this day and age, there are cameras and motion sensors that detected my presence the moment I crossed through the gates at the bottom of the hill. But as of yet, there's no evidence of anything moving inside.

I can't help but think of the passages I've read. Of Sam and Jen coming up to that old empty Tudor mansion that only holds ghosts and phantoms. Childish, I know. Especially when my own personal demon waits outside the SUV of our murdered sheriff at the end of the driveway.

Shifting the weight of my ax in my left hand, I pull my eyes away from the demon and the cruiser and march up the steps to the imposing front door. There is no iron gate portcullis between me and the door, but that does little to alleviate the feeling I'll have as much luck getting inside this place as I would storming a castle. Of course, there's a big, black cast-iron door knocker that reminds me of the one on Scrooge's door. This one doesn't turn into Jacob Marely's face; it's already a skull with a ring set into its jaw. Using it seems intimidating, invasive, and presumptuous. Thankfully, I spot a modern doorbell. One that is hooked up to a camera, an internet connection, and a cell phone app. That confirms my suspicion that despite all the mansion's medieval trappings, Eventide's security system is state-of-the-art. Which means he already knows I'm here. Which means there's no point in being coy. I push the doorbell.

Aware that someone, presumably an assistant or a maid or a butler and not Eventide himself, is now looking at me through the doorbell camera, I fidget. Back at the end of the driveway, the Demon-Zoey paces outside of the stolen sheriff's SUV. Shifting my eyes from the door, the doorbell camera, the demon watching me from the end of the driveway, and the ax clutched in my hand gives "escaped mental patient" more than "innocent hockey player/pizza saleswoman." The time spent waiting for a response seems like an eternity. I'm trying to come up with another plan when noises thump from the other side of that thick, oak door. Deadbolts twist in their mounts. Latches come undone. The demon still waits. The door cracks open.

The one and only HHR Eventide stands at the threshold, stiff and erect. Again I'm struck by his stature and presence, more so here than in the dimly lit bookstore. He's as poised as a brick wall and as handsome as a classic painting to be hung on it. Those dark-lined eyes look down on me and exude an aura of enigmatic wisdom. His stoicism betrays no emotions. He isn't surprised, isn't angry, isn't happy, but passively amused if not wholly aloof. Does he remember that cryptic message he scribbled in the library book? Wearing a pinstripe black suit with a narrow black tie that's only slightly loose around the collar, he looks ready to walk into a Manhattan 5th Avenue board meeting. The only sign that he's working from a desk inside his home is the pair of slippers on his otherwise bare feet. Is this how he dresses every day? In his hand, he carries a chrome, six-chamber revolver with a long shiny barrel. Is this how he usually answers the door?

"Miss Abigail Hendrix, if my memory serves me correctly," he says my name. *My name*, first and last, as if he had his finger pressed to the Yellow Pages.

"I'm so sorry to bother you," I stammer. Whatever plan I dreamed up since two law enforcement officers were murdered at my doorstep never went this far. The sight of this impeccable man, holding a gun, dressed to the nines and in bath slippers has erased any idea of what I might say. My mind is as blank as a chalkboard washed with water. "I know you like your privacy. But… But you wrote something in my book and… And I need your help."

"So I see," he says in that even-keel, smooth-as-glass voice.

His eyes look straight forward, over my head, down to the gates guarding his property. The demon who looks identical to my sister is still there, waiting outside the sheriff's Ford Explorer. I figure his next move is to either fire the gun aimed at my stomach, call the police, or slam the door in my face and leave me to deal with my problems on my own.

"Won't you come in?" he says and ushers me into his home with an open palm.

At a loss for words, I move slow and lethargic like molasses poured from the bottle. The best I can do is nod in response as I step through the doorway and beyond him into a massive, vaulted foyer. The door closes thick and dense behind me. All noise from the outside world is muted. There are no drafts in the mansion. There is no music. No blaring TV or clatter or footfalls of others. It is silent inside. When he shuffles his feet behind me, the slippers make soft shushing sounds against a granite floor.

"Please excuse the revolver," HHR Eventide says.

I don't turn back to face him. His words register, but my eyes are busy taking in the grandeur of the home in which I find myself. My attention is pulled between the elegance of his voice and the elegance surrounding me. This isn't a foyer but an entrance hall with a grand staircase on one side and a lit fireplace on the other. The fire crackles and pops. It's warm in here. Dark-stained moldings, wainscoting, and the balustrading of the staircase give a rich old-world charm. Laurels and pinecones are carved into the polished rosewood casings above the doorways to my left and right. A crystal chandelier bathes the room in a soft, dusky glow. The walls are decorated with classical oil paintings and European game mounts. A stuffed pheasant is captured in mid-flight on the wall opposite the front door. Above the fireplace, an antique double-barreled shotgun hangs under the white skull of an elk with huge antlers. It reminds me of the demon from under the tunnels and sends spider legs up and down my arms.

"There are dangerous things about," he says. "But you're safe in here. If you'd like, you can set your ax in the umbrella stand."

Finally, I face the man. In the same manner in which he welcomed me inside, he now gestures with an open palm, fingers held tight in a row, to an umbrella stand next to the door. With the other hand, he tucks the revolver inside his suit jacket and into a shoulder holster not unlike the one Zoey uses. Similar to the one Demon-Zoey uses too, for that matter. The fact that I'm still carrying the ax has slipped my mind until his eyes fix on it, expectantly.

"Oh. Yeah. Of course," I say and slide the ax into the cylindrical can that also holds a single, black umbrella. Because of course all of this is normal and natural, and I absolutely know what I'm doing. Never mind that I keep my pink collapsible umbrella in my glovebox and have never used an umbrella stand in my life. Never mind that I've never been in a place so luxurious. Never mind that my favorite author is in the same room and has elected to keep his weapon. Never mind the demon outside. Never mind that I feel like I've been teleported far from my stale, humdrum hometown into another dimension. Everything is normal. Everything is fine.

"Let me get you something to drink," he says, doesn't ask, and walks that tall, spindly frame through the doorway to the right.

I follow him into a bright and sprawling kitchen made of white and black checkerboard tiles, marble countertops, brass fixtures, and a massive six-burner gas stove with cast-iron grates. The appliances are modern and stainless steel but match the classic feel of the rest of the room. A knife block with chrome handles rests on the counter. The window above the sink is stained glass. A scythe with a long rusted-brown blade and an even longer wooden handle so weathered it looks like driftwood hangs above the window. An antique decoration that matches the room's aesthetic, but who can see one of those things and not think of the Grim Reaper?

HHR Eventide goes to work retrieving a glass from a cupboard, filling it with ice from the freezer, and topping it off with water from the tap. As he does this, he says, "When Edgar G. Huntington first had this manor built back in 1926, the kitchen was isolated from the main area of the home, relegated to the servants. There was a separate dining area and work area for the hired help, a lesser house hidden inside the larger home, never visited by the original owner. But I changed all that, of course. Do you know that in most urban dwellings, hosts tend to receive and entertain guests in living rooms and dining rooms? But in more rural areas, folks tend to gather in kitchens? An architect friend told me that, and I kept that in mind when I moved here. Hence, I removed the barriers between the servant and resident portions of the house and had the large breakfast bar installed to accommodate those more agrarian tendencies of my new neighbors."

I sit on one of the stools at the high counter. He's on the opposite side as if he's a bartender and I'm a regular. He places the glass of ice water I never asked for on the counter before me. The scythe hangs over his head like a guillotine.

"So, what brings you to my home, Miss Hendrix?" he asks.

"How do you know my name?" I say.

"From the book signing, of course," he says, and smiles for the first time, as if I'm silly for asking. Then he goes to his refrigerator and pulls out two stainless steel bowls. One larger. The other small. "I know you, Abigail Hendrix. And I knew your father as well."

"You knew my father?"

The larger bowl is filled with dark red cherries. The other holds whipped cream. Because of course he doesn't have a plastic tub of Cool Whip like the average citizen of Woodduck.

"Edward was one of my dearest supporters," he responds, and it's weird hearing my dad's name come out of his mouth. No one called him "Edward," especially not me. Friends, co-workers, and acquaintances all called him "Eddie" or "Ed." But somehow, I think that would sound even stranger coming from HHR Eventide.

He dips one of the cherries into the whipped cream and plucks it from the stem with his teeth.

"But... But he was just some guy," I say. "You have millions of fans. Why would you know me or my dad any more than–"

"Well, you both lived here, in my newly adopted hometown," Eventide says. He's smiling now, and the red of the chewed-up cherry stains his teeth. His smile feels practiced, forced even, but that doesn't bother me. As a matter of fact, for the first time all day, I feel a sense of relief. The rarity of his expression makes me feel special, like he's giving me something he wouldn't give to others. As if all the darkness in the world has removed the joy from this man's life, but my simple presence has brought it back. "I try not to think of everyone I come across as either a reader or not a reader, a customer or not a customer, a fan or not a fan. Just as you shouldn't think of me as only a writer. Humans are complex, multifaceted creatures, so much more compelling when they're not pigeonholed into those rather limiting, binary categories. I've found you and your father very interesting indeed. The fact that both of you were dedicated readers of my work is only a dollop of cream on top of an already wonderfully sweet dessert. Ein sahnehäubchen, as they say in the Old World." At that, he pops another cream-topped cherry into his mouth. He slides the bowl my way, offering the cherries and cream to me.

"But the only time we've ever met was just a few days ago," I say. "There were a hundred other people there."

"I apologize, my dear. I forget how bright you are," Eventide brandishes his more familiar photo-op smile. "The truth is, I recognized something in you the first time I saw you. A capacity for great things. A talent. It was '*Avoir un coup de foudre*,' as the French say.

"I became aware of both you and your father shortly after I moved to this quaint and quiet hamlet. You were walking him into the church on Fifth Street the first time I saw you. First Lutheran I believe it is. He went inside and you walked to the park across the street. You were reading 'Interlude of Envy.' Not an hour later, he rejoined you, looking rather sour, and the two of you walked home. One of his failed attempts at temperance, I suppose. But you caught my eye that day. You had an undeniable glare of determination. As you do now. Beauty and strength folded together in a forge."

He pauses as if lost in my eyes. "So many questions for me," he says, dismissing the moment. "But so far, you haven't answered any of mine. You knocked on my door. We sit in my kitchen. Yet you haven't told me what has brought you here."

I realize then that we're sort of jockeying around each other, giving up bits of information only as necessary, piece by piece, like boxers who only lower their gloves to sucker their opponents in for a knockout blow. He was right about that day last summer. I walked Dad to an AA meeting at First Lutheran, and it didn't go well. But I'm not going to confirm his suspicions. That day is none of his business.

"Someone was chasing me," I say. "They chased me all the way to your driveway."

"So I saw," he says. "Someone? Or...?"

Did he know Zoey as well? Did he mistake the demon at his gates for my sister?

"I don't know if I can explain," I say. "There are people... There are *things* in this town that shouldn't be. Bad things. Strange things. Things not from... Not from around here."

"We're often afraid of people we don't understand," Eventide says.

"No, it's not like that," I correct him. "I'm not talking about people from different countries or people with other religions. These *things*... They're like something out of one of your books."

"We're often afraid of things we don't understand," Eventide says, delivering that line and that smile again. "Did you know how close I came to failure early in my career? When I first released 'The Coffin Nail also Turns,' and 'The Storming Sea of Souls,' almost no one bought them. The critics were ruthless. My agent wanted to end our contract, and my publisher nearly dropped me. But then I handed them 'The Towers of Silence and Sand,' and everything changed. See, Miss Abigail, in writing that book, I had to research some strange and ancient things, and I came to understand the world in a much deeper way. Sometimes, things we don't understand, dark things, frightening things, can later come to benefit us. After all, look around you. Look at what the darkness has done for me."

"You don't understand what I'm trying to say. There's... There's..." I hesitate to tell him everything. Of course, I hesitate. This man has been my crush, my idol, and my fantasy for years and years. Now I'm in his kitchen where I should be making pleasant conversation and eating his cherries and welcoming him to the town and offering to show him around. I've imagined meeting and having conversations with and having more than just conversations with this man a thousand times over. Now I'm going to tell him about the horrific things that come up from my basement? A secret I've kept from everyone in my life?

"It's okay," Eventide says and rests his palm on top of my hand. "The world is a strange place and often seems cold and lonely. But you are not alone. Please," he says and proffers the cherries and cream again.

By now, I'm obligated to partake. So I do, dipping the big, black cherry into the cloud-white cream.

"Sometimes, all we need is another person who understands our demons," he says.

That word. It's the exact word I've been trying to avoid. It is the secret I've kept since the day of my father's death. But again, what should disturb me, comforts me. Because he's right. It's been so lonely, so restricting, so imprisoning to keep all of these horrors to myself. If I can tell him, if he'll believe me, if he can help me... The idea is softer than the whipped cream and sweeter than the cherry.

I chew and swallow.

"They come from below," I say. Still, I pick my words carefully so they can be received metaphorically if he chooses. "When I'm at my weakest. When I'm the most greedy or selfish or scared... They come."

"And when they come, do you embrace them?" he asks.

I laugh at that, an uncomfortable huff devoid of mirth. "I don't think we're talking about the same things anymore."

He nods. That smile is there, but it's different. A knowing smirk rather than a pleasant grin. A smile smiled for only himself. "I assure you We are." Then it changes back to that charming, just-for-me smile. "Tell me, if you could have anything in the world, what would you take?"

"I just want my old life back," I sigh. All that pent-up fear and tension has me feeling like a steam tank ready to blow its rivets. Saying those words opens a release valve.

"And what did you have before that was so wonderful?" Eventide says. "You're a curious person, Abigail. Certainly, you'd like a more unique and exciting existence. Travel and adventure. Money. A large home. An interesting partner. A different life?"

"I mean... I suppose that's why I read your books," I confess. "Because you take me into different lives full of things normal people take for granted and other things only extraordinary people can acquire."

"You, Abigail, are far from a normal person. And neither am I," HHR Eventide tells me. He sets his other hand on top of mine now so he's clasping my hand in both of his. "And thank all the spirits above and below for that. I can show you wonderful things, Abigail. They might be dark and strange and even ugly upon first sight but..."

What he's offering me is a life I've only dreamed of. Not a life lived vicariously by reading stories and books others have written, but a life worthy of being written about. A life of wealth and luxury, every day spent walking through a new place and speaking new languages and trying new foods and meeting new, interesting, and beautiful people. A life free from fear and want and loneliness and jealousy. A life experienced by a thousand characters but never myself. Those two hands holding mine, they could carry me away from every problem I've ever had. But I can barely feel them. Instead, I feel two fists clenched around my spine as if a python is coiling around my torso. And I know what that feeling means. It heralds the embodiment of all my weaknesses. The Demon Lust. The Demon Greed. The Demon Selfishness. It's coming.

I yearn to stay in this place with this man and ignore all the problems outside of this amazing home, but that's not possible. Something that looks like my sister murdered two officers on my front step and has me trapped here. Things are rising out of tunnels all over town, attacking Eric and Jason and people who have nothing to do with my weaknesses. And now, I'm conjuring more of them out of the deep.

I pull my hand away.

"I'm sorry. It's just... Do you have a basement here?" I ask him.

"A basement? Naturally." That I-know-something-you-don't smirk returns to his face. "There's a wine cellar accommodating over two hundred vintages from a span of four hundred years. And... older things."

"What do you mean, older things?" I ask, stiff in my spot at the breakfast counter, like a prey animal not wanting to admit to itself a predator has it spotted.

"What do you need, Abigail?" he asks. "Tell me how I can help you."

"I need my ax," I say and bolt for the front door, leaving him there in the kitchen with his cherries and cream.

In the reception hall, I rip my ax from the umbrella stand. The cylinder tumbles over and rolls across the dark wood floor. Eventide follows me, but I don't give him time to elaborate on what he is trying to tell me. The crush of an encroaching demon strangles my spine. If there's a basement, or a wine cellar, or anything below the ground here, I hope I can cut off what is coming up before it's too late. But the grand staircase only goes up. Not down.

Rather than running past him and back into the kitchen, I go the other way so he can't stop me. I'm running through rooms that have names from a game of Clue: a study, a parlor, a ballroom... There are white lacquered walls leading up to rounded molded corners and muralled ceilings. There are leather chairs and a globe opened on a hinge to reveal a decanter full of brownish liquor and matching rock glasses. There's a bear skin rug. There are room-wide, floor-to-ceiling bookshelves and old paintings nearly as large. In the parlor, there's a polished, white casket positioned under a bay window. The lid is closed, so I assume it's a decoration. A prop. A conversation piece. A homage to Count Dracula? Then I find a stairwell. One path leads up to the second and third story. The other leads down.

Hanging on a null post carved from rosewood in the shape of a giant acorn, I wheel around the turn and down the stairs.

"Abigail!" I hear Eventide call me. He knows his way around this place, and while I probably took the longest way possible to find these stairs, he's behind me having hardly walked at all. "Abigail, can I have a word?"

There are things about this place that aren't right. There are things about Eventide that aren't right, but I don't want to admit it. I want this place to be perfect. I want it to give me everything I've been missing in my life and take away everything I've been suffering. And oh god, do I want to accept everything Eventide is offering me. But first, I need to see what's in the basement.

When I reach the bottom of the stairs, I'm not in any dull, concrete, and mildew-layered cellar. I'm in a den with plush carpet, racks of bottles of alcohol, two billiards tables with stained glass chandeliers over each, plush couches, and a TV that spans the width of the far wall. An average man cave if the average guy was worth fifty million dollars. But I don't see any wine. What I do see across the room is another door. I run between the two pool tables and rip it open.

Another set of stairs leads deeper into the earth. No more richly stained rosewood. The walls here are made of thick, cyclopean bricks. The steps too. As I plunge down the stairs, it smells like fresh soil. Earthworms and compost. A little bit like rot and decay too. When I reach the bottom, I see the hundreds of bottles of wine he boasted. It's not a large room, but it holds four arched sconces packed from floor to keystone with dusty bottles and wooden casks.

My hot sweat chills in the cool air. Just like in the tunnels underneath town, I'm below the frost line and cooled by that permanent fifty-degree subterranean temperature. Above me, Eventide's slippers scuff against the rough carved blocks of the stairs.

"Did you find what you were looking for?" Eventide asks from above.

My eyes flitter about the small room. There are no demons. Not yet. But I still feel that clench around my vertebrae all the same. They're close, just behind a veil, ready to break through at the slightest falter of my virtues. That radiation-like buzz courses over my skin too. A whiskey shiver that won't go away. A low-grade electron hum of a brewing tornado. When I look at the floor rather than the walls of wine bottles, I see why.

Five clay bowls rest on the floor. Charcoal lines connect the bowls and form a star about five feet across with the bowls placed at each point. And I'm standing in the middle. The bowls... they're like the one I found in my basement before Sheriff Graham and Deputy Ruiz showed up at my door. There are things like letters swirling around the brim of each that twist down to the bottom to a rough drawing of things not quite human.

"It was Goethe who wrote, 'If the pentagram gives you pain, then tell me, Son of Hell, how did you gain entry? Are spirits like you cheated?'"

I look up the stairs. "What the fuck is that supposed to mean?"

"Careful, my dear," Eventide says. "They're listening to everything we have to say."

"What are these? Where did they come from?" I say, all pleasantries gone from my voice.

"Incantation bowls," Eventide says. "Handmade by Hebrews of antiquity, sold to Zoroastrians who feared evil spirits were entering their homes. See, the incantations etched around the bowls lure evil spirits to the center. The bowls were buried, upside down, under the doorstep of those ancient Persians' dwellings, so as to trap the demons there and keep them out of their homes."

"So why are these ones right side up?" I ask, fearing the answer.

"The dark ones have given me fantastic gifts, Abigail," Eventide says with that knowing smile. "They have made me who I am, and if you want to be like me, you'll embrace them too. See, you're not the only one who can call them up from their black abyss."

The bowls rattle against the irregular blockwork of the floor. I spin around to see them disappear as if crude oil leaked up over top of them, but the black is so pure, it has no shape or depth. The spots where the bowls sit at each point of the pentagram aren't so much covered in an opaque fluid as much as my eyes are blind in the places where they had once been. And those black blind spots are spreading wider and wider. There are demons below those pools of midnight, and they're coming through.

A tentacle rises and twists like a vine growing up a lattice in sped-up time-lapse. The tip of a raven's wing spears out of another hole. Hooked claws of a panther's paw curl around the black and dig into the floor's stone blocks. A monstrous lobster claw climbs up behind me, and I send my ax head through its fragile shell. It hisses as it retreats. I have time to chop into the skull of an emerging hogshead, splitting the bone, but the tentacles, paws, and wings are encircling me. I can't fight them all, not in this cramped wine cellar.

I bolt up the stairs, my ax clutched tight to my chest, and plow into the man standing there in a black pin-striped suit and slippers. He stops me in my tracks and holds me by both arms. HHR Eventide casts his deep eyes down on me.

"Can you control them yet, Abigail?" he asks. "Have you learned to play with your demons?"

Chapter Twenty
The Courtyard

If Eventide isn't expecting me to react violently, he doesn't know me as well as he thinks he does. I shove him as hard as I can with the shaft of the ax. His feet scramble backward, clearing him of the doorframe. While unspeakable things climb out of those inky black pools below, I charge into the billiards room. Not that I'm safe here. I won't be safe until I'm back above ground, out of Eventide's mansion, far away from this place... and probably not even then.

From the billiards room, I'm racing up the steps to the main floor. As frantic as my run was to find that wine cellar deep below the surface, I couldn't keep a mental map of the mansion's floor plan. It's all a maze of gothic stage dressings and classic luxury of a level I didn't know existed in Woodduck. When I enter a vast dining hall, I find a ridiculously long rosewood table and an elaborate array of plates, bowls, glasses, and an extravagant number of forks, knives, and spoons, all laid out for two. Huge windows and glass patio doors look out onto the sprawling courtyard behind the house. In the center of the courtyard is an imposing statue and fountain of angels on horseback with spears and shields. Everything out there is blanketed in a layer of crystalline snow. Everything is still and calm.

Outside seems safer than inside, so I use the ax like a battering ram and smash the head into what I assume is a locked handle. The French door bursts open. The cold of the waning afternoon rushes in. Somewhere behind me, deep inside the mansion, Eventide is singing my name. I'm sure those things from below are on his side, like attack dogs awaiting his whistle to sic. Thinking clearly, perhaps for the first time since I saw two dead law enforcement officers on my front stoop, I quietly step outside and ease the French door shut behind me.

The cold hits me as instantly as electricity. Daylight is dying almost as quick. I didn't bother to grab my coat when I fled my house, but I don't intend to stay out here for long. All I need to do is find the path back to the front of the house, get in my Volt, and get away from this place. With any luck at all, the Demon-Zoey is long gone.

I bet the thing smiled wide when it saw me step inside of Eventide's mansion. That's why it didn't follow me up the driveway. Because it wasn't chasing me; it was corralling me, and as soon as I came here, its job was done.

My boots crunch across the snow of a brick-paved terrace overlooking the courtyard. The wind cuts across my ears, deafening me to anything else. I want to be out of view from the dining room as soon as I can. Much like the interior of the mansion, I don't have time to map out all the twists and turns of this courtyard. It's a maze of terraces, stairs, walkways, statues, fountains, hedges, and dead gardens buried in snow. I take a flight of stairs leading down into the tangle of paths and shadows.

The mansion's wings surround the courtyard on three sides. On the far side of the courtyard is a vacant servant's quarters and a pool house. Beyond those buildings to the south, further from town and my car, is the infinite expanse of the Great North Woods. Hedges, sometimes trimmed into simple rectangular rows and other times expertly sculpted into orbs stacked on top of each other block my view. The statues greeting me at each turn are angels at war. They wear Roman breastplates and greaves, carry spears, and flaunt wings of doves. Their faces and bodies are beautiful, but with a glint of harshness in their bored-out pupils. Knowing what I know now, they're more likely to be angels of the fallen type. I slip past them down to the lowest of the terraces. The path opens to an oval brick patio and the elaborate fountain I'd spotted from inside. The water has been turned off for the winter. The basin is filled with snow and ice.

The angels are carved in white marble and sit upon rearing, snarling horses with flared nostrils.

Multiple staircases lead down to this place, it seems as if every path eventually leads to this spot, but there are also more hedges and statues to hide behind. I sneak out of sight from the dining room windows and duck behind one of those statues. Could be Gabriel. Could be Lucifer. I have my guess which.

"Abby?" the voice of my sister, inquisitive not accusatory, echoes off the mansion's surrounding wings.

Shit. I'm not alone with Lucifer. I press my back against the pedestal, hoping I'm hidden from the Demon-Zoey. Across the courtyard, a door opens. From around the snow-covered shape of an orb-hedge, I see something distinctly inhuman inside the mansion. When it steps out on animal legs, it shape-shifts into a thing that looks entirely normal. From the opposite wing, another door opens. Another demon steps out. Its boar's head, tail, and wings turn to mist and what is left is the shape of a person. I hear but don't see a third door open, claws step out, and a door close behind it. That makes a total of four.

Behind layers and layers of clouds and trees, the sun dips below the horizon. The darkness deepens.

"Abby, let me help you," Zoey's voice calls to me. "After all, we're sisters."

We're anything but. I know it. The thing pretending to be Zoey knows it too. But these things only deal in death and lies. My numb fingers grip and regrip the ax. I'm not sure, but I feel like the sound of its voice came from the back side of the courtyard, up and to my left. Peeking from my hiding place near the statue and seeing no demons, I dash across the sunken oval, around the ornate fountain, to a similar statue that guards the opposite steps. I hold tight to my new hiding place and wait.

A foot crunches snow. Then another. The clack-clack of Zoey's high heels. The demon is just up the stairs from me. It knows I'm close, but not exactly how close. I want so badly to sulk further around the statue's pedestal, further from view, but the snow around my feet will betray the smallest shuffle. I'm stuck here, frozen in place as sufficiently as the warring angel above my head.

Another footfall crushes snow on the steps around the corner. Then another. It's coming down into this sunken oval patio. But it's moving slowly, trying to hide the sound of its approach, not singing out to me anymore. Six more patient footfalls follow, getting lower and louder each time. To keep from seeing the puffs of steam coming from my mouth, I hold my breath. It steps into view.

The thing looks everything like my sister, from the impractical high-heeled shoes to the suit pants, to the suit jacket, to the handgun held at its waist, up to the eerily familiar face. I see her in profile. She's not looking my way but to the fountain. *It*, I remind myself. It is looking forward, not *she*. This thing is not Zoey. It is *not* my sister. I should *not* hesitate.

Heaving the head of the ax up to the twilight sky, I must grunt because Zoey's face turns my way. Just the face. Not the gun. The ax head sings down from the early stars. It cleaves into the flesh of its forearm. Bones snap. Skin rips apart. A hand still holding the gun tumbles down into the snow. Black blood sprays the white snow. The demon wails louder and higher pitched than any human ever could.

If the other demons didn't know where I was before, they know now. I waste no time but draw back my ax for another strike. Part of me expected the demon to revert to its true, subterranean shape after I chopped off its hand, but the thing retains Zoey's form. I don't allow that to give me pause. I saw what this thing did to Sheriff Graham and Deputy Ruiz. It will tear me apart with its bare teeth if I let it. With the ax head cranked behind my shoulders, I sling it sideways into the Demon-Zoey's sternum. Molten tar bursts out of that red blouse. The demon wails as it crumples down into the snow, but the screeching doesn't last long. It drains down to a single quivering note, then surrenders to the courtyard's deathly placid hush.

The thick black blood, more blood than could be contained in a normal human body, gurgles up from the pit in the center of this thing's chest. It bubbles over the body and into the snow. I back away out of disgust. While keeping that molasses-like muck off my Red Wing would be nice, there are three other demons still scattered through the paths and hedges. As if I'd rung a dinner bell, they're certainly coming my way now.

I trudge through the black sap and run away from the fountain and back up the steps. That was a mistake. Standing down the path, looking me dead in the eye, is Jane from The Book Bazaar. She's dressed as she always is, in an elaborate patterned dress with layers of shawls and scarves and beads and wooden jewelry. It doesn't suit her look the way she's carrying that chrome-handled butcher knife, with her elbow up and her fist by her ear and the tip of the blade aimed straight at me. Because, of course, this isn't my eccentric hippy friend who runs the cozy, dusty, bookstore downtown. This is a thing born in Hell and brought up with pure sin and corruption.

The Demon-Jane hisses.

Behind me, a boot crunches through snow. A creature that looks like Lilith Littlebird, my serene and stealthy boss, is creeping up on me. She's short and round and wears a nice pullover sweater just like Lilith would wear, but this isn't her. If it were, I wouldn't have heard it creeping up on me. Just like the Demon-Jane didn't come from The Book Bazaar, the Demon-Lilith didn't come from Accounts Receivable. It's holding the scythe from Eventide's kitchen, and contrary to everything Lilith has ever been, it looks mean. Aggressive and murderous, and even as worn and rusted as the scythe is, I have no doubt it will separate my head from my neck if I give this demon a chance.

Eventide chose these demons specifically and then armed them with whatever he had lying around his home. It's a game to him, to confuse me and make me hesitate before killing them. But this is a showdown and the one with the least amount of sanity is going to win. All I have to do to come out on top, to lose my mind that is, is allow myself to admit what Eventide has done to me. He lured me into his home, he did his best to seduce me, and much worse, he summoned up infernal beasts from hell to come and kill me. He is nothing like what I thought he was.

Demon-Jane hasn't stopped hissing, and when she takes a step closer, my mind is made up on which one of them to deal with first. Anger floods my mind. Sanity slips free and I charge straight for the creature pretending to be my friend. I'm screaming and I have my ax wound up over my head, the blade hanging behind my shoulders. A stride away, I catch a glimpse of panic in the demon's eyes. The ax is already arching down. A moment later, the handle smashes through the forearms trying to block the blow and the blade sinks through the skull and into whatever excuse for brain matter resides inside of this thing's head.

What looks like the body of my friend collapses down to the pathway, bringing my ax with it. The handle slips from my cold hands and clanks against the bricks next to the butcher knife.

Behind me, the Demon-Lilith takes slow steady strides my way. I snatch the handle of my ax from the walkway, but it won't dislodge from the Demon-Jane's skull no matter how hard I yank. I'm dragging the corpse across the bricks, but the goddamn ax won't come free. The Demon-Lilith's strides grow longer and quicker. Her smile grows wider. The scythe rises, eager to slice through my throat.

I'm left with no choice but to abandon the ax. My mind is set on vaulting over the stone banister into the garden below when my eyes land on the butcher knife Demon-Jane had been holding. I pluck it from the thin layer of snow. As the Demon-Lilith charges, I fling it in her direction, just to fend her off. What happens next is the coolest James Bond ninja thing I've ever pulled off. The blade spins end over end until it plunges into the Demon-Lilith's neck, just below its chin. The scythe is forgotten. The demon is clawing at the blade sunk up to the hilt into its throat. Gallons of that inky syrup gush down its chest and to the ground. It falls to its knees. Its growl hasn't stopped, but now it's drowning in thick wetness, gurgling, coughing, and choking. The horrid creature disguised as my sweet and kind boss falls forward. Its stolen face smacks hard against the bricks and the impact shoves the handle of the knife deeper until the tip of the blade punctures through the back of the neck.

Three down. One to go. One demon and HHR Eventide.

"Okay," I whisper under my breath. "Now where's Hank?"

"My dear, Abigail," Eventide calls to me from the mansion's French doors. "Haven't you been listening to what I'm trying to tell you? Haven't you read a word of my prose?"

His silhouette stands before the lit interior of the house, but he hasn't spotted me yet. I drop below a retaining wall and let evening be my ally. In the dim, I slip further from the terrace where he stands. My ax is still lodged into the Demon-Jane's head, but I know it's too valuable to abandon. Creeping out from the retaining wall, I'm able to set the sole of my boot against the Demon-Jane's head and wiggle it back and forth until it's worked free. Taking it with, I flee deeper into the courtyard, around hedges and statues and the dead husks of garden plants. Eventually, I find myself at the edge of the oval center patio with the big fountain of horseback angels in the middle.

From across the courtyard, I can see Eventide plainly. And for the first time, I see him for what he is: not a talented and mysterious author extraordinaire, but a madman filled to the brim with evil and arrogance. I don't know if he can see me, but I sulk deeper into the shadows of another statue all the same.

"Don't you understand, my Abigail?" Eventide says. "These beings... They're a blessing, not a curse. You merely need to learn to control them. Use just a drop of your imagination and think of what you can accomplish by replacing all of your competitors, your oppressors, and your enemies with these willing and obedient servants."

So, he called them from Hell. He set the incantation bowl in my basement, and I suppose in the tunnels as well, so I'd call up even more. All of this, from the very beginning, was his doing. My dad's murder. Jason. Deputy Ruiz. Sheriff Graham… All of this goes back to HHR Eventide. Peeking around the statue pedestal, I still see him in the door frame. The handgun the Demon-Zoey dropped rests in the snow just a few feet away, but I doubt I can hit him from here.

"I've had my eye on you for a long time now, Abigail," Eventide's voice booms across the courtyard. "Ever since that day I spotted you in the park, I've had you on my mind. I picked you out. Above all of the other potential partners here in this pathetic little town, I chose you. Just imagine everything we can accomplish together!"

There's a noise to my left. The last demon. I can't see it yet, so with any luck, it hasn't seen me either. I'm tempted to rush out to the gun lying there in the snow, but I'm not sure I even know how to fire it. Do I need to cock it? Is there a safety? The only thing I know about guns is what I've read in books! Instead of going for it, I stay hidden near the statue of a fallen angel and try to control my breathing so I can maybe hear the demon's.

"Come out from the darkness, Abigail," Eventide says. "Come by my side and I'll show you how to play with your demons."

He's baiting me. He knows my only advantage is my stealth, so he's goading me to respond and give away my hiding place. But I know better.

"Or, refuse me, and I'll unleash all the legions of Hell upon you," he says. "Join me, or you can join your dead father."

"Don't you talk about my dad!" the words burst out of my lips before they are thought. "He was a good man! Better than just good. He was a hero. He was a great father and more of a man than you'll ever be."

Call it stupid; I don't care. Some things can't be allowed to go unchallenged. And this piece of shit? This hack novelist? This wanna be Stephen King? This phony Lovecraft? He does not get to talk about my dad. Forgetting all about the demons lurking around us, I stand up from my crouch and march for the upper terrace where he looks over the courtyard. If Eventide is the start of all of this, my ax can be the end of it.

Unfortunately, the last demon hasn't forgotten about me.

As soon as I'm out of the shadows, the shape of a man, it's too dark now to identify who this demon is supposed to be, storms around the fountain and comes at me. It has the antique, double-barreled shotgun from above the fireplace. Just as I duck, startled into a crouch, it fires. Buckshot burns through the air above my head. I swing my ax, recklessly, without an aim point, in the direction of the gun. The flat of the head smacks against the stock, knocking the shotgun away. That doesn't slow down the demon. It attacks me with fists and elbows, pummeling me the same way a drunk in a bar would beat me to a pulp. I'm trying to ward off the blows with the handle of my ax, but then a big, thick fist collides against the side of my head.

I don't remember falling. Just find myself lying in the snow with the ax resting against my abdomen. My head is fuzzy. My brain hurts. My ears ring. I'm in no shape for solving puzzles, but I know he clocked me good and knocked me to the ground. And if I want to avoid another blow like that, I better get my head straight.

The demon is taking its time, strolling back to the place where it dropped the shotgun. As I struggle to pick myself up, it retrieves the gun. In the dim light, while the rest of its face is covered in shadows, its teeth shine an evil rictus. It swings the barrel my way.

"No!" I yell out of instinct, not because I think it will listen.

But it does stop. Like a rabid dog remembering a command from a cruel master. It holds the shotgun, barrel pointed but not aimed, muzzle low enough so that if it fires, the spread might hit the patio instead of me. Its burning ember eyes are locked with mine, but it doesn't move.

"Stay right there," I tell it, because if it listened once, maybe it will again.

A deep Rottweiler growl rinses from its guts. Aggression and obedience debate inside its mind. Somehow, that growl is familiar. I recognize it as a source of more humane words, but I can't place it. Who is this demon pretending to be? Hank? Jason? The man in the green seed jacket? Whoever it is, I know this thing is not a fellow human citizen of Woodduck. It is a hell-born creation hiding behind a familiar face.

I dare to glance away from the last living demon here in the courtyard to spot the handgun below me. But only a glance. If I don't maintain a steady glare with the demon, whatever control I have over it will slip away. And I'm right. In the split second I look for the gun below me, the shotgun rises. It's no longer pointed at the ground but at the dead center of my chest.

"No!" I yell and the demon freezes once again.

But the growl grows louder. There's impatience in it now, as if when it can get no louder, it will break free from this trance. It's now or never.

I drop my ax. I dive for the gun. My fingers scoop it up. Buckshot rips through the cold night air, high, missing me again. I spin the grip of the handgun so it points at the demon. If there's any cocking, or taking off a safety, or anything else that I have to do, I'll be dead. I line up the three white dots on the sights with the demon's body and squeeze the trigger.

The gun bucks in my hands. The flash blinds my eyes. The bang deafens my ears. The bullet punches a hole in the middle of the demon. I fire again and again and again. The impacts flare blaze orange like fire. Black ooze gushes out of the holes, draining the demon of whatever is inside of it. That all-too-familiar human shape topples over backward and falls lifeless onto the courtyard.

Slowly, I get my feet back underneath me. The Demon-Zoey's handgun is warm. The barrel smokes like in an old western. Nothing around me moves.

Eventide is still here, watching all of this play out. I swing the gun that way but only fast enough to spot his backside, running into the safety of the mansion. I fire anyway. The bullets smack against the brick exterior, not aimed well enough to even break glass.

From somewhere inside, he flips on floodlights. The entirety of the courtyard lights up as bright as noon. I turn away from the shine and the mansion. When I'm able to reopen my eyes, I see the human shapes of the demons I've killed.

At my feet is a thing that looks like my sister. And just beyond it, with bullet holes punched through his plaid flannel shirt, is the man who didn't deserve the hand he was dealt. Who too often had to go it alone. Who wanted to be a better man in spite of all his demons and flaws and weaknesses. Who did his best to raise us. Who failed as often as he tried. At my feet, dead again by the gun, is my father.

Chapter Twenty One
Unlikely Aid

All the emotions that spilled out of me the day my dad died drown me again. Memories flood down my throat and fill up my lungs, replacing all the air. I'm right back there in my living room, with Dad in his recliner, his gun hanging from his fingers, and a hole bored through his chin and out the top of his head. I can smell the iron-like flavor of blood and the chemical residue of burnt gunpowder. Behind my eyelids, I see the horror that first emerges from my basement steps. I smell the familiar mildew of the basement and the sulfur of hell. Sheriff Graham holds me in the driveway while paramedics wheel out the body. His jacket smells like old leather. His neck has the tang of cheap aftershave. I shiver from head to toe. Maybe from the cold. More likely from my mutinous nerves.

I try to repress the shaking, but it's more than just nerves. It's guilt. It's shame. It's disgust. It's never left me. If I could go back and do things differently... If I had said something... If I had done something... If I had done the right thing the first time and stared down the demon crawling up the stairwell and met it with an ax and chopped its ugly head off instead of just running away. If I hadn't allowed it up, maybe he wouldn't have let the demon into his mind, and it never would have had the chance to convince him to do what he did. If I hadn't done what I'd done. If I hadn't run away...

If.

A strange, desperate idea comes over me.

Maybe if I go to him now, maybe I'll find that everything I believe to be true isn't. Maybe this is my father. Maybe he's still alive. Maybe I can help him. Maybe things can be different.

Insanity, any sane person would call it, but while I'm in its grasp, insanity is inescapable.

Motion catches my eyes and mercifully pulls my gaze away from the body at my feet. Floodlights from the house burn my eyes, but I can see that Eventide has fled. To his kitchen or his master bedroom and four-poster bed, or his safe room or maybe down to his wine cellar that isn't a wine cellar at all but an occult worship dungeon and portal to Hell. He's been replaced by another. It's human in form, and for reasons I can't admit, it scares me more than an entire horde of upright pigs, arachnid amalgamations, things with wings like bats, broods of vipers all bound together at the tails, abominations on two legs and four legs, or ghouls on thousands of legs. It knows me, knows my weaknesses, knows my failures, and knows how to defeat me. It has been the one in charge of all the others. In those flames in its eyes, I know it has already envisioned my demise. Perhaps Eventide wanted to seduce me, but this thing, this dread, wants to eat me alive.

And I know it. This is the demon that killed my father.

I have my ax. I have the empty gun in my hand and the shotgun at my feet. There's a scythe and a butcher knife between me and the doors to the mansion. All the tools I should need to finally sate my vengeance. But I no longer have the nerve. The vision of my dead father has robbed me of it. I want nothing more than to slaughter the demon in human form just inside those doors, and then hunt down Eventide and drag him from his bed or vault or dungeon and show him what I really think of his books. But the thing on the other side of that glass embodies all my fears and failures. It is the thing trapping me in this town. It has enslaved me in its game of demons and watchtowers. It owns me. My feet carry me backward, away from the terrace and the corpses at my feet.

For the second time in my life, when I should stand my ground and attack, I run instead.

Around hedgerows, down narrow paths, up marble steps, I find myself running around the drained and snow-filled pool. Between the pool house and the furthest end of the wing is a pathway and a gate. I don't know if the demon behind me is chasing me, but my own shame compels me just as fiercely. I don't look back. Once I'm through the gate, I find a pathway cleared of snow and ice that leads me around the manor house and back to the front driveway.

My Chevy Volt is where I left it. I have the keys. I know it will start, and regardless of what awaits me in the rest of Woodduck, I want to drive it as far from this place as possible. I'm halfway across the brick driveway when headlights blind my eyes. My ears fill with the roar of an engine and the wail of brakes. A car screeches to a stop between me and my Volt. The headlights shine up at the mansion and I'm able to lower the arms shielding my vision.

It's Zoey. Or it's a thing that looks like Zoey. She's standing outside the driver's door of a blood-red Chevy Camaro, a car that looks like it was etched from rubies. She's wearing a black suit with a blue blouse under the jacket. Her lips are still red and her eyes are almost as hot. It looks like my sister, alright.

I'm holding up the ax and the gun to block the shine of the headlights. When I lower my arms, I point the gun at the thing standing outside of my sister's car.

"Abby? What the fuck are you doing?" she says.

"Are you really you?" I say. "Are you really my sister?"

"Abby, you fucking nut case, who I am hoping didn't actually murder two law enforcement officers on her front step… Of course I'm your fucking sister. Now put that gun down before I grab you by the hair and make you punch yourself like when we were kids," she says.

"Zoey!" I cry and run to her. Because, yeah, this is Zoey. No doubt about it.

We're sisters and we've known each other through the good and the bad, but I've also been accused of murder and was just pointing a gun at her, so I don't hold it against her when she doesn't hug me back.

"Thank God you're here," I say. "There's things I need to tell you. And I really need your help dealing with them."

"Yeah," Zoey says. "No, duh. Now get in the fucking car and let me get you out of here."

"But my car…" I start.

"Fuck that piece of shit. Call USAA and get it towed later. Now get in the Camaro," Zoey says.

I obey. As soon as my butt hits the ultra-low bucket seat, Zoey's launching the car into a tire-melting hundred and eighty-degree skid. Once we're pointed back down the driveway, she does something with the pedals and the shifter, and we're rocketing down the twisting narrow driveway. I don't know if the dangers of driving on icy roads have ever given her pause, or if she just goes through a half dozen brand new cherry red Chevy Camaros every winter, but she holds nothing back. Working the steering wheel like a Formula One driver, she swerves around each turn until we're barreling toward the gate and the abandoned Ford Explorer. There's just enough room around the front of the SUV for Zoey to thread us through the needle. Then we're racing north along Hill Road, back into town.

"We have to go to my house," I say over the engine noise.

"Are you fucking crazy?" Zoey fires back. "Do you not realize that you are wanted for three murders? Two of which happened right fucking there? We are *not* going to your house!"

"Zoey, we *have to* go to my house!" I say again.

"Abby!" Zoey yells, but I don't let her carry on.

"I didn't kill those people. As for the two that died on my doorstep, I know I didn't do it because I watched you do it," I say.

"Abby, if you're going for some insanity plea, now is *not* the time to practice your courtroom antics," she says. "We need to get you somewhere safe, and we need to find you a *really* good fucking lawyer."

"The things that killed those people, they're still out there," I say. "The guy in the seed coat. The demon that killed Jason. The demon that killed Dad. I already killed yours, but who knows how many more have slipped free from Hell and are wandering through town."

Without warning, Zoey slams on the brakes. The Camaro immediately skids on the ice-packed road. We twist to the left and right as she deftly works the wheel to keep us out of the ditch. A good quarter mile later, we come to a stop.

"What the fuck are you talking about?" Zoey screams at me. "God damn it, I'm your sister and your life has literally gone to shit around you, and you won't tell me what the fuck is actually happening! God, fucking, damn it, Abby. For once, will you talk to me and tell me what is going on?"

"Dad didn't kill himself," I spit back. "Not without help he didn't. Something came out of that basement. Something not human. Something from the Bible or the Quran or the Torah or a book even older than all of them. I don't know, but I saw it coming up the stairs, and I was scared, so I ran. Didn't even say goodbye to Dad, assumed he was too drunk to care, so I left. And I let it have its way with him."

"Are you being serious right now?" she asks in a way that tells me she doesn't a word I've said.

"I don't know what they are. Ghosts. Monsters. Demons, I guess. I don't know," I tell her. "One came up the basement steps the night Dad died. It killed him. They've killed others. They infect people's minds. Eventide has been using them this whole time–"

"HRR Eventide is wrapped up in this? Now that, I believe," Zoey says.

"They come whenever I'm at my weakest. When the guilt of how Dad died gets the better of me, when I'm consumed by shame, when I hate myself, when I remember I let that first one get to him."

"Abby," Zoey says my name, and for once, there's not a hint of sarcasm in her voice. "It is not your fault what happened to Dad. No matter what you think you saw and no matter what you think you could have done. That was not your fault."

"Don't lie to me," I beg. "I'm not stupid. You've blamed me this whole time. I saw it on your face at the funeral and every time since then. And I see it in your absence whenever you're not around."

"Abby, no! You have more right to blame me than I do to blame you. I'm the daughter who ran away. Not you. You're the daughter who stuck around. You're the daughter who tried getting him into AA. You're the one who looked after him. You're the one who never gave up," Zoey says. "As for me? I did everything I could to distance myself from this town. To pretend like I'd never even heard of Woodduck. And after Dad died? The truth is, the guilt was so heavy, I chose to ignore it rather than deal with it. It was easier to hate this town, to hate Dad, to pretend to hate you. But, Abby, you're my little sister. I love you."

I dive into her, wrapping my arms around her shoulders. If the car was still moving, we'd be in the ditch. But we stay there, stationary in the middle of Hill Road, while I soak Zoey's fancy suit with my big salty tears. And this time, I feel her arms come around my shoulders too. And soon, my shoulder is wet too.

"Well?" Zoey says, expectantly. "Are you going to say it back?"

"I'm sorry," I say instead. "I'm sorry I thought all those terrible things about you, that you thought you were too cool for me and Dad, that everything you had going on down in the Cities was more important than us, that you didn't love me. I'm sorry I didn't try harder. I'm sorry for how I treated you."

"And?"

"And I love you." And then the waterworks are back on, and that's all we can do for a while.

Eventually, Zoey peels me off of her. "Love you too, sis."

"Then you gotta believe me," I say. "I can explain everything, but I have to show you something in the basement of the house."

Chapter Twenty Two
What's in the Basement

Before we go back to the house where two cops were murdered and where Suspect Number One lives, Zoey insists we have someone scope it out first. So we meander around the edge of town while we use her phone to call Eric.

As the phone rings and rings, I'm certain I got the number wrong, or that he's decided to be done with me after I'd become a murder suspect, or that one of the demons has gotten to him. My nervous system shifts into a higher gear with each buzz of the ringtone. When the phone clicks to life and I hear his voice, I'm washed in relief.

"Eric and Sons Electric, this is Eric Erickson, younger Eric, not Old Man Eric," he says.

"Eric, this is Abby's sister, Zoey. We haven't met but–"

"Oh, we've met. You were the one raising Cain up on the second floor of the courthouse over some fine or whatnot," he says through the car's speakers.

"Yeah. Okay. Fine. Whatever. That's not important right now," Zoey says. "I'm calling because we need your help."

"We?" he asks.

For a moment, I'm convinced that he believes I'm guilty, if not for the librarian who was killed while we slept arm-in-arm, then certainly for Sheriff Graham and Deputy Ruiz.

"Eric, it's me," I say. "Whatever they're saying on the news, don't believe it. I didn't hurt anybody. You know me. You know I wouldn't have done–"

"Abby? Oh, thank god!" Eric says. "The news is saying you were kidnapped or killed. They're saying that whoever's done this has to be someone from out of town. And after what we saw under the courthouse? Abby, I've been driving around all over the place looking for you. You had me scared to death! I even thought about going back down into those tunnels but…"

"I made a few calls to the press," Zoey tells me. "Told them the BCA has reason to believe it's someone from out of town. Helps to start framing the story as soon as possible." Then, to Eric, "Listen, Abby's with me and she's safe. But we need you to do something for us. We need you to drive by the house. Crime scene investigators might still be there. Might be a plain-clothed officer in a car or a van watching the place from down the block. We need you to go there and check things out. Abby says there's something in the basement she has to show us."

"I'm just a few blocks away," Eric says. "Be there in a jiff."

We stay on the line and don't have to wait long.

"Lights are off," he tells us. "Nobody is parked in the driveway."

"What about along the street?" Zoey asks. "Any cars that look out of place? Anybody hanging out, just watching traffic?"

"In this weather? If anybody was watching from a car, they'd have to keep the engine running so as to not freeze to death," Eric says. "There's yellow tape around the yard and across the front door, but otherwise, the house looks the same as usual."

"Good. Park down the block and go inside," Zoey says. "Don't turn on the lights once you're inside but pay attention if it feels like anybody is watching you as you go."

"If it feels like someone is watching me? Oh, that's not going to creep me out at all," Eric says. "Okay. Heres I go."

As we wait for Eric to finish his recon and report back, Zoey cruises closer and closer to my place on 7th Avenue. I listen as he shuffles and pants and eventually cracks open my front door.

"Okay. Yeah," Eric says. "The place is empty. I didn't see anybody in the street, but I feel like I walked over half a dozen graves or so while my grandma was watching me do it."

"Perfect," Zoey says. "We'll be there in a minute."

She hangs up. I cringe. More demons have come up from that basement than anywhere else, and now Eric is in there alone in the dark. But a minute later we park behind his work truck, a block from my driveway. Just as Eric described it, the street is empty and dark. No one waiting in an idling vehicle. No lights on inside the house.

"You're absolutely sure we have to come here?" Zoey asks.

"Yeah, I'm sure."

"Girl, don't ever say I wouldn't stick my neck out for you."

"Fine. Let's just go already," I say and pop open the car door.

We trot down the street like a pair of soldiers afraid of snipers. She's eyeing every car and window as we go. When we make it to the house, sure enough, there's yellow police tape stretched across the front yard and an X over the doorway. Going through the big garage door isn't an option, so we're forced to use the front door. I try to ignore the darkened blood stains on the concrete steps and stucco siding. I open the door, and we duck under the yellow X.

"Jiminy freakin' crickets!" Eric says when we come inside. "Can we turn on a gosh darn light yet?"

As soon as I'm inside, those phantom hands wrap their grip around the base of my spine. A moment later, Zoey shuts the front door behind us and the house is as dark as the tunnels, a blackness too absolute to distinguish between humans and demons. Maybe Zoey's right and we should leave the lights off, but there's no way I can withstand the blackness a second longer. I hit the small light over the sink, and it fills the kitchen and living room with a dim glow. Zoey and Eric are standing there, both looking to me for answers. Thankfully, for once, I have them. Or at least I have the start of some answers.

"Come on," I say. "Follow me."

I toss the empty gun in my sink. I bring my ax.

I'm not afraid of what I might find behind the door leading downstairs. After all, it wouldn't be the first time I've faced down a demon, and now I have my two best friends at my back. So naturally when

I open the door, there's nothing but a plain old staircase leading down into a very boring basement. Nevertheless, it feels like wild dogs are gnawing at my backbone. And that electric buzz has the hairs on my arms standing on end again. I flip on the lights and lead them down to the concrete floor.

"We expecting a tornado or something?" Eric says, nervousness thick in his voice.

I don't blame him. I can feel that pressure in my spine that tells me danger isn't far away. The electric hum of the bowl stands my hairs on end.

"There," I say and point to the strange and ancient bowl sitting near the drain, right where I'd dropped it.

It looks similar to the bowls in Eventide's wine cellar, with the strange symbols or letters starting at the rim and circling down and toward the center where there's a rudimentary drawing of a demon. A human face, albeit with four canine teeth. Clawed hands. Twisted horns. Hooves. This bowl, like the ones at Eventide's, is turned right side up.

"What, were you eating cereal down here?" Eric says. It's in his nature to try to joke his fear away, but now? No one is laughing.

"It's an incantation bowl," I say. "From Israel or maybe Iraq or Iran… I don't understand the history, but they used to bury them under their doorsteps, upside down, to trap evil spirits and keep them from coming into their homes. But this one, the way it was set here, right side up, it's guiding the demons up from below, right into this basement."

"I don't get it," Zoey says, but she's not looking at me or the incantation bowl. Always the detective, she's inspecting the walls and the nooks and crannies of the basement. "Why would you put that down here if you knew–"

"I didn't," I say. "But it's been down here since before Dad died. Someone came down here and purposely put it this way."

"Who would do that?" Eric asks.

Zoey and I answer him at the same time, "Eventide."

"That's where I found the Sheriff's missing cruiser," Zoey explains to Eric and me. "It's where I found you, running away with that ax and empty gun in your hand."

"Okay," Eric says, still with a bit of a forced snicker in his words. "But how would Mister New York Times Best Seller HHR Eventide get into your basement?"

Zoey shoves her weight into one of the cinder blocks set into the wall of the foundation. It pops an inch out of the mortar as if on a spring. A door-sized section of the wall eases inward, revealing a long, dark tunnel beyond it. Cool, stale, fifty-degree air flavored with the ever so diluted but still distinct stench of death wafts into the basement.

"We heard rumors about these tunnels since we were kids," Zoey says. "So, when I finally got my badge and could con the Woodduck Records department into letting me see the maps, and while I was up here getting a birth certificate anyway… Well, I pulled the plans and learned that everything we'd heard was true. We knew they ran between the courthouse and the Sheriff's department and all around downtown. What I didn't know, what I didn't even suspect, was that when they were built, Mayor Huntington had a tunnel dug specifically for him. A tunnel that connected his home to the home of his mistress. A tunnel that runs from this very basement all the way to the mansion where HHR Eventide now lives."

"He had these things, these incantation bowls, in his wine cellar too," I say. "He uses them, or the demons use them, as a gateway from Hell. All it takes to wake them up is greed and lust and wrath and pride, gluttony and envy, sloth…"

"So, just the things that everybody feels and does every fucking day of their lives but nobody wants to admit," Zoey says. "Shit, Abbs. Did you really think all the things that make us human made you something worse than the rest of us?"

"I know everybody deals with those things too, but Eventide knew Dad and me. He stalked us. He told me all about how he watched me bring Dad to AA," I say. "Coming back from war, losing his wife, drinking… Eventide knew what he had in Dad. Dad and I both had a larger dose of guilt and shame and regret than other people, and he saw that as an opportunity to take advantage of us. He sicced the demons on Dad, and when they were done with him, Eventide let them have their way with me. Lonely, scared, guilt-ridden me. Said I had a 'talent.' Maybe what he meant was I had a vulnerability. A susceptibility he could exploit."

"When you say demons…" Zoey leads me on.

"I am not being metaphorical," I say. "I mean the literal hooves and horns kind of demons."

"Yeah. She ain't kidding," Eric says. "I wouldn't believe her if I hadn't seen 'em for myself. Ugly things. Huge things. The kind of things I don't think we want to mess with."

"There's more of these bowls in those tunnels," I say. "Near the courthouse is my bet. I think I kicked one the first day I brought you down there and broke another one when I was coming to find you, but it was so dark, I couldn't tell."

"And these demons… They're behind the murders?" Zoey says.

"Jason, Sheriff Marty. Deputy Ruiz. Dad's suicide. Everything," I say.

"Okay…" Zoey says, only taking a moment to come to terms with what I've told her. Then, as is her way, she's ready to get to work. "So what's the plan?"

Her back is to the opening of the tunnels. Eric is nearest the stairs, just under the single light bulb dangling from the ceiling. I step toward the middle of the room. Toward the incantation bowl. I flip my ax around to lead with the flat, blunt end.

"First, we smash the bowls, starting with this one right here. Then, we go after Eventide," I say.

"If you break that bowl, there's no going back," Eric says.

"Smash it, Abbs. Smash it now," Zoey says.

I don't wait but heave the ax head over my shoulder. It should be an easy thing, smashing this fragile clay pottery into a thousand pieces, but just as I'm about to bring down the ax, the lightbulb over my head pops. There's a brief shower of glass and sparks before the whole basement is covered in inky, opaque, darkness. And then the demon is there in the middle of us. Bones crack and skin rips as it expands up above us. Zoey hits my eyes with the beam of her cell phone flashlight. Through the glare, I see the demon. Even as light-blinded as I am, I know this one. The one with the pretty human face but the long goat horns, fur-covered shoulders, and fangs for teeth. The one that killed Dad.

My ax still hangs over my shoulder, ready to strike, but before I get a chance, the demon lashes out. I'm knocked off my feet. My head meets the floor, and explosions ignite across my field of vision. Zoey fires her gun, but it's just one more flash in the fireworks display. There's a howl. A scream. In the whirling, inconsistent light of Zoey's flashlight, I can't track exactly what's happening. She's thrown aside, away from the entrance to the tunnels. Boots against concrete give chase.

I'm slow to pick myself off the floor. My hand is searching for my ax and coming up empty. Zoey is searching the floor too, panning her light for her gun. The demon is gone. And along with it...

"Eric?" I call out.

It's just me and Zoey in the basement. There's no sign of the man who'd taken me out on a date, who'd trusted me in the deepest, darkest parts of Woodduck, who'd made love to me on my couch upstairs.

"Eric!" I'm screaming now, into the tunnel, only for my torn voice to be swallowed by the dense porous walls. "Eric!!!"

Zoey pulls me away from the entrance. My muscles go weak, almost limp, and it's all I can do to keep from falling to the ground. She stands, fierce, in front of the door with her gun and flashlight aimed into the abyss.

"No!" I shout and wrap my arms around her, pinning her hands to her sides and all but tackling her to the ground. "It has Eric. You'll shoot Eric."

We're turning like figure skaters away from the entrance to the tunnels. The light from her phone is at her thigh, panning as we spin, the only light down there with us. Meanwhile, she's babbling over and over again, "What the fuck. What the fuck was that? What the fuck! Holy fucking shit!"

And then another light shines from across the room, just as stark and colorless as the light from Zoey's phone.

"Abby?" Eric says.

I let go of Zoey and by the light of their phones, I see Eric standing at the entrance to the tunnels, pointing his phone back toward us. I run to him, almost tackle him, but pull him away from the tunnel.

"Oh my god! I thought it took you! I thought I lost you!" I'm wailing into his ear.

"It's okay. I'm alright," he's telling me. "It ran off. Back into the tunnels. I think it took the bowl when it skedaddled out of here."

"And you *chased* it?" Zoey asks.

"Well… you know… just kind of seemed like the thing to do," Eric says.

"Boy, do you know how to pick 'em," Zoey says.

But I'm still hugging Eric. And even though the buzz of the incantation bowl has left my skin, the squeeze around my backbone is stronger than ever.

"It hasn't gone far," I tell them both. "I can feel it. The demon. It's close."

Chapter Twenty Three
Returning Alone

It's asking a lot for anyone to believe this story. That physical demons are coming out of clay bowls placed around town by a best-selling author and big-time celebrity? That this world-renowned author has specifically targeted a local homely accountant who's currently wanted for triple homicide? To ask anyone to believe that is a lot. The only bigger ask would be to assist said homely account to commit a fourth murder, that of the big-deal famous author in his own haunted mansion.

Zoey has her security clearance, her prestigious job with the BCA, and prison time to think about. As for Eric? We still haven't been on a second date. So, when I go back to HHR Eventide's towering, Flemish Renaissance Revival mansion at the end of Hill Road, I go alone.

I park Eric's work truck next to my Volt in front of the mansion. How I'll get the vehicles back from here isn't the most important thing on my mind right now. For as many demons as I've killed, not once have I had the slightest inclination to inflict that same lethal brutality on a human being. Of all the commandments and pillars of faith and virtues I've tried to keep during these past months, surely "Thou Shall Not Kill," ranks pretty high on any comprehensive list. But this is the man who killed Dad. And others. And has unleashed an unknown amount of suffering and misery wherever he's gone. This is what I'm thinking about as I walk up to Mister HHR Eventide's door.

That big cast-iron ring hanging from the mouth of a skull waits for me to bang it against the metal plate, but I have a strong suspicion he already knows I'm here. Before I reach for the knocker, I hit the "SEND" on the burner phone. No turning back now.

While my hand is still reaching for the knocker, the door opens. And just like so many times before, when the door opens, an agent of Hell is standing on the other side. No physical monster with snarling teeth, talons, claws, and scales like a dragon. The thing standing across the threshold from me is a tall and thin man dressed in a pin-striped black suit and bath slippers. No doubt there is a revolver under that jacket, and if I was carrying it, I believe he would probably ask me again to place my ax in the umbrella can. But I don't have my ax or the gun I'd plucked from the snow in his courtyard. I come unarmed, and what drives me crazy is that he expected me to return, unarmed, starving for his embrace. Otherwise, he wouldn't have opened the door, or if he had, he would have had that gun aimed right at my guts when he did.

"Do you understand now, my dear Abigail?" HHR Eventide says to me in that slick-as-butter voice of his. "I'm the only one who can help you. I'm the only one who can show you the way."

"Yeah. I understand," I tell him. "You're the only one who truly understands what I've seen and done."

"Come in, my child," Eventide says, fixing me with those black-laced eyes. "I've been waiting for you."

I step into Eventide's mansion. All the wealth and decadence that awed me the last time I walked through this door is still here: The richly stained rosewood, the ornate moldings, the classic paintings, but the gold has lost its glitter. The shotgun is missing from the fireplace mantel, probably still lying outside in the snow. When the door shuts behind me, I've never felt more alone and isolated in my life. I turn around and just like before, Eventide is standing between me and the door, cutting me off from it as if it were an escape route. I'm not surprised or offended. After all, the last time we saw one another, I was in his backyard killing the demons he had summoned. All things considered, he's being an extremely hospitable host.

"You said you can show me how to control them. How to use them for my own benefit," I state, don't ask.

"Of course," Eventide says, all patience and confidence as if everything will come to him in the fullness of time. "But first, allow me to pour you a cup of coffee. The evening is late, and we have much work to do."

He glides past me, leading me toward the kitchen again. Along the way, he doesn't check over his shoulder to see if I'm following. He just knows that I will. The kitchen is clean and well-lit, just like before. The only thing that's missing is a butcher knife from the block and the scythe over the sink. The coffee is already brewing, the pot nearly full. The machine hisses as the last few drops land in the carafe. It's as if he knew not only that I would come, but when I would arrive, down to the second. China cups hang from hooks under the cupboards. He retrieves two and goes about pouring.

"Do you take cream or sugar?" he asks with his back to me.

"I didn't come here for coffee," I say and still haven't told a lie, but I'm eyeing that knife block and its remaining blades.

"Of course, you didn't," he says but goes ahead and pours a small amount of plain white cream from a small porcelain pitcher into my cup. He gives it a stir and extends the cup to me. "But I do enjoy being a proper host."

I take the cup, bring it to my lips, but set it down on the breakfast counter. "Show me," I say.

He sips from his steaming cup but doesn't respond.

"Show me how to control them," I say again. "Show me how to conjure them up from below, not just by accident but when and how I want. Show me how you use them."

"My dear Abigail," he says. Both cups are resting on the counter, props in this little theater of ours. "The powers granted to me from below are so much larger than what you have in mind. The demons are just the beginning. Certainly, I can call them at will, by name, and send them out to do my bidding. But they also inform me. Through the connection… You've felt the connection between yourself and the ones you've called up from below, yes?"

I nod. The pressure that grips my spine when they're coming up from underground. And that leash that pulls me toward them, wherever they are.

"Through the connection, they keep me well informed and aware of things I'd normally have no knowledge of," he says, and a new source of fear crawls up my spine when I hear those words.

"What sort of things?" I ask. I'm playing prop with the cup of coffee again. Holding it, bringing it to my lips, setting it back down again, using it to play cool, as if everything is as it should be, and I've expected every twist in this conversation.

"Well, I used them to get to know you and your father. And I know you tried to smash the incantation bowl I placed in your basement," he tells me. "And how you and your sister and that friend of yours plan on smashing all the bowls I've placed underneath this town. Those artifacts are centuries old, Abigail. I spent a good deal of time researching them and went to great lengths to acquire them. Each one is truly irreplaceable."

My heart is thumping under my breastbone now. My nerves feel like I've had a dozen cups of coffee instead of only sniffed at one. I want to ask him why. Why did he put those bowls there, right side up, to send demons to my father and me? What did we do to deserve it? But instead, I ask a more timely and pertinent question. "What else do you know?"

A smile grows on his face. He only has two smiles. There's the public aloof-and-mysterious smile he wears in his author photo and to all his events. The one so practiced he can make millions of fans and readers believe, myself included, that it's meant only for them. And there's the smile that says he knows what I don't, that he's always known more than me, and that he has always maintained the upper hand. That's the one he wears now.

"I know your sister has a map of the tunnels, and she and your friend are using that map to come here, to this very manor. And upon your signal, they are to come out of my cellar, having smashed the bowls and shot dead any demons they've found along the way, so that you can kill me, uninhibited," Eventide says and takes another cautious sip of the hot coffee. "Did I get all of that correct? Sometimes the sensations coming from my demons can be a bit ambiguous and ethereal."

My face and hands grow cold as the blood drains away. Eventide must see it too. That know-it-all smirk of his spreads wider.

"You can send that text message now if you'd like," he says. "The one that lets your sister know you're in the house and she can come out of the tunnels and into the wine cellar and smash all the bowls. I'm afraid she won't find the wine cellar as free of obstacles as you hoped, but any good plan takes these sorts of contingencies under consideration, now doesn't it?"

Coffee tips out of the cup and onto my hand, burning it. I hardly notice. From under the floorboards, I hear muffled gunshots, screams, and the scraping of claws and talons.

"Does it not?" Eventide asks again, his grin making its way into a poorly repressed laugh.

I throw the coffee cup at him. The scalding fluid splashes over his face, steam-cleaning that smirk right off. As he cries out and tries to wipe the burning coffee from his eyes, I bolt out of the kitchen. I have to get to the wine cellar. Zoey and Eric are both down there, just as Eventide said, and something else too. Something familiar, but of unfathomable evilness. I can feel it grinding my spine into dust.

The last time I ran for the basement, I had no idea where I was going, and I'm not any better off now. The mansion is a tangled cluster of rooms and hallways and dead ends. But it's not as if Eventide has used his connections with the demons to twist his home into an ever-shifting maze. It has a floor plan. Some of these rooms, the reception hall, the parlor with the casket, are familiar to me. The staircase leading down to the basement billiards room is just ahead. I see it and rush for it.

When Eventide steps out of an adjacent door, blocking my path and pointing a gun at my face, I think, maybe I'm wrong after all. Maybe this place is some sort of shifting and shuffling maze, rearranged for its current owner to cut me off from where I need to be. Regardless, the site of the barrel of the revolver aimed at my face sends my boots skidding to a halt. Before I can think, before I can tell my body to do otherwise, I'm walking backward, away from Eventide, away from the chrome revolver, away from the stairs, and away from the sounds of my sister swearing and firing her own gun over and over again.

"You misunderstand the situation, my dear Abigail," Eventide says. He doesn't line up his eyes with the revolver's sight. This close, he doesn't have to. Instead, he glares at me over the barrel. "I don't want to hurt you. I want to save you."

"Save me from what?" I say although I'm not interested in his answer. My mind is spinning, trying to find a way to escape, trying to figure out how to get into the basement and save Abby and Eric from whatever it is that's going on down there.

"From a conventional life, of course," Eventide smiles. He's walking toward me, forcing me further from the stairs and deeper into the parlor. "From this town. From that hovel where you dwell. From all of the people and places and jobs that have led you to believe you're nothing but a boring, lonely, insipid accountant not worthy of a promotion."

"On the morrow, I leave for Zurich. From there, Vienna, Munich, Berlin, Paris, Amsterdam, and London. We can return to this residence if you wish, or any other you fancy. I certainly understand if you have no desire to ever set foot in this town again. Join me, Abigail. You have such a skill in calling up these servants of the darkness. Together, you and I, we can be so much more than you ever imagined."

"What about them?" I nod to the sounds of Zoey and Eric battling for their lives in his basement. The gunshots have stopped. I can still hear Zoey growling and swearing. Nothing of Eric.

"You have to forget about them, Abigail," Eventide says. "Think of them as memories from a previous life. Fond memories, if you like, but nothing you'll want to go back to once I've shown you everything we can be."

My back knocks into something hard. Not a wall. My eyes flash away from Eventide to see what it is. The casket. The stupid Dracula-esque prop I spotted the first time I'd raced through these rooms. Only this time, the lid is open and the subterranean smell of earth and rot and decomposition wafts up from what lies inside.

It's Eric.

His corpse, I mean. Not the living Eric, full of bad jokes and incessant smiles. Not the Eric I saved from the tunnels or the Eric who made love with me on my couch or the Eric who chases away the demon from my basement. This Eric, this very human Eric, is dead. And has been dead for much longer than a few minutes or a few hours. Days, this corpse has rotted. The skin is yellowed wax paper stretched over bone. Jaundice. The eyelids are sunken. Hollow. The lips are pulled back to reveal blackening teeth. Not a yellow lab grin but a junkyard snarl. He wears the same clothes he wore when we first met. Jeans. A leather tool belt with a pipe wrench in its holster. The tan duck coat with the brown collar. A t-shirt underneath that's soiled and oily now. Even the maroon and gold Gophers hat lies on the silk bedding next to his head.

What was supposed to be a glance, a check for threats behind me, has now stolen all of my attention. I'm facing the casket, trying to comprehend what my eyes are telling me, walking backward away from the horror laid out on silk in the ivory coffin. I bump into Eventide's chest first. The barrel of the gun prods my kidney, but I can't bring myself to turn.

"Are you beginning to understand now, Abigail?" Eventide whispers in my ear. As one hand holds the gun jabbed into my back, the other rests on my shoulder. "You've already embraced a demon, taken it into your home, and gained carnal knowledge with it."

"Eric is... Eric is..." I want to tell him that Eric is alive and fighting alongside my sister. That he's a good man and could never be something so rotten and decayed as the thing before me or as evil as what Eventide is trying to explain to me.

"He's been dead for some time," Eventide says. "Ever since you allowed him to go alone into the tunnels under your office. You've come to know the thing that came from the incantation bowl I set in your basement. The thing you first saw just before your father passed away."

The abomination with the twisting horns and mangy fur-covered shoulders. The beast with the flail of tails. The thing that just attacked us in my basement. The thing that killed Dad. It was Eric.

My stomach is full of spoiled milk. The hand on my shoulder might as well be leeches or a stranger's vomit or the black bile of the demons themselves it nauseates me so much. I pivot to face Eventide and, pushing off the casket, shove him with one hand, hard, in the chest. He snickers and keeps the gun leveled at my chest. At this point, I don't care if he shoots. I've only gained a few feet of empty space between the two of us, but at least he's not touching me anymore.

"You can't escape me, Abigail. Where else will you go?" he says.

I'm pinned against the casket again. It lists on its metal stand. My hands, one lands on the polished white sidewall. The other slips into the casket and lands on Eric's decomposing thigh. It feels hollow, dusty, and fragile. Revulsion shoots from my palm to my guts. My hand slips off the dead leg, and it lands on something cold and hard. The pipe wrench still slung in the tool belt. A big, heavy bastard covered in rust and as heavy as a hammer.

Eventide approaches a step closer, smiling all the while.

"I'm only going to give you so many chances, my dear," he says. "Eventually, I'll have to concede that you're incapable of learning the things that I have. And if that time comes–"

The time has come, for sure, for Eventide to learn a thing or two. It only takes a nudge of the handle to slip the pipe wrench out of the holster. My fingers find the grip of it, cold steel and rust. Before Eventide can finish his latest salvo of bullshit, I bring it out of the casket and around in a big wide arch. When the weighted steel jaws of the wrench meet Eventide's weak chin, a jolt runs up my forearm and little white bits shoot across the room. Teeth, I notice as they bounce against the carpet.

As he staggers backward, he's spitting more white rocks into his palm. When he looks up at me, confusion and anger have replaced his smarmy smirk.

"You bitch! You brog my toof!" he says.

It was more than just one. But correcting him on that point isn't important. What matters most right now is the revolver in his hand. I wind up, bringing the wrench over my shoulder the same as if it were an ax, and send it down as hard as I can into his forearm. The sound of his snapped radius and ulna isn't that different than the sound of a wooden bat sending a baseball to the upper deck. The revolver clatters to the floor. As my eyes watch it land, I notice those stupid bath slippers he's still wearing. I lift one heavy Red Wing high and pile drive the heel down into the slipper. Between his pain-induced howl and the thud of my boot driven into his foot, I don't hear the crunch of broken bones, but I feel their initial resistance give way as my heel sinks closer to the floor. His fingers crinkle in anguish. But I'm not done with him yet. All these demons he's saddled me with? If I haven't learned a damn thing along the way, I've learned how to fight. Ax or no ax, he's no physical match for me. I pull a fist back by my ear and drive it into his face. This time I aim a little higher, sending a right hook into his left eye. My hand explodes in pain, but his face goes slack. His eyes roll up, showing me blood vessel rivers cutting through the whites. Then he teeters over, landing flat against the floor like a dropped plank of wood. The back of his skull cracks loud against the hardwood.

Eventide doesn't get up. I snatch his revolver off the floor. From the basement stairwell, my sister is still screaming.

Chapter Twenty Four
Something Elder

I scramble down the stairs, tethering myself to the null posts to keep my speed around the turns. Taking the steps three at a time, I'm to the billiard's room in a few strides.

What I find before me is a battlefield caught in a standoff. Bullet holes decorate the walls. The big TV at the end of the room is cracked and flickering nonsense rainbow patterns. The pool tables are shoved from the center of the room. One of the stained-glass lamps is shattered. Bottles of whiskey and scotch lay broken and bleeding their contents onto the disheveled Persian rugs. But I don't smell the booze; I smell the hellspawn.

If I dragged it outside, the demon would take the form of the old farmer wearing an ugly green seed jacket and missing a hand. But down here, it's the same tangle of tails and limbs and claws I'd last seen inside the county courthouse. The leviathan is massive, consuming all of the space between the floor and ceiling. Black eyes glisten from its dragon-like head. Its beak screeches when it sees me, making my ears bleed. Its tail sways like a cobra. Countless claw-tipped limbs linger near the ceiling, eager to lash out. Several of those leathery tentacles have Zoey wrapped up, almost mummified. Her arms are pinned to her sides, forcing the barrel of her smoking gun toward the floor. Unlike our last meeting, the leviathan shows no signs of retreating or holding back.

"Abby!" Zoey screams from its grasp. One of the tentacles curls around her forehead and forces her chin up. Another long tubular limb, this one severed and ending it an oozing stump crawls across her exposed neck.

But I got a gun too. A revolver. An old-fashioned gun a cowboy or a '70s detective would use. No safety. No clip or magazine. Nothing fancy going on here. Just a trigger and bullets. I point it at what I assume is the leviathan's heart. When I pull the trigger the cylinder of bullets rotates and the hammer winds back and snaps forward. The gun with its curved handle kicks in my hand and I almost drop it. But I hang on and fire again. The noise and flash of the blast deafen and blind me to the world. The leviathan wails and dribbles black ooze from the center of its mass, but the beast doesn't collapse to the floor or let go of my sister. Instead, it slouches closer to me. My ears ring, loud, louder than Zoey and the hiss of the demons, muting only partially the next shots as I squeeze them off one after the other.

"Abby!"

I hear Zoey yell between shots and underneath the constant tinnitus whine. The gun is so much louder here in the enclosed basement than in the courtyard behind the house. But I can hear her call my name, just barely. Hers and another familiar voice.

"Abby!"

I spin away from the leviathan, my sister, and the broken TV. Before the door leading down to the wine cellar is the demon I've come to know as Eric. Only this time, I know better.

"Abby! Stop!" he pleads. His palms face me as if he's a traffic cop. As if he's human. "That's not your sister. It's one of them. One of those *things*!"

So he noticed the gun I'm pointing at his face. Maybe he notices the cylinder full of bullets slowly turning into position. Maybe he notices the hammer creeping back as well.

"Abbs, that motherfucker is not who you think he is!" Zoey yells from behind me. "Shoot that asshole in that stupid fucking–" her words shift into screams, and then I hear slippery wet muffling as one of those appendages coils over her mouth.

"Abby, it's me," Eric says. "Listen to me on this one. You gotta trust me on this. That's not–"

The gun fires. Same bang. Same flash. Same screech ripping holes in my eardrums. But after this shot, things get quiet. A wisp of smoke clears from the end of the barrel. Beyond it, Eric in his duck coat and tool belt and jeans stands stiff. His jaw is slack. His eyes roll up. A black dot about the size of a nickel sits in the middle of his forehead. He's got nothing more to say.

Even the leviathan seems to have gone quiet for this short moment.

"Nice fucking shot, baby sis," Zoey says behind me.

Eric's body… this demon's body that had been posing as Eric, this demon who took the place of someone who was more than likely a great guy, but I'll never get to know, this demon that murdered the real Eric… it hasn't toppled over yet, but it's on its way. The chin drops to the chest. The weight of the torso lists over the toes. For a moment, I can see a hole in the back of his head much larger than a nickel, the size of a tea saucer maybe. Then the body curls forward, almost like the Demon-Eric is going to do a summersault, and when it's halfway to the floor, everything changes.

The dangling dead arms grow in width and strength. The duck coat rips apart at the seams. The arms are now black legs that end in hooves. Horns stab through the skin of the Demon-Eric's lower back, twisting as they rise. The human form has doubled over on itself and is surrendering to a much larger and darker shape. New arms, demonic arms, exploded from the human ribs. The new body is nude but glistening black fluid. Its penis is no longer flaccid but stiff and aimed at the ceiling. A human head emerges from shoulders thick in black matted hair. The face is handsome. Beautiful even. Perhaps matching one of those marble fallen angels standing under a blanket of snow in the courtyard.

This is the first demon I saw climbing up the basement steps. The one I didn't have the guts to kill then, and the one I didn't have the nerve to kill the last time I was here. This is the demon that encapsulates all of my mistakes and cowardice and guilt and shame and regret. But now I fully understand that this is also the demon that killed my dad. Not me but the ugly beautiful thing before me and all the sick vices it imbues. Despite what I saw when I came home and found my dad dead in his recliner. Despite what I saw lying in the courtyard, dead again from the gun. Now I understand. Now I have my sister by my side. Now I have my nerves.

"I remember you," I tell it.

"Oh, cursed child," the demon says. "I have known you, but you have not yet come to fathom me." His voice is the sound of pain. When it speaks, even the whining in my ears is consumed. "I am Belphegor, Amon, Mamon, Asmodeus, Beelzebub. I am Hates, Poseidon, Yama, Iblis, Osiris, Anubis, and Ahriman. I am Evil. I am the leader of legions. I am the prince of lies. Call me Lucifer, but I am known by a thousand names and from a multitude of nightmares. I was birthed from the wound Cain delivered unto his brother Abel. I am the bastard son of a billion sins, the result of every rape, the manifestation of murder and war and genocide. But what's worse, is that I am your personal demon, my essence specifically curated to match your sins. Your destruction is my completion. And you think you can be rid of me with a thirty-eight-caliber hollow point?"

"I kill fuckers like you between chapter breaks," I growl.

"Abby, look out!" Zoey screams from around the wet, flesh of a limb.

Instead of looking out, I fire. There's one blast, I have no idea where the bullet goes, and when I squeeze again, the gun clacks dry and inert. Before I can test it and pull the trigger again, hoping it was just one empty cylinder, tentacles like black mambas slither over my shoulders, around my hips, and corkscrew up my ankles. A long length of that salamander skin twists around my arm holding the gun, then around my hand. It crushes my fingers together. The handle of the gun slips from my grip. It clunks against the floor. Then I'm lifted from my feet and those snake-like limbs begin their mummification process.

The leviathan has us both. The pressure around my spine isn't a ghostly thing anymore but a physical threat that can rip me apart at any moment. Meanwhile, the Demon-Eric, Prince of Bullshit or whatever else he wants to call himself, creeps closer. He wants to smell me. Taste me. Perhaps devour me. I can feel the rage and lust and jealousy permeating from him. And that crush of his presence. All those times before, whenever Eric was around, not the real Eric, but this abomination wearing his skin, the strangulation of my spine was always present. Why hadn't I realized it before? How had I been so stupid?

"Your shame…" the demon says as it inhales. "…is divine!"

"Such barbaric exploits!" Eventide bellows from the bottom of the stairs. Of course it's only after the hellspawn has us wrapped up nice and tight that Mister HHR Eventide, horror author extraordinaire, future customer of Schmidt's Dentistry and Orthodontist, and puppet of unspeakable evil, limps into the billiard room. His left eye is swelling up good and he's holding his palm to the side of his jaw, keeping in what loose teeth still cling to his gums. Sure, Zoey and I are probably about to die, but at least I have the satisfaction of nailing that son of a bitch in the face before my light is snuffed out. "Did you truly believe you could get the better of me through physical violence?"

"It's been working for me so far," I say through tight teeth. The coils constricting around me are getting tighter, making it harder to breathe, let alone speak.

"Yet here you are, ensnared by the leviathan and eye to eye with the face of your failure," he says. The Demon-Eric is smelling my neck, first on the left side, then on the right. I can see Zoey on my right, still alive, but covered in those spiraling tentacles everywhere but her eyes. "You've done very well with all of the previous demons that have come your way. In that, I concede your point. You've been quite successful in sectioning these beings into useless, lifeless mounds. But your ax or that gun or a wrench won't help you here. And since you stubbornly resist my tutelage, you leave me with no choice, Abigail, but to destroy you."

Zoey's mouth slips free. "Nobody calls her Abigail, dipshit! And what's the HHR even stand for? Harold Hairy Rotten Ass?" Then a severed limb slips its leathery muzzle back in place and she's all muffled screams.

"Very clever, I'm sure," Eventide says. "And what about you, Abigail? Do you have some vulgar quip to sling my way? Or are you beginning to understand the cost of rejecting my offer?"

"Fuck you," I say, because there's no point in pretending to be pure or pious or perfect anymore. The demons have risen. And now that I know they could only come up because of the cursed artifacts that Eventide set below my home and my work, a flood of guilt drains out of me. Relief washes in to replace that horrible, gut-twisting self-hate. It truly isn't my fault what happened to Dad. Of course, Zoey and Sheriff Graham and everyone else under the sun have been telling me that, but right now, on the verge of my death, I let myself believe it. It wasn't me. It was the two human-like fiends, Eventide and the Demon-Eric before me. They are to blame for all the deaths and sorrows, and maybe they'll be responsible for the death of me and my sister too, but when I go, I feel like I can go with a clean conscience, for the first time in a long time.

Eventide is standing out of reach of the leviathan that has Zoey and I entangled. The Demon-Eric has paid him no mind. But now, Eventide raises his palms and aims them at the demon holding us, as if using his hands to communicate with it. It occurs to me that that's exactly what he's doing. He's had some level of control over these things from the very beginning. At any moment, he'll give the leviathan the command to kill us. I feel it, the way he's reaching out to it. It's similar to the grip that's been at the base of my spine for so many days. It's like the connection that pulled me through the tunnels, to the deer demon, to the spider demon, to the Demon-Eric all dressed up in his electrician's sheep's clothing. What Eventide is doing, it's not complicated. Nothing more than nudging a terrible thing to be more terrible. Like rolling a boulder to the lip of the cliff and letting gravity do the rest of the work to bring it crashing to the bottom.

"Don't you see? These wonderful and awful creatures have given me everything. Before I discovered the bowls, before I discovered what they could conjure, I was an abysmal failure. Relegated to a life of mediocrity and obscurity! But with the demons, I replaced those who stood in my way until finally my greatness was revealed to the world. I've achieved everything I've sought to achieve. I've laid claim to my every desire. Every desire, so far. Every desire, but you. You can still join me. We can stand at the top of the world, shoulder-to-shoulder, hand-in-hand. But this is your last chance, Abigail," he says my full name intentionally now, mocking me with it. Maybe it seems childish, but it aggravates me anyway. "Save yourself. Save your sister. Come to my side. Or die."

The coils tighten around me, squeezing the air out of my lungs, pressing my arms and elbows into my ribcage, and cutting off blood to all my extremities. The same thing must be happening to Zoey because she's grunting and straining against the tentacles wrapped around her. A clawed hand strokes my hair and slips around the back of my neck. The too-beautiful face of the Demon-Eric spread its mouth open wide. Fangs as curved and narrow as a cobra's drip with saliva.

I'm free of guilt. Free of shame. Free to die. Free of damnation. But my absolution doesn't come with surrender. Not now when I know what Eventide has done to Woodduck, to Sheriff Graham and Deputy Ruiz, to Jason, to Dad. And what he intends to do to all the other people outside of this place. Something in his ramblings finally clicks in my mind. All this time, he's been telling me how he's attached to these abominations, and how I could connect with them as well. Those lines tugging at my mind in two different directions, to the pair of demons in the room, are still there. The pressure condensing my spine is somehow more than the squeeze of the physical tentacles wrapped around me. It's a connection between me and the demons. Not just these two, but legions of others. Lesser demons. Stranger demons. Stronger demons. Older demons. I reach out for the strongest connection and find something truly horrific. A particular entity that is elder to the thing before me claiming to be Lucifer, Beelzebub, Osiris, and Hates all rolled into one. A thing older than the very concept of "demon." A creation not from under the Earth, but beyond it. A thing of the abyss, which can never be removed or erased because it is the void itself. Something more ancient than religion. Older than the Earth. Elder to time itself. And all it needs is a little nudge to come tumbling this way. The incantation bowls still rest on the floor of the wine cellar. I can feel their electric buzz.

I suppose with the Demon-Eric turning on Zoey, she never had a chance to smash them. Which suits me just fine.

The entity I've reached to out and found... I have no idea how it might fit through the crude portal the bowls create, but I know it's coming.

And just like I've connected with this elder beast, I feel Eventide as well. I'm able to connect with the leviathan and the Demon-Eric, and while he's also connected with them, I'm able to creep inside Eventide's mind. It stands before me, as easy to enter as an open door. I slip inside, just for a moment, and finally, I see him for what he truly is: an unliked and unloved child who had to cheat and lie his whole life to gain a minimal amount of affection, and finding that route to satisfaction unrewarding, turned to garnishing the adoration of strangers. And when that proved equally unfulfilling, he chased after artistic accolades and the accumulation of material positions. And when that path was barred to him, he sought out the unholy powers he could only dream of on paper. All of which made a wholly dissatisfied, angry, distant, judgmental, miserable man who could, at best, export his misery onto others in failed attempts to alleviate his own. But all that is below his active mind. In his super-ego, he sees himself as one of the most talented and deserving individuals on the planet, and the only one who has the means and the clear path to achieve greatness. As for me, sure there's a sexual attraction, but mostly I'm like everyone and everything else he's ever come across: a tool he can use to achieve his goals. The only thing he fears, the only thing he sees as potentially stronger, wiser, and more powerful than himself, is the elder entity slowly rising through the wine cellar.

I beckon it to the surface with all my pride, greed, wrath, envy, lust, gluttony, and sloth. I drag it up with hatred and malice and murderous intent. I use all the things I shunned for so long like a bait fish, hauling unspeakable evil up from depths deeper than space and time.

Tremors shake the mansion's foundation. As subtle as a hum to begin with but growing in amplitude and frequency every moment. As my connection with the entity grows stronger, I want to recoil from it, as if my mind is touching hellfire and I know instinctively to snap away from it lest be consumed in its appetite. But I have to keep it leashed for a little longer.

"If only you would have listened to me, Abigail," Eventide says, believing this to be his last spoken regret before he condemns us to the fate of the demons who hold us.

"Actually," I manage to utter from my compressed lungs. "Actually, HHR, I have been listening."

The truth is the man standing before us isn't special. He's not uniquely talented, or overwhelmingly willful, or more intelligent or articulate or creative than half the population of Woodduck. He holds no special grasp on the power he wields. He clings to it desperately, like a rider about to be thrown from a bronco. So, I step in and take the reins.

The pressure constricting around me loosens, not completely, but enough that I can breathe again. It gives Zoey room for her to work out the arm which holds her gun. Her elbow comes clear of the gray-black twist.

The barrel of her gun follows. She swings it my way. With her mouth still muffled and strangled as it is, she can't yell at me to duck or get back, so she aims real carefully.

When she shoots, the handsome face of the demon in front of me explodes. Skin and nose and white cheekbones are spread between his ears like intricate sand art dropped before the glue can set all the grains in place. All the pieces are still there, the colors of it still present, but rearranged so it's no longer something beautiful. Zoey shoots again and this time, the bullet smacks against its temple where the left horn meets the skull. More colors now. More fluids. Orangish and yellowish and clear fluids that are meant to stay below the pretty picture. The horn flops over, barely clinging to its peeling scalp. The clawed hand caressing my head goes limp. The demon's corpse flops to the carpet.

All distractions gone now, I reach out, deeper into those connection lines. The floor underneath us shifts and cracks. I can't see the cellar, but I sense the wine bottles rattling from their places and shattering against the stone floor. The seams of mortar between the incantation bowls are ripped asunder. The walls come undone at the corners, exposing raw earth.

"No! What are you doing?" Eventide shouts, and through the psychic connection, I feel him fight back. When Eventide senses this rough beast I've summoned, he's finally afraid.

The leviathan roars and squawks and wheezes from its dragon mouth. Its free limbs and tentacles lash out. They tackle the nearly headless body of the Demon-Eric. Some crawl toward Eventide, threatening to grapple him as well. Some of the phalanges restrict tighter around me while others flail loose. It's conflicted, confused, angry, and immensely dangerous. It must sense my connection with it, and through that connection, the larger, more dangerous demon from deeper than the depths of Hell. It's afraid.

"You're insane! You have no idea what you're doing!" Eventide yells at me.

Fear floods his mind. He lets slip his mental grip on the tether to the leviathan, leaving me its lone master. I command it to release us. Immediately, the tentacles unravel from our bodies. Zoey and I fall to the ground while the leviathan thrashes the body of the Demon-Eric against the floor and ceiling.

There, lying on the thick Berber carpet of the billiards room, I can feel the subterranean rumble shake my bones. The elder beast is coming, and I have no intention of stopping it. As a matter of fact, I search my soul for all the anger and selfishness and hate and lust and revenge and all the things I've repressed for so long and let it boil over. I've been cheated. I've been shunned. I've been lied to. I've been attacked. And the whole time I've played nice. I've minded my Ps and Qs. I kept my nose to the grindstone. I didn't swear or fight or drink or fuck. I played the nice girl, but I won't do it a second longer. No more Mister Nice Girl.

The quake grows so severe it's hard to stand, but I scramble to my feet all the same. Behind me, Zoey reloads her gun and goes to work emptying it again into the leviathan. My focus is on Eventide. He makes it two steps up the stairs before he stumbles, maybe because of his broken foot or maybe because the foundation of the mansion is shifting a foot in either direction underneath him. Regardless, I take advantage of it. He's on all fours climbing up the stairs when I get my hands on him. I fill two big fists with the fabric of that pompous, pin-striped suit jacket. It rips, almost freeing him from my grasp, but the moment I sense him slipping away, I dig my fingernails into his face. Rather than losing all the skin from his face, he twists underneath me. My hands move to his neck and clench down tight. His eyes bulge and his mouth gasps like he's a fish on land. His face turns scarlet red. His whole world exists inside of my arms.

"I've learned to control my demons, HHR Eventide," I tell him. "Don't you want to stick around and play?"

Behind me, an explosion sends chunks of brick and mortar across the billiards room. The elder beast, the god of death and abyss and loneliness has arrived. It's not an evil thing. It is a thing beyond morals. A thing that existed before good and evil. It is a thing of absence. A hollow, vacuumous being that only exists to devour and consume. It is a nothingness diametrically opposed to creation, existence, life, and love.

It is also a thing of infinite size and shape. The narrow confines of the wine cellar are too tiny for its mass. It bursts through the walls and earth below the billiards room, leading with claws and teeth and beaks and tentacles and wings. The thing is an amalgamation of every horrid thing the world has ever seen, blown up to gargantuan proportions and painted in the thick mucus-like black blood of all the lesser demons that came before it. The sight of it, my mind can't comprehend, can't understand, can't contain, it's so horrid. It's as if I'm seeing pain itself, the visual equivalent of gluing my palms to a hot stove. If I stay mentally connected to it for long, I'll lose my mind.

Zoey's in full flight now, only hesitating when she comes alongside me and Eventide. She grabs me and yanks me off from him. I resist, and when she rips me away from him, my nails drag long red gouges through the skin of his neck.

"Party's over sister!" Zoey yells. "We gotta go, like right fucking now!"

The leviathan's tentacles are chasing after us as well, climbing the steps to escape the most dire threat ever conjured. Eventide twists and paws at my ankles from below, but he's too weak to get a hold of me and slow us down. We race up the stairs to the main floor, leaving him behind to deal with the consequences of his own greedy actions. Side by side, we weave through the various rooms of the mansion. Floorboards snap and splinter upward as we go. The elder beast is making more room for itself. I don't look back. At one point, Zoey almost takes a wrong turn, but I grab her and stop her before she does. This time? This time I know where I'm going, and it's straight for the front door.

We burst out of the mansion like it's a prison break. Barely staying on our feet, we spill down the front steps. We don't stop there but put as much distance between us and the mansion and the horrors inside of it. Minnesota's wintery bite greets us. We welcome it as a reprieve from Hell. Light spills over the cusp of dawn.

"Abigail!" Eventide's cry stops me in my tracks.

I'm almost to Eric's work truck, our ride out of here, but instead of jumping in with Zoey, I turn around.

HHR Eventide stands in the entrance of his home. His hands grip the doorframe, trying to hold himself from being dragged back into the recesses of the mansion. A single tentacle tightens around his waist. Behind him, walls collapse and a thing too horrible to exist on this plane rises. A hundred thin black tentacles swim through the air behind him.

I'm holding onto the doorframe as well. Not with my hands, but with my mind. I press against the threshold, against the will of the elder. As it presses outward with all its vileness, I resist with all the love I have. I can't let it escape the mansion. I won't unleash any more of its brand of misery onto the world above.

"Save me!" Eventide begs. "You called it up from Hell! Cast it away! Please!"

I say nothing, but for a quick moment, I let my grip on the elder slip. In that brief moment, a horde of twisting writhing phalanges shoot through the door frame and turn into human hands in the pre-dawn light. I forbid them to go any further. The hands land on Eventide's chest, shoulders, hips, arms, legs, and face, covering him in palms and eager hungry fingers. His screams are gagged by those hands as they pull him back inside.

Chapter Twenty Five
Day Break

When day breaks and night's shadows flee, no one comes to the mansion at the end of Hill Road. No one has any reason to believe anything of note has happened there. It's only the home of a self-absorbed, attention-craving author who should be gone on the next leg of his world tour. There's no reason to believe he has anything to do with the murders of Jason, Sheriff Graham, and Deputy Ruiz and the disappearance of one, Eric Erickson. Law enforcement from the neighboring counties, the state patrol, and yes, the BCA are all over the rest of Woodduck. So are the news vans and the reporters. There are so many of them now, we can't go back to my house. And there's no way I'm going to work either. That place is a hive of chaos.

So Abby uses the BCA-issued computer in her Camaro to look up the address of Eric Erickson, and we go there. It's a recently built three-bedroom split-entry on the newer side of town. It has a basement, a walk-out with big windows, and a sliding glass door with a view of the backyard. A door to sunlight rather than condemned tunnels. Still, we search the basement for any strange clay bowls decorated with cryptic writings and crude drawings of demons. We find none.

"I don't want to wait until things cool down," Zoey says. "I think we better go down into those tunnels with some good headlamps and a pair of sledgehammers and smash every single one of those bowls."

"There's a shed out on Hill Road that leads into them," I say. "We can use that. And I'm sure there's plenty of tools we can borrow in the garage."

We're marching upstairs to Eric's living room and dining room. The morning is bright. The sun reflects off the white snow so sharply, I squint when I look outside. But it's good to be up here, above ground, in the light. It's a shame what happened to the man who used to own this house. He was innocent of everything. Maybe the most innocent man I'd ever met. Or maybe that's what the lying demon disguised as the electrician tricked me into believing. Regardless, he didn't deserve his fate.

"I still have the map from the Records department," Zoey says. "It won't take long."

"I don't think we'll need it," I say. I can feel them now that I know what to look for. That hum. The buzz. The magnetism. It's different from the connections I made with the demons but similar. Just as tangible. And there are other things out there on the other side of the veil. Better things than demons. Benign things. Malevolent things. Even good and beautiful things. I suppose I could always make these connections. That's why Eventide targeted Dad and me from the start. Our vulnerability. Our susceptibility. Our openness. He used our empathy against us.

In the end, Eventide was a hell of a teacher. He showed me how to reach out to those things, to affect them, to manipulate them, to steer them, and if necessary, how to send them back to Hell. The leviathan and the elder beast are deep below the mansion on Hill Road, and most likely Eventide went with them. But there is one more being that twists its essence around my backbone. The last of the surviving demons to have replaced a murdered human here in Woodduck. I can sense it, it can sense me, and it waits for my instructions.

Zoey is making calls to her connections at the BCA and other law enforcement agencies. We've already practiced our story and locked in the details. But before we can go to the police and turn ourselves in and start making statements, with lawyers present as Zoey insists, there's one last thing I have to do.

Well, not *me*. After all, I have something that can do things for me.

The Demon-Jason has been lurking in the crawlspace in an abandoned mobile home in the trailer court on the north end of town. It has wanted to get deeper, to return to where it came from, but it is an evil thing, and I could care less what it wants. And I have business for it to tend to.

At my behest, it crawls out from its burrow, through the snow, until what looks like a college kid turned homeless drug addict emerges. Its Adidas hoodie and Converse shoes are covered in dirt and ice. Its exposed skin is cracked and frozen to the shade of candle wax. Begrudgingly, it walks out of the trailer court and finds the sidewalk along Highway 210. Then it turns toward the courthouse, but before he gets too far, under my command, it shapeshifts.

Its shoulders shuffle and the hoodie falls away but never hits the ground. It just sort of stops existing. Under the hoodie is a black pin-striped suit jacket. The college kid's posture stiffens. His frostbitten face grows smooth. His unkempt hair melts into a freshly combed, greasy, black quaff without a lock out of place. If it was wearing baggy blue jeans before, no one could have said so. His pants are now a black pin-striped silk that matches his jacket. Maybe it was a filthy college kid who staggered out of the trailer park in his tennis shoes, but it's the one and only HHR Eventide who marches into the courthouse in his bath slippers.

Because of who he is, or, who he looks to be, the reporters who fill the big granite hall swarm him. Lights and cameras and microphones aim for his clean-shaven, stoic countenance. There are cops there as well, and although they're initially not as interested as the press is with the local bigshot writer, once he starts talking, he gets their attention quickly enough.

The reporters are asking him questions, but he doesn't answer any one of them. Instead, he says, "I have a statement to make that I'd like everyone to hear." The clamor dies down, with just a few reporters still trying to get their questions in. Then, the demon in a pin-stripe suit speaks because I will it to speak. "Everything that has happened in this town over the past few days is my fault. I'm here to confess to the murders of Jason Jones, Sheriff Graham, Deputy Ruiz, and Eric Erickson. You'll find his body inside my mansion, already in a casket in the parlor. I'd like to go to the police now."

And that's when the reporters get loud with their questions and impatient for answers. The thing that looks like Eventide says no more. If it says anything beyond that, I don't care to eavesdrop and listen. Once the police have him in handcuffs and are hauling him to the holding cells in the Sheriff's Department, I disconnect.

When I open my eyes, I'm back in Eric's kitchen. Zoey and I are sitting around his table. She's been keeping a careful watch over me. But I come back to her as if waking up from a light rest.

"There," I say. "It's over."

"Good job, sis," Zoey says. "You're amazing, and I love you. Sorry it took so long for me to say that."

Emotions overwhelm me and keep my words trapped in my throat. We hug for real this time, without alcohol and with both of us awake, honest with each other for the first time since I can remember.

By the time Eventide goes to trial, the snow is melting, the days are longer, and birds are starting to come back from down south. Spring comes late in Minnesota. It's May before the last mounds of dirty snow melt away from the gutters and corners of parking lots where it had been plowed and piled up over the long winter.

I don't follow the trial. It's on TV and Zoey even testifies, just to make sure the demon in Eventide's skin is properly dealt with. She also uses her connections to ensure the cells where they lock him up are all above ground. As for me, I made my statement and submitted it as evidence, but I have no desire to go on the stand and try to stick with our lies under cross-examination. It's not much of a trial anyway. Since I let go of the demon, it hasn't spoken. Its lawyer, strange to think a demon could have a lawyer, but maybe not so strange when you really think about it, is going with an insanity plea. It's his only option with a client that has confessed to four murders and hasn't said a word since and, if I'm being honest, has the reputation for being a weirdo to begin with.

I returned my copy of "A Black Heart Unbroken," signature and all, to the library. And, since that's where I work now, I don't even charge myself a late fee. My position at the Woodduck Public Library is only temporary. In the meantime, I talked with the budget office and showed them some ways to divert more funds to this critical civic resource. Should be a nice bump in inventory, services, and payroll. The old ladies should have no problem finding a qualified candidate to replace me now.

It doesn't feel great taking over Jason's position after he was brutally murdered in the street. This isn't a story of "all's well that ends well." Innocent people are dead. My dad is dead. Everything that was once good in Woodduck is tainted by the terrible things that happened here. A man who should have been a happy and successful American author of the same caliber as Stephen King, HP Lovecraft, Nathanael Hawthorne, and Edgar Allen Poe (in my opinion anyway) is most likely suffering eternal and unspeakable torment. But his greed earned him his fate. I don't read his books anymore. Threw them all in the recycle bin shortly after he was dragged to hell where he belongs.

As for me? I know now that I'm not sinful, weak, greedy, selfish, or lustful any more than anyone else. I know I can be kind. I can forgive. I can admit my mistakes and try to do better. And I can love.

Back at the old house on 7th Street, the last piles of snow melt. The gutters rush with water. The door leading into the tunnels has been walled off and sealed shut. The basement and the tunnels are free of any ancient clay bowls. There's a realtor's sign in the front yard.

I don't feel bad for Eventide. But for Jason? Graham? Ruiz? Eric? The thought of those lives cut short keeps me awake at night. Because the real demons, the real nasty ones you can't kill with just an ax? They linger, long after you thought you'd put them in their graves. And they show back up, never attacking exactly, but making themselves known in the most unwelcome of times. During good times, they poke their head in to remind you that things can never be that good for long. And during bad times, to sort of press their thumb on the scale and make whatever you're dealing with just a little bit worse. And they never RSVP. Never let you know they might swing by. Demons never knock. They barge in, graves and deadbolted doors be damned.

So my ax is coming with me. The one made of wood and steel, sure, it's coming with. But so is the real ax I used to kill all those real demons. The ax that splits my mind from its darker thoughts. The one that reminds me of the good times with Dad and the good times yet to be had with Zoey. An ax not of wood and steel but of patience and kindness and truth that always protects, always hopes, always perseveres. And although love can fail from time to time, I hold a wet stone close at heart to keep my ax razor sharp.

There's a person I miss more than all the rest. Someone who's death, I still remind myself regularly, I couldn't have prevented. Not under any reasonable scenario could a person expect to see what I saw in the stairwell and know it wasn't a hallucination, a nightmare, a strange shape in the shadows that couldn't be safely dismissed. But maybe if I had found ways to make stronger connections with those still living, things would be different. I loved my dad, and I wish every day that he was still with us. He was strong and caring, and he was dealing with things I still can't imagine.

But spring is here. The air smells like wet dirt and sprouting grass. And Eventide left me with a gift. Not a book or a signature, but a means of reaching out and asking for help. Zoey and I are still polar opposites, but we're going to take a shot at splitting the rent in her Minneapolis loft apartment. Maybe with a little glue, our broken pieces will fit together. I figure I've given enough to Woodduck. Or done enough damage. As for this house, some memories, some trauma, some things are okay to let go. Zoey has been coming to visit me in the meantime, while I build up the courage to submit myself to the bustling, chaotic metropolis. Whether I have the courage or not, the time has come to leave. Soon, a moving truck will pull up to the curb and the movers will hike up my steps and ring the doorbell. Despite everything that has happened in this old home, from mourning a mother I never knew, to losing Dad, to the demons crawling out of the basement, I'm still attached to it. Before I can let it go, there's still one more thing I have to do.

The house is bright. All my books and blankets are in boxes. There's a cooler full of condiments and half-frozen McGregor's Buffalo Chicken Pizzas next to the fridge. The Christmas lights still hang from the eave outside my living room. I figure the next owners can keep them. It's quiet in here. I sit on my couch, close my eyes, and stretch out with my soul. It takes time and effort. It's as if I'm searching for the right puzzle piece in a box full of them from across an empty field. But I'm patient. And eventually, I make the connection.

At first, the sound is distant and muffled. I stay where I'm at, my eyes closed so tight the tears of hope can't escape, and stay focused. The thump thump thump of heavy work boots grows more distinct with each step up the stairs. Only when I'm sure I have a tight hold of the connection, that I won't lose it and it won't slip away, and when the boot steps are almost to the top of the stairs, do I move from the couch.

    I sprint around the end table, knock over the ax left resting there, and race through the kitchen to the door leading down to the basement. I'm not the least bit afraid of who is on the other side, and I know he can't stay long. As soon as I reach the door, I throw it open and hug Dad as hard as I possibly can.

About the Author

Joe Prosit writes sci-fi, horror, and psycho fiction. His novels include Bad Brains, 99 Town, 7 Androids, Zero City, and most recently Look What You Made Me Do, a psychological slasher horror. He has published many short stories in various magazines and podcasts and compiled them in his short story collections title, Machines Monsters and Maniacs, all of which can be found at www.JoeProsit.com. If you'd like to find the man himself, he's regularly on the road at cons and events all across the Midwest or lost deep in the Great North Woods. He lives with his wife, kids, and dog in northern Minnesota.

Prefer to read on your device?

Go to this link and enter in the password: Ru@BadBrain? to download your free eBook version that is included in the purchase of this book.

Made in the USA
Middletown, DE
08 February 2025

70493130R00136